HUNTED GIRL

CAROLYN RIDDER ASPENSON

Severn River
PUBLISHING

HUNTED GIRL

Severn River Publishing
www.SevernRiverPublishing.com

ISBN: 978-1-64875-122-6 (Paperback)

ALSO BY CAROLYN RIDDER ASPENSON

The Rachel Ryder Thriller Series

Damaging Secrets

Hunted Girl

Overkill

The Chantilly Adair Paranormal Cozy Mystery Series

Get Up and Ghost

Ghosts Are People Too

Praying For Peace

Ghost From the Grave

Deceased and Desist

Déjà Boo

The Holiday Hills Witch Cozy Mystery Series

There's a New Witch in Town

Witch This Way

Who's That Witch?

Another Witch Bites the Dust

Greatest Witch of All

The Lily Sprayberry Realtor Cozy Mystery Series

Deal Gone Dead

Decluttered and Dead

Signed, Sealed and Dead

Bidding War Break-In

Open House Heist

Realtor Rub Out

Foreclosure Fatality

The Pooch Party Cozy Mystery Series

Pooches, Pumpkins, and Poison

Hounds, Harvest, and Homicide

Dogs, Dinners, and Death

The Angela Panther Mystery Series

Unfinished Business

Unbreakable Bonds

Uncharted Territory

Unexpected Outcomes

Unbinding Love

The Christmas Elf

The Ghosts

Undetermined Events

The Event

The Favor

The Magical Real Estate Mystery Series

Spooks for Sale

Selling Spells Trouble

Cloaked Commission

Join Carolyn's Newsletter List at

CarolynRidderAspenson.com

You'll receive a free novella as a thank you!

PROLOGUE

Detective Tommy Mancini stood with his palms in front of his chest. His expression went blank for a moment, but not before she saw the hatred darken his eyes. A man stood in front of him, pointing a gun only inches from his head. Rachel Ryder quickly pulled her gun from her purse and aimed it at the man's back. Before she had a chance to speak, Detective Mancini shook his head slightly. She took two steps forward, moved to the car parked across the street and darted directly in front of the man with the gun. Detective Mancini took a step forward and said something, but the rush of adrenaline in her veins made it impossible to understand.

The man stepped closer and pressed the muzzle against the detective's head.

"Stop! Police!"

It was just a moment. A simple moment of hesitation.

A flash of light. Rachel caught her breath as the explosion echoed through the alley. Tommy Mancini crumpled to the ground.

It takes only one and a half seconds for a trained police

officer to react. For Detective Ryder, it was a gut reaction from hard-core training and years of preparation, yet in that moment, she failed. She pulled the trigger repeatedly until she cleared the magazine, taking the man down with a spray of shots covering the middle of his chest. She jerked the gun, released the magazine, and reloaded as the shooter's body stiffened. As his muscles collectively relaxed, he fell on top of her husband.

1

I stared down at the pale, scabbed face peeping out of the pile of wet leaves. The black sky and tall trees made the wooded area even darker. I flipped on my flashlight and held it toward the body, as if the small light could banish the man's demons forever cemented into what was left of his soul. From the looks of him, those demons had captured his soul long ago. "Looks like our buddy's been here a while." I carefully touched his forehead. "He's cold, but I'm not sure. The temperature could be delaying rigor."

Bishop coughed into his jacket sleeve. "God, the smell is awful. How can you breathe?"

Thanks to the temperature, the vic didn't smell all that bad. Mostly, it smelled like he took a dump in his pants, but that was probably pre-death. Death defecation isn't as common as people think, and it doesn't happen as a person dies. It happens during the process of rigor mortis, which, as I'd mentioned, was delayed by the temperature. "Consider yourself lucky. We could have found him in August."

"Jesus. Don't curse us like that."

"Here's a pro tip. When you've seen as many of these as I have, you learn to breathe as little as possible. Here." I pulled a tissue from my jacket pocket. I kept a wad of them for this exact thing. I handed him the tissue. "Use this."

He rolled his eyes. "What the hell am I supposed to do with this?"

"Rip off a few pieces and stuff them in your nostrils. It'll soak up some of the stench." I took another tissue and did it myself. "Trust me, it helps."

"You look like an idiot."

"Do what you want, but at the moment, all I smell is clean tissue while you're over there choking on dead guy stink."

He ripped off a piece of tissue and followed suit. "Have you always been so heartless?"

"So I'm told." I got back to business. "Did you check for an ID?"

"Just got here a few minutes before you."

"So that's a no?" I shifted my weight between my legs, not holding back my smile. "What's the problem then, partner?"

"No problem. Just thought we should wait for the tech to get here and have a look."

"Right." Rob Bishop was a pretty good partner, but his small-town experience didn't afford him the gritty stuff I saw daily working homicide in Chicago. We spent most of our time handling home break-ins better served through the patrol division rather than the criminal investigation division, but Hamby, Georgia, wasn't Chicago. That was a double-edged sword for me. I missed the adrenaline rush of a murder investigation, but I'd begun to almost enjoy the small-town life.

Bishop and I worked through our differences, the fact that we came from completely different worlds our biggest mountain to climb. His world consisted of women who stayed at home and had their nails done while he investigated minor crimes. I carried the weight of serious crime victims on my shoulders. Rape victims, homicide victims. The stuff of *Law & Order*, only real. Though our worlds didn't match, we'd worked hard to find the middle ground, and after some bumps and bruises, we'd learned to trust each other. Partners couldn't exist without trust.

I did a cursory check on the victim. His thin, beat-up jacket wasn't enough to keep him warm during Georgia's early spring nights, but given the rest of his appearance, I guessed he had other things on his mind. I carefully dusted off some of the leaves covering his body. The syringe lying next to his hand and the band wrapped around his arm told me the guy had shivered all right, but not from the weather. "Looks like a standard OD. Poor guy." Assessing the victim and knowing the why—in this case, an obvious drug addiction—made any investigation easier.

"He can't be helped now." Bishop took a step back. He's never said much, but as a top-notch detective, I've learned he struggled with addicts. Maybe they just hit a little too close to home? We hadn't been partners for long, and I still had a lot to learn about him.

"I disagree. We are his voice. He can no longer speak for himself, so it's our job to speak for him."

He nodded once, clearly feeling like he was being lectured.

I sighed. "I didn't mean to—"

"No, no." Bishop shook his head. "You're right. It's our job."

"Then let's do it. What do you think?"

He nodded.

No detective likes to stick their hands inside a dead addict's pockets. We don't particularly like sticking our hands in any dead person's pockets, but the risk is higher with an addict. I knew too many officers pricked by dirty needles. I had no fear approaching an armed suspect, but making me stick my hands into the dirty pocket of someone whose life goal was to get high by whatever means possible felt above my pay grade. Unfortunately, my superiors didn't agree. I grabbed a clean pair of gloves, and as I slipped them on, blew out a breath and gathered my nerve. "I'm going in." I swallowed hard as I crouched down to the victim's side. "Right front pocket first."

"Got it," Bishop replied.

"Clean," I said.

I've handled every kind of dead body imaginable. I've cleared dead animal carcasses from the road. I've cleared human carcasses from the road. I've unearthed body parts, found what we called sinkers in Lake Michigan, and unlocked long-dead and longer-trapped victims from bolted closets. If you tallied those up along with the number of autopsies I've witnessed, you'd have to borrow a hell of a lot of fingers to count how many dead bodies I've seen. I consider myself a pro, but it never gets easier. Death isn't pretty. It's heartbreaking and lonely for everyone involved.

We had a partial view of his face but not enough to make an ID without changing the head position or removing even more of the leaves to check his other pockets. "Can you take photos?"

"Did you miss the flash going off?" he asked.

"I'm a little focused here because my partner doesn't like to play in the leaves."

"Bite me, Ryder."

"Just keep your camera on. We might not know the guy, but there's always a chance, and we need the scene recorded."

"I'm not new at this."

I glanced back at my partner. "Sometimes I wonder."

He made a *pfft* sound.

"His left pocket is tucked beneath him. I'll need to rotate him to the side to check it. You ready?"

He crouched down beside me. "Go for it."

I checked his pocket. "Nothing." I stepped over him and checked the other pocket as Bishop took photos. "This one's empty too." I set him back in position and swept the leaves from his head, then stood and examined him carefully. "Wait. I think I know this guy." We'd still need an ID, but a basic identification would open possible investigative doors even before Ashley from the crime scene investigation unit arrived.

Bishop took a closer look. "Damn, I think I do too." He sighed. "Jesus, he looks bad."

"Years of drug use is bad on the complexion."

He glared at me. "Always the smartass, aren't you?"

No, I thought. That was self-preservation. Sarcasm was my magic wand. It gave me the ability to do what I do and still sleep at night. At least most of the time. "This is the homeless man who sits on Windward and State Route 400, right?"

"Yeah. Poor guy." He sighed. "I just gave him twenty bucks three days ago."

I moved the leaves from his left arm and got a better look at the band he used to inject his last dose of heroin, then I eyed my partner. "That helps us establish a timeline, so good for you."

"Fuck! I just paid the guy to overdose."

"Three days ago?" I shook my head. "Ain't no way this guy held onto your money that long. Hell, he probably got himself a fix ten minutes after you gave it to him." I scraped away more of the leaves from the needle lying next to his hand. "Why doesn't Hamby have homeless shelters? Maybe he could have gotten help." I knew the odds of an addict getting high in the woods wanting help were slim, but timing mattered, and if the city had shelters, this guy might have taken the leap. Improbable, but still possible.

I checked his front pants pocket and pulled out a receipt from McDonald's dated a few days ago, then held it up toward my partner. "Looks like your money went to a Big Mac, large fries, and a large coffee."

"At least he got something in his stomach."

I knew that made him feel better. I gently lifted the man's arm and carefully checked around it. "No ID, though. I'll call the homeless shelter in Alpharetta. See if they recognize the guy from a description."

Bishop nodded.

The wind picked up, and the few leaves left on the trees rustled in the light night breeze. The pine trees swayed, allowing a hint of the moon's dim glow to reach us. The sounds of the small wooded area surrounded me. A tiny animal scurried past, crunching on sticks and leaves as it made its way to cover and protection.

"Who called this in?" I asked.

"Public Works was out here prepping for tomorrow's road work. One of them had to pee. Saw the body and made the call."

"Probably best he didn't catch the guy in the act."

Bishop looked at me with defeat plastered across his face. "He was beyond help. I've talked to him a few times, and there wasn't a lot left up there. I felt bad for the guy. That's why I gave him the twenty. He was skin and bones, and I thought he'd buy himself a meal. I should have just brought him Chick-fil-A instead."

"Hindsight's twenty-twenty, isn't it?"

Over the past year, Hamby and the surrounding towns have seen an increase in homeless people and cons pretending to be homeless. They focus on the exit ramps from State Route 400 and big box parking lots, particularly the ones along Windward Parkway, where their audience is captive. It's hard to say no to a man standing next to your car window staring at you, and these guys knew that.

After countless complaints from residents, our illustrious city council voted to, as they said, *eliminate the vermin* from the streets, and in an effort to do so, removed the trees lining the entrance and exit ramps on 400. In their defense, the areas were littered with trash, and the requests for money at the busy intersections were dangerous to everyone, but it wasn't a solution. The homeless just moved to other locations in town. "Our city council doesn't have a clue."

"About?"

I stepped back from the body. "The homeless. Cutting down the trees hasn't stopped them. They just move to places like this where they still die alone." I hated what happened to our mentally ill, our homeless, and our addicts. Yes, there were cons taking advantage of what they deemed an opportunity, and there were ways to handle them, but the homeless required a better alternative than removing the only shelter they could find in the middle of the colder seasons.

No one is more than a few steps away from homelessness or addiction. Everyone swims through life above a powerful undercurrent of fear and insecurity. Some are strong enough to keep their head above the water, stop the current from pulling them down. Others are too weak and are eventually sucked down into the bowels of the water, unable to push their way to air. The man under the leaves hadn't been strong enough to withstand the pull.

2

The soft, growing wail of sirens seeped into my ears. I stepped back from the body, and even though I didn't believe in God, prayed for the man's soul. It was hard to believe in a peaceful afterlife when the current life was mostly hell.

I switched my small flashlight from one hand to the other and aimed it at the body, traveling a slow circle around the area in search of anything to help tell the story of the man's final moments, ones filled with poison that led to eternal blackness. I wondered what those last few minutes were like for him. Were they sprinkled with a combination of anticipation, regret, and then, finally, joyous relief only to be followed by nothing, or did he even have any time for that before the darkness hit?

Did his heart race as he walked through the woods in search of the perfect spot to feed his addiction? Did he feel the pointed branches of the winter trees scrape against his thin jacket and even thinner skin? Or did the ever-beckoning call of the high trump everything else? More. More.

More. Had that driven him to his death? Was he running from something or running to something?

I scanned the ground for footprints but saw nothing other than a few broken sticks and flattened patches of weeds. "How common is this spot for the homeless?"

Bishop sighed. "About as common as the rest of them, but it's one of the few where they didn't remove the trees completely, so it's probably been more active as of late."

The area touched a small, wooded section of land yet to be purchased and developed into something like another useless strip mall featuring a nail salon or dry cleaners that would be out of business in a couple years. If they lasted that long.

I listened to the sounds of State Route 400 and Windward Parkway, still buzzing with traffic even at the late hour. Engines roared as cars and trucks drove by, their drivers unaware of the death seeping from the wooded area along the side of the road. A life was taken there, yet no one would leave a cross because nobody would know. And nobody cared.

"It still amazes me how you refuse to follow procedure."

Bishop laughed. "Might as well get used to that, Doc."

I shook my head. "I am following procedure."

Doctor Mike Barron, Hamby's new and improved medical examiner, a primary care doctor in town who specialized in forensic pathology for fun—his words—was a stickler for the rules and liked to get on my case when he thought I broke them. "You called it an overdose."

"It is an overdose."

"Technically, it's a death investigation," Bishop said.

I narrowed my eyes at him. "I know *that*. I didn't say the guy was murdered. I said he OD'd." I wished I could take back those words when I heard them out loud. "Okay, fine. Technically, it's a death investigation, but the band on his arm and the syringe next to his hand are strong indications that he overdosed, so sue me." Just because the man died from an overdose didn't mean he did it himself, so I got their point. Begrudgingly, but I got it. "And you." I pointed to Doc. "You've been here a month. You're still getting your feet wet, so be nice."

"I've been at my job for more years than I like to count, and I've worked on various cases with the Hamby PD for a while now. I've earned my badge."

He had me there, and he knew it. "Duly noted."

He smiled, then crouched down to examine the body. "Odds are it's self-inflicted, but let's see what we can pull from his equipment."

Obviously, I thought, but didn't dare say it. And that was progress for a big-mouthed, half-Italian female detective from Chicago. My gift and curse was speaking my mind, mostly at the worst moments possible, and working in a small town with the good old boys' club meant I had to work hard at keeping my mouth shut. "Already checked his pockets. No ID."

"Let's hope he's on AFIS," Barron said.

"I'm guessing he is," Bishop replied.

AFIS, the automated fingerprint identification system used by law enforcement, digitizes, stores, and analyzes both criminal and non-criminal fingerprints. When I applied for the academy, they took my prints, so they're in the system. My mother wasn't a cop, but she owned a weapon, and her prints took up space in the ether of AFIS. "Odds are he's been arrested before," I said.

Bishop nodded. "Most of the addicts have been at one time or another."

Chief Jimmy Abernathy pushed through an overgrown cluster of dormant wild azalea bushes, swearing as a random pine tree branch whipped him in the face. "Damn it! When's the city going to clear this area?"

I didn't think he expected an actual answer. "Maybe you can file a workers' comp claim?"

He shook his head and glanced at my partner. "Where we at with her snark meter?"

"About a ten," Bishop said.

"Hey now! I'd say I'm at a four at best."

Everyone laughed but the medical examiner, and he didn't have much of a sense of humor on the clock.

I respected Chief Jimmy Abernathy. He'd been on my side during a tense battle with the previous chief and most of the politicians in town, and his assistance in handling the investigation garnered him a lofty and well-deserved promotion. Of course, half the department went down in flames from the fiery explosion of that investigation, upping his shot for the job, but he deserved it. And I deserved having a chief who respected and supported me. It made my job a hell of a lot easier.

"So, what do we have?" Chief asked.

"Looks like an overdose," Barron said. "But we'll go ahead and have the scene recorded just in case."

The chief nodded.

"He doesn't have any ID, so we'll run him through AFIS and see what we can find," Bishop said.

Jimmy nodded and spoke to Barron. "Think it's a straight-up OD?"

"I don't like to make assumptions."

I dropped my head back and groaned. "He wrapped his

arm and shot up. I'm pretty sure you wouldn't be assuming he overdosed."

"While that may be the case, I will wait to determine cause of death until after I perform the autopsy."

Jimmy narrowed his eyes at me.

"And we shall sing praise to that final call," I said.

Barron crooked his head to the left. "Why would you sing when someone is dead?"

The chief shook his head. "That was pretty bad, Ryder."

Bishop agreed.

"I was being sarcastic."

The chief smirked. "Y'all can sit on this for the night. Ashley will handle the scene, but she won't be done until tomorrow morning anyway. Get your notes typed up, then head on home." He asked the medical examiner when he would begin the autopsy.

"In the morning. I can call you with my preliminary findings once I perform the initial exam, but a final report could take weeks."

We all knew that. It was how the system worked. Only in very rare moments did medical examiners push for lab work to be returned quickly. Those rare moments were often the key to an investigation, but asking for that with a probable OD wouldn't get me anywhere.

"Be back early, though. We can start the groundwork on this so we're ahead of the game," Jimmy said.

"Yay." I removed my latex gloves as we walked back to our cars. "Sounds like another exciting day at the Hamby PD."

"You know it," Bishop said.

The Hamby PD housed all street patrol and other law enforcement that didn't warrant a closed door or even a few partial walls in a large room surrounded by the higher-ups. The pit, as it was called, consisted of slick sleeves—law enforcement slang for patrol officers and the department's clerical staff. Paper pushers—commanders, staff sergeants, and the rest of the powers that be—sat behind closed doors in their real offices with actual walls. Detectives had cubbies, but they were small and inefficient for any kind of truly private conversation.

My cubby was located on the far side of the pit, so every time I entered, I had to walk past a pit full of eyes focused right on me.

Bishop walked next to me, doing a poor job of not laughing.

"Why do they do that?"

"Do what?"

"Seriously? That's how you're going to play this?" I shook my head. "Thanks a lot, partner. They stare at me like I've got some infectious disease and they don't want to catch it, and you can barely contain your laughter."

He smirked. "I wouldn't go that far."

I fell into the chair in his cubby and groaned. "Things were better for a bit, but the stares are getting on my nerves."

"I promise you, they don't think you've got an infectious disease."

The look on his face told me he knew what they thought. "Spill it, partner."

He pressed his lips together. "You feel like donuts? I could use a Boston cream."

I straightened in the chair. "Just say it. I'm sure I can handle it."

"Okay," he said. "But don't shoot the messenger."

I glared at him. "Stop stalling."

He whispered, "Some of the guys here might be under the impression you bat for the other team."

I furrowed my brows. "Bat for the—I'm sorry?"

"You know, swing for the girls?"

"Please speak English."

He exhaled. "They think you're a lesbian." He held up his hands. "Of course, I've told them you're not."

My face instantly heated. I gripped the chair arms. "Seriously?"

"Remember, don't shoot the messenger."

"Why the hell would they think I'm gay?"

He stared at me, brows raised. "Are you really asking that?"

I pursed my lips and said, "Yes, I'm really asking that."

"You're a female detective in a small Southern town. Think about that."

"We're long past the women's rights movement, partner."

He crooked his head to the left and shrugged. "I'm just telling you what I'm hearing."

I exhaled. "Whatever. I know I don't talk about my personal life much, but some of the guys know about Petrowski. They know I'm a widow." Saying that out loud made my stomach hurt.

"It's just guy talk. Don't let it bother you. They'll forget about it soon enough."

"Right. They're talking about me behind my back. That can affect my job."

He chuckled.

"What?"

"You affect your job just fine on your own."

I crossed my arms over my chest. "I know, but I'm allowed to."

We both laughed.

I stopped laughing and held up my finger. "What exactly makes them think it? Because I'm a female detective? Is this place really that sexist?"

He exhaled. "I didn't say it was rational."

"Because it's not."

"Listen, you're a woman. You wear your hair in a bun—"

I cut him off. "You're seriously not saying my hairstyle indicates my sexual preference over the fact that I'm a—was married to a man."

He spoke calmly and enunciated his words, which annoyed the hell out of me. "I'm just telling you what I'm told. May I please finish?"

I waved my hand in the air. "Be my guest."

"First of all, the fact that you're a widow isn't common knowledge. Yes, some know, but as you're aware, we lost a lot of our team with the Light investigation."

"So, you're blaming me for the department's sexist behavior now?" I rolled my eyes. "Wow."

"I'm not blaming you for anything. I'm saying we have a lot of new officers who might not know your backstory yet."

I pursed my lips. He was right, but still. If word got around that I batted for the girls, why wouldn't the fact that I was married make the rounds too? "I still don't get it. Hair isn't an indicator of sexual preference."

"It's probably a combination of things. Your hair, your clothing—"

I glanced at my jeans and work boots. "My clothing?"

"The few times you've come out with us socially, you take shots with your beers, and you wear jeans and boots. The only time anyone's seen you dressed up was at Lawton's fundraiser, and let's be honest, you could barely walk in those heels."

I knew drinking with the guys, something I rarely did and then only under duress, would come back to bite me in the ass. I dropped my head back and sighed. "I've had exactly three shots in the three times I've gone out with you all. Three, and not three at each bar, but three collectively for all three times. And I've had one beer at each place. You know I don't drink much. Obviously I've only done that to make these assholes more comfortable around me, but that's clearly a big fail on my part. And as for my clothing, seriously? I'm a detective. Why do I even have to say this? Real female detectives don't dress like the ones on TV. Trying to chase down a suspect in heels is killer on the calves, not to mention the lower back. And male cops wear work boots, so what would you suggest I wear?"

"I'll repeat, don't shoot the messenger."

"I'll repeat, these guys are idiots."

"Did you say that before?"

"I don't know."

He smiled. "Listen, I'm not defending them. You're a badass, and people respect you, Ryder. They do. They just don't *get* you. You're not the typical Southern woman, and they don't know how to handle that. Think about it. You killed the guy who murdered your husband, and then you hunted down the criminal who hired him. That's as badass as it gets. And then here you investigated a murder that everyone, including me, believed was a suicide, and ripped the political structure of this town to pieces. Women here bake cookies and hold Tupperware parties. They don't kick ass and take names."

"So when they do, they must be gay."

He shrugged. "The South hasn't quite made it into this century, especially the police."

"That's pathetic."

"I don't disagree."

"So, what am I supposed to do? Hire a hot young male escort and trapeze around town with our arms interlocked? Let him nibble on my ear while I blush and laugh gleefully at his flirtatious behavior?" The thought of that made me want to throw up.

He laughed. "I'd pay good money to see that."

"You're an asshole."

"But I'm your asshole for ten hours a day."

"Thanks for the reminder." I stood. "And for the record, I don't own any Tupperware."

He laughed as I stomped back to my cubby, flipping the onlookers sitting at their desks the bird on my way. I swallowed back the urge to scream something about their personal sexual preferences.

Chief Abernathy called me and Bishop into his office. "Good news. Ashley's got a positive ID on the vic."

"Great," Bishop said.

Jimmy nodded, but his face showed trepidation instead of pleasure. "That's not all. She recovered another set of prints at the scene."

3

Bishop's smile disappeared. "Brad?"

Jimmy nodded.

"Shit," Bishop said. "Not again."

"Who's Brad?" I asked.

Bishop dropped his head and shook it. "Son of a bitch!"

Jimmy said, "Brad Pruitt. Andy's brother."

Ashley knocked on the partially open door.

"Come on in," Jimmy said.

"Chief Abernathy stopped by the lab and asked if I'd gotten anything, and I was just on my way to bring this to y'all, but Sanders grabbed me en route."

"I wish y'all would stop calling me chief," Jimmy said.

"With all due respect, sir," Ashley said, "it's your position."

He nodded. "Still getting used to it, I guess."

I smiled. I'd become friends with Jimmy's wife Savannah over the past few months. She was my only female friend in Hamby, actually. She'd confided in me about Jimmy's promotion and how for the first month he came home every night in disbelief that a captain had been appointed chief.

He deserved it. He was good at his job, and he was a good leader.

"I'm with Ashley," I said. "You're the chief, so you'd better get used to it." I glanced at her. "The Roswell shelter sent a fax this morning. The picture matched Randall Jeffers. Are they correct?"

She nodded and handed us each a copy of her findings. "I can verify the deceased is Randall Jeffers, age thirty-nine. Five arrests, all misdemeanors, and no convictions. All in Fulton County. Alpharetta and Roswell, to be exact."

"Guy probably just wanted the jail's hot meals and warm beds," I said.

"Have you ever slept on a jail bed?" Bishop asked.

"Anything's better than a night in the cold."

"She's got a point," Abernathy said. "Ashley, please go on." He looked straight at Bishop.

"I recovered a partial from the syringe. I ran it through AFIS and got a match belonging to Bradley J. Pruitt."

I stared at Bishop, but he wouldn't make eye contact.

Ashley handed us the last page of her report. "Age forty-six. Ten arrests in Fulton County. I didn't print out the ones from Forsyth or Dekalb, but I can if you'd like. Currently sitting on three active warrants for possession, trafficking, and, of course, dealing. All felonies and all in surrounding cities here in Fulton."

Bishop's jaw tightened. "Son of a bitch."

Jimmy's eyes softened. "Sorry, Rob."

I tilted my head to the side. "Damn."

Ashley raised her hand. "I'm a little confused."

"Andy Pruitt is doing work on my house," I said. "Bishop referred him."

"Andy's my best friend. Brad is his brother and an

addict." He dragged his hand down his months' worth of facial hair. "This isn't good."

"I had no idea," I said.

"Andy doesn't like to talk about it."

Ashley spoke so softly, I could barely hear her. "The ME hasn't completed the autopsy, but that doesn't mean—"

"Additional prints can mean a few things," I said.

"Yes, but there's more," she said.

"And that is?"

"Dr. Barron found a skull pendant and chain in Mr. Jeffers's left shoe."

"Probably stole it and was hiding it," I said. "One of the first places they use. If they have socks, which is rare, they'll use those for storage."

"That's so sad," Ashley said.

I nodded.

"I'll call Barron," Jimmy said. "Bishop, can you talk to Andy and find out where his brother's staying? We need to bring him in."

Bishop groaned. "We'll take care of it."

Jimmy nodded once. "Do that and get back to me. I'll keep y'all on the investigation, but keep in mind, the lines are already blurry. We may have to hand it over to Harry and Sanders. Understand?"

Bishop nodded.

"Loud and clear, Chief."

"Damn, I can't get used to that." Jimmy smirked. His effort to lighten the mood was completely lost on Bishop.

"Let's go, partner. I've got some heterosexualing to do."

Ashley raised a brow. "Did you just say—"

I held up my hand and headed toward the door. "Investigating. I said investigating." I felt both Jimmy's and Ashley's eyes drilling into my back on the way out.

Bishop knocked on my cubby's pseudo-wall as I finished up the rest of my paperwork on a small drug bust off Windward from earlier in the week. "You ready?"

I closed my laptop. "Yup. I'll buy coffee." I walked through the pit with my head held high, making sure to make eye contact with everyone staring at me. Each one of them glanced away as I did, just like dominos falling in a line.

Bishop shook his head. "It'd be funny if it wasn't so pathetic."

"Pit full of pussies."

"Nice talk for a lady."

"Hey, I never said I was a lady."

"Noted."

"Did you talk to Andy?"

He shook his head.

"He's at my place," I said. "Why don't we head over there after Dunkin'?"

"I spoke to Allison, his sister. She gave me some info. I thought we'd start there. If we can't locate Brad, then we'll talk to Andy."

"He's worked in my house for two months now and I had no idea he had a brother or a sister, let alone a drug addict brother. Any other family members I should know about?"

"Parents are dead. It's just the three of them now."

"Oh, wow. Did you tell Allison why we need Brad?"

He shook his head.

"What'd you say?"

"Just that we needed some info on an investigation."

"Got it."

He kept quiet for the rest of the drive to Dunkin'. I held

back from asking any questions for the time being. Sometimes it was best to let stuff sit and process before going balls to the wall about it. I knew my partner well enough to know he'd talk when he was ready. If that didn't happen soon, I'd nudge him. I was all for processing a situation, but we had a case to solve, and it couldn't go cold because Bishop had to get his feelings in check.

He pulled into the Dunkin' Donuts drive-thru line, gripping the steering wheel so tight his fingers turned white.

"You sure you should be handling this?"

He stared at the car in front of us.

"Hey."

He turned his head in my direction, then spoke with a stern, completely unemotional tone. "I'm sure."

"Okay then." I adjusted the seatbelt jabbing into my neck. At five foot five, the Charger's seatbelt shouldn't be a choking risk for me, but there I was. I moved the hinge farther down the strap to relieve the tension on my larynx. "How 'bout them Bulls?"

He didn't respond, his fingers still as white as a hospital bedsheet.

"So, go on any dates lately?"

His jaw tensed. The car in front of us finished its order and pulled up to the window. Bishop rolled the Charger forward. "What do you want?"

"Large black coffee, please." I handed him my debit card.

"I've got it," he said. The snarl on his face was enough to stop me from arguing.

"Where are we going?"

"One of the extended stay hotels in Forsyth County. Can you call the sheriff there, let them know we're coming?"

"I'm on it." I called the sheriff's office and gave them a heads-up since the hotel was on their turf. McFarland

Parkway was the dividing line for Fulton and Forsyth counties and wasn't in Hamby, but Brad Pruitt's last known residence was at the off-brand, rent-by-the-week hotel just past State Route 400. The courtesy call would keep the other departments off our back if need be. "They're good. Sending an assist just in case. You want me to handle this?"

He shook his head. "I'm fine."

"Duly noted."

Bishop pulled into the lot and parked in front of the main entrance. I scanned the lot, committing what I could to memory. "This place is a pit," I said, pointing to three boarded-up windows on three separate first-floor rooms in a row. Crime scene tape hung from one side of the farthest window. "Looks like FoCo Sheriff's been here recently."

"FoCo? Did you just call the Forsyth County Sheriff FoCo?"

"Heard it in the pit recently."

He nodded. "Place is filled with addicts and homeless, FoCo's finest." He accentuated FoCo when he spoke.

A bell dinged when we walked into the office. The front desk clerk had seen better days, days that fell somewhere south of the 2000s. The scars on her hollowed-out cheeks were from meth picking, a nervous side effect of extensive drug use commonly attributed to meth. Her browning teeth confirmed her habit. I watched her hands for the slight shake, then took two steps back from the counter and kept my hand on my weapon while Bishop handled the conversation. Meth addicts were the hardest to deal with, especially if they needed a fix. They angered easily, and their irrational emotional swings weren't easy to predict. This one clearly needed a fix, so better safe than sorry.

"Help you?" She chomped on a ball of gum as she spoke, and tiny droplets of spit began coating the counter. Beads of sweat pooled on her temples, and her eyes popped like it took all she had to maintain her cool. They shifted between me and my partner.

Paranoid much?

Bishop flashed his badge. "We're here for one of your customers."

"Name?"

He scrolled through his phone for Pruitt's mugshot. "This guy. Brad Pruitt. You know him?"

Her eyes shifted to mine and then back to Bishop's. "Not familiar with the name, but I can check." She used her dirty sleeve to wipe the sweat from her forehead.

Instead of typing into the computer, she flipped through a yellow legal pad, nervously humming between chews, and then shook her head. "Uh, I...no. He's not here no more. We kicked him out for non-payment three days ago." She turned the paper around and showed us the pen line through his name, with the words *no pay* written beside it.

Mighty fine system they had.

"Have you rented his room?" Bishop asked.

That time she had to check the computer. She tapped the keys with two fingers and stuck her face close to the screen. Girl needed glasses. "Not yet."

I thought as much. Seven cars were parked in the lot when we drove up, and though most of the time weekly renters didn't have vehicles, the place didn't look full.

"We'd like to take a look at the room, please."

"I'm not allowed to show rooms if you're not a customer."

I stepped to the side and walked behind the counter.

"Hey, you're not allowed back here."

I ignored her and picked up the legal pad.

"You need a warrant for this!"

"Not if it's in plain view," I said, and began moving toward the key hooks on a bulletin board.

She blinked.

"Call your manager," Bishop said.

"We don't got no manager. We got an owner." She dialed the number and put it on speaker phone. Bishop spoke to the man.

"Let 'em in the room, Lisa," the owner said.

"Sure thing, boss."

She pulled a key off the rack and walked us around to the back of the hotel and up the creaky metal stairs to room 246. She handed Bishop the key. "Make sure to lock up when you leave. If I'm not at the desk, just leave the key in front of the computer." She quickly made eye contact with me before turning away.

I have a way of making people uncomfortable.

Bishop waited for her to walk away, then widened his eyes and said, "Not a tweaker."

I laughed. "Nope, not at all."

Law enforcement call meth heads "tweakers" for several reasons, but mostly because they're paranoid and jumpy, and she was a lot of both. The fact that she still had a job meant her addiction was still somewhat manageable, but judging by her face, it wasn't long before she'd cross the line to helpless.

Bishop angled himself to the side of the door while I stood behind him with my gun drawn. It might have seemed a little dramatic, but addicts and rent-by-the-week hotel calls could go multiple ways, and better safe—and prepared —than sorry.

He knocked on the door. "Brad, it's Rob Bishop. Open the door."

No sound came from the other side of the door, so

Bishop put the key in the lock and twisted the handle. When he pushed the door open, the smell of rotting food hit us like a brick. I swallowed to stop my gag reflex from going into overdrive.

"Jesus, why don't they clean these rooms right away?" I asked.

"I get the feeling Lisa's responsible for it, and she's probably not in any rush."

I held my arm against my nose and eyed the disgusting room. "This is nasty."

Bishop laughed. "Where's your tissue?"

I secured my weapon in the holster and pulled a tissue from my jacket pocket, then ripped it in half and handed him a piece.

"You don't even flinch from the smell of death, but rotten food has you turning all sorts of green," he said, chuckling. "I lived in the dorms in college. This place is nothing compared to those."

I stuffed the tissue pieces into my nostrils. "Some smells get to me, others don't."

"That's some strange compartmentalizing."

I shrugged, then glanced around the room, careful not to step on any of the pizza boxes, beer bottles, or cheap scotch bottles scattered around the floor as I kicked a path to the back of the room. Andy's brother went a step above addict into hoarder territory. "Damn, poor Andy."

Bishop walked over to the small desk and used the hotel key to lift a newspaper and push it aside. Several used syringes lay underneath. "Brad never cared about hurting his family. Andy got over that years ago."

I slipped on a pair of disposable plastic gloves and walked over to the desk. "I'll take too stoned for five hundred, Alex." I took photos of the items on the table while Bishop snapped a pair of gloves over his large hands.

He moved the newspapers off the desk, revealing more needles, mostly unused. "Don't see that often. These things are gold in an addict's world."

I nodded. "Looks like someone left in a hurry." Clothes lay all over the room—on the bed, floor, dresser, chair, and desk. Piles of clothes, not just a few thrown here and there. I checked the sizes for a few, all men's mediums except for two women's sweaters with holes in them. "This is Ralph Lauren. Dude dressed well." I moved around to the other corner of the desk, took a photo of a standing Taco Bell bag, then pushed it aside to photograph the scribblings on a notepad. *CB 12:30.* "CB 12:30. That a place or a person?"

"Brad's involved with—or was, last I knew—a woman named Caroline Bryant."

I nodded. "Bet we get to hang with her soon."

He laughed. "I'm not taking that bet. I don't know where she's living these days, but it shouldn't be too hard to find her." He dug into a pile of garbage on the floor. "Take a look at this." He held up a gold necklace with a skull pendant. "Same thing Ashley mentioned the medical examiner found on Jeffers. I guess gaudy is in."

A lead brick settled in my gut. I held out my hand. "May I?"

He handed me the necklace. "It's all yours."

No, it wasn't mine, but it was definitely meant for me. It was a message that my past was part of my here and now. "Shit."

4

He continued searching through the room. "We need patrol here. They can gather everything and bring it to the station just in case we need it for later. We shouldn't be wasting our time with this trash." He clicked the mic on his shoulder and contacted dispatch.

"Forsyth's sending someone, remember?"

"They're taking their time."

I followed up his request with a call to Forsyth, who said their deputies were two minutes out. Then I got back to the skull, examining it carefully. I knew the piece. I'd seen similar ones hundreds of times, but twice in one day wasn't a coincidence. "This is a Mexican gang necklace." My mind flashed back to the night of Tommy's murder and the necklace draped around the killer's neck.

Bishop maneuvered his way through the mess. "You think? I see shit like this all the time. Kids think it's cool to wear this crap."

He was right. The skull trend was big, but the brick settling in the pit of my stomach swore it wasn't just a trend. "Brad Pruitt's forty-five, right?"

"Forty-six."

"How long's he been using?"

"About ten years."

"He mix his hits?"

He shrugged. "Mostly heroin, I think, though he once said he used meth occasionally."

"That's two entirely different highs."

"I know. I don't get it."

"Did he have some kind of injury? Something that got him addicted in the first place?"

"No. Best guess is it was an emotional thing."

Poor Andy. I've seen hundreds of families destroyed because of addiction, but it's always more personal when it's someone you know. "I doubt the necklace belonged to him. He's a little old for the trend." Drugs didn't care about age and neither did drug addicts, so it was entirely possible Brad Pruitt was connected to someone who'd wear a skull necklace. It was also possible he'd stolen it thinking he could sell it for cash for his next fix. I ignored the brick settling in my stomach.

"What're you thinking?" Bishop asked.

I cleared the fog enveloping my brain. "Just checking off boxes."

He nodded. "You said Andy's at your place, right?"

I stared at the painting above the bed but didn't actually see it.

"Hey." He gently removed the necklace from my hand and set it on the desk. "You okay?"

I nodded. "Yeah, of course."

"You sure?"

"Mm-hmm."

The door to the small room opened and two uniformed deputies from Forsyth County stepped in.

The taller of the two smiled. "Got a call to assist y'all?" When he examined the room and realized what that would entail, he said, "Holy shit."

The other guy covered his mouth and nose.

As Bishop introduced us, the two deputies eyed me up and down, examining me intently. Cops sizing up cops wasn't unusual, but that didn't mean it was comfortable for female law enforcement.

The taller of the two deputies exhaled as he scanned the filthy room again. "Sheriff says he's happy to take this over, but if you want your own people to collect any evidence, we're good with that."

I told them we'd have our team handle it. Mixing evidence collection between counties was an icy slope to walk down. "We're working a suspicious death, and this could be related."

"Not a problem," he said. "The sooner I can get away from the smell, the better."

"Understood," Bishop said.

"Any information on the three rooms in the front of the building?" I asked.

The deputy nodded. "Drug trafficking bust. Six arrested."

Bishop and I nodded. "How long ago?" I asked.

"Three days. Cleaned out most of the hotel during the arrest."

"Either of you here for the bust?" Bishop asked.

"I was," the other deputy said.

Bishop removed his phone from his blazer pocket and swiped on the screen. He held up the phone. "Did you see this guy?"

The deputy examined the photo carefully. "He wasn't part of the bust, but I can't say he wasn't one of the people staying here. Most of them took off after they figured out what was going on."

I chastised myself for not paying better attention to the cities around us. Chicago was different. Districts were components of a bigger picture, but smaller cities were independent entities that shared information when needed. The best way to keep tabs on the surroundings was by connections at other departments or the local news. I'd dropped the ball on all of it.

The taller deputy examined the photo. "I was here on another call two weeks ago, and this guy was in the room." He glanced around Brad Pruitt's room. "Not this one, though."

"You bring him in?"

He shook his head. "There was a fight. He wasn't part of it. He didn't have any drugs on him, and he was outside when we arrived, so we couldn't confirm his involvement. He insisted he was walking by when it all went down."

"What about this guy?" I showed him Jeffers's mugshot.

He nodded. "He was here."

"Was he part of the fight?"

"Put him in lockup for the night. He was passed out in the bathroom."

"So, no charges?" I asked.

"Wasn't worth it."

I understood that. Drug busts were a dime a dozen and backed up the jails and courts, so we picked our battles carefully. Both Georgia and Illinois shared the three strikes law, but those first two strikes had to be felonies. The third could be something as simple as stealing a pair of socks from a drug store, and those kinds of third strikes weren't worth the paperwork.

Ashley walked in and smiled. "Oh. I see some overtime

hours on my next paycheck." The girl had the most cheerful disposition ever, especially in the field. She swore it was because of her daily yoga, but I knew the truth. Crime fascinated her.

I could relate to that.

She set down her bag, opened it, and got to work. "Anything in particular I'm looking for?" She directed her question to the taller deputy, her cheeks flushing.

I covered my smile with a fake cough.

"We're not staying, ma'am."

"We've got several syringes." I walked over to the table and pointed to the necklace. "And this." I glanced at Bishop, who raised his eyebrow. "This is Pruitt's room, so we're looking for anything that might connect him to Jeffers." I put my hands on my hips and stared at the garbage on the floor. "I'm sorry."

"Not a problem. I'll have this done in a few hours."

I admired Ashley's positivity. I stopped back at the hotel office while Bishop leaned against his Charger and smoked. I handed Lisa the key.

"Do I need to clean up in there?"

I pursed my lips. "We've got a crime scene tech in there now. It'll take her a while, but you're probably going to need a small dumpster."

"Is the guy dead?"

"No one's in the room."

"Oh, but is he, like, dead now? Is that why you're here?"

"This is an active investigation. I'm not at liberty to share the details."

"Can I just ask one more thing, please? And that's it. I promise." She tapped her fingers against the counter, then picked at the beads of yarn pilling on her sweater as she bounced on the balls of her feet again, and it wasn't from too much caffeine.

"I can't promise an answer."

"Is it about the...the drug bust before? The one with the Mexicans?"

I shrugged. "It might be a few days before we clear the room, but we'll make sure to let you know."

"Yeah, yeah, that's cool. I get busy here, you know, helping and shit."

I raised my eyebrows. She got busy, but I doubted it was because she was helping people and shit. "The neighbors will start complaining about the rotting food smell soon, so be prepared."

"I fucking hate this job."

"Supports your habit, though, right? At least for now?" I flipped to Pruitt's mugshot and tried another angle. Holding up my phone, I said, "You use with this guy?"

She smiled. "Heroin isn't my thing."

"Needles work for meth too, honey."

She tilted her head to the side and huffed. "What do you want from me?" Her posture was straight, and she spoke quickly. "I told you I didn't know the guy."

"You don't need to know someone to shoot up with them."

"Okay, yeah. I...I've been in the room, but he took off after that bust. Freaked him out, I guess."

"He say anything to you before he left?"

She pressed her lips together and ran her hand through her greasy hair. "I told you, I barely knew the guy."

"Interesting use of past tense." I walked around the counter again.

"Hey!"

"In plain view, remember?" I leaned against the counter,

keeping a reasonable amount of distance between us and making sure she saw my sidearm. "Twenty minutes ago, you were jonesing for a hit, but look at you now. Maybe I should grab the county deputies up in 226?"

"I'm not high."

"And I'm the Queen of England." I smiled. "I'm going to ask you one more time. Do you know where Brad Pruitt is?"

She exhaled. "I told you he left after that bust. That's all I know, man."

"You said he was kicked out for non-payment three days ago, so which is it?"

"I mean, yeah, officially, but..."

"And you know this how?"

She picked at a scab on her hand. "He came to me, asked me to keep an eye on his stuff. Said he'd be back with cash to pay the bill."

"And?"

"And he gave me a deposit, so I've kept the room like he left it. He said he had shit to get out of there."

"How much cash did he give you?"

"Am I under arrest? I want a lawyer."

I laughed. "I don't give a shit about you. It's Pruitt I care about."

"He gave me some ice, said it was good stuff."

"He say where he got it?"

"I don't know, something about a new distributor coming in from out of state, I guess. What's it matter? The stuff was shit anyway."

"Then it looks like he owes you, huh?"

"I don't care about his shit, but I don't plan on cleaning it either."

I handed her my card. "You see him, you let me know, okay?"

"Whatever. I don't need no trouble."

"You help me, and you won't get any."

I lit a cigarette and stood next to Bishop.

He watched me inhale and hold it for longer than I should have. "You know that shit'll kill ya."

"Hypocrite."

He shrugged. "We're all going to die somehow, but I thought you quit."

"I did."

He nodded once.

"Lisa and I are best friends now."

"You seem to have a lot in common."

"She confirmed Pruitt left the night of the bust, but he asked her to watch his stuff, paid her with some ice he said came from a new distributor out of state."

He flicked his cigarette to the cement and ground out the fire with his steel-toed boot. "That's not good."

"Nope. There's going to be a drug war in them hills, sugar."

He stared at me. "Was that your attempt at a Southern accent?"

"How'd I sound?"

"Like shit."

"Probably should lower your expectations, then."

"Tell me about the skull pendant."

I blew out a breath of smoke. "What about it?"

He lit up another cigarette. "You seemed pretty interested in it. Mean something to you?"

"Nope," I lied. "Just a popular symbol for a gang in Chicago, that's all."

"Right."

5

Andy stood in the middle of a ladder on my small porch. He reached up with a paintbrush and dabbed a bit of paint on the trim, then smoothed out the glob with slow, calculated strokes. Van Halen played loudly from his earbuds.

Bishop tapped my arm and then held his finger to his lips. I nodded as he stepped forward and gently nudged the back of Andy's leg. I took a step back also, keeping my body rigid and preparing for him to fly backwards off the ladder, but thankfully, he didn't. He simply removed an earbud and laughed. "Not this time, asshole."

I really liked Andy.

He climbed down the ladder, smiled at me, and shook his head at Bishop. "I was putting in my plugs when I heard your car pull up. You're an old man driving a muscle car. You know people think you've got a small dick."

I bent my head to cover my smile, then changed the subject before the fight started. "They're buds, not plugs." He was right about Bishop's Charger. The engine was high-school-shop-guy loud. "Hey, you talk to your sister?"

He looked at Bishop. "She left me a message, but I haven't checked it yet. She okay?"

His smile faded and his shoulders stiffened. "She's fine. It's Brad we're looking for."

Andy's face mimicked his best friend's. "So, you called her first? What'd he do now?"

Much like families of law enforcement, families of addicts often prayed for the best but expected the worst. It wasn't an easy way to live, but it worked.

Bishop's expression changed from concerned and uncomfortable to his detective face. His eyes narrowed just enough to show the fine, crinkly lines sprouting from their sides, and he pursed his lips, which highlighted years of smoking lines even under his graying scruff. "Have you heard from him recently?"

Andy sighed and shook his head. "Not for a few months. Come on, tell me what he did."

"We don't know if he did anything," I said, and it was true. "We're investigating a case and would like to talk to him about it."

He set the paintbrush over the can of paint, then wiped his hands on a cloth he'd hung from the ladder. "What kind of case?" He looked to Bishop. "Stop beating around the bush. What's my brother involved in?"

Bishop sighed. "A man was found in a wooded area off the highway. Looks like an overdose."

"What's my brother got to do with that?"

"His prints were on the needle."

His eyes widened. "You think Brad—"

"We just want to ask him some questions," I interjected. Bishop wasn't exactly playing hardball with his best friend, but he wasn't being sensitive to the situation either. I wouldn't go as far as to say I'm sensitive, but the guy had been good to me, and I wanted to ease his frustration. If I've learned anything in my time as a cop, it's that the family isn't responsible for the actions of one of their own.

"Okay." He eyed Bishop carefully. "Addicts share that stuff all the time. Doesn't mean my brother's involved in the guy's death."

"We have to follow the evidence, and right now the evidence points to having a conversation with Brad," Bishop said.

"We tried to locate him at his last known residence, but he took off in a hurry a few days ago," I said. "Asked the girl at the front desk to keep an eye on his stuff."

"That by-the-week dump off McFarland?"

I nodded. "He's officially out for non-payment, but he gave her some ice to keep his stuff." I sighed.

He tilted his head. "Ice?"

"Crystal meth. It's one of the many street names for the stuff."

"Learn something new every day."

"Much of it we shouldn't have to, but this is the world we live in now."

"I'm sorry. I don't know what to tell you," Andy said. "My brother and I didn't sit around and talk about his problem." He removed his Braves baseball cap, rubbed the top of his head, and then put the cap back on. "I really can't give you much." He picked up the paint brush, tapped it lightly on the paint can, and then set it inside a can of paint remover. He swirled it around the inside of the can as he said, "I haven't talked to him in over a year and couldn't care less if I never heard from him again."

He didn't look at us as he spoke, which made me wonder if he was lying. Even though addicts destroyed families, relatives often couldn't help but protect them when the cops came around. I couldn't understand it until the mother of one told me she'd rather her son get high at home where she could protect him from both cops and criminals. I empathized with her dilemma. "Have you had run-ins with any of his associates lately?" I asked.

Bishop kept his feet planted firmly on the ground. I knew he was uncomfortable, but he'd have to get over that or risk being removed from the case.

"If you mean have any of his buddies come looking for money lately, no. I think my sister said someone came into her boutique looking for him a few weeks back, but she told him to leave."

I made a mental note of that. If Pruitt owed a dealer money, that person would be back, and would go to the weakest link first. Since their parents were dead, that weakest link was Allison.

Bishop removed a small spiral notepad from his pocket and took notes. "Did she describe the guy?"

Andy shook his head. "We don't usually go into that kind of detail."

"Why wouldn't she tell us?" I asked.

"She's protective of him. I don't get it, but it's her choice."

"What can you recall of the conversation you had with her?"

"It's the same one we have every time this shit happens. Some thug came around saying Brad owed him money or had something that belonged to him. She told him she doesn't associate with Brad and asked him to leave. End of story."

My partner flipped the notepad closed. "Is Allison at work today?"

Andy shrugged. "You talked to her. You tell me."

I cringed. I understood why Bishop was white-knuckling

his steering wheel earlier. Dealing with Brad put stress on his relationship with Andy.

"Andy, we're trying to help your brother."

He sighed. "Let me text her and see."

I eyed Bishop as he watched his friend's every move. I was missing something. Something my partner sensed, or maybe just two men momentarily at odds.

"She's there doing inventory, but she's not sure how long it'll take." He responded to her text. "Told her you'd be coming by."

"Great." I smiled at my handyman, who was quickly becoming a friend. "If we find out anything, we'll let you know, okay?"

"If you find his body, let me know. And the only reason I'll care then is to do right by my parents. They'd want him buried with them." He pulled on a plaid fleece shirt and began buttoning it. "He's been dead to me for years."

6

I rubbed my hands together as we drove through town, waiting for Bishop's raised blood pressure to return to normal. I stared out the window at the mini-mansions lining the streets, wondering who actually needed a six-bedroom house and all that extra space. I'd driven this street hundreds of times already, and I still couldn't fathom needing so much.

"Allison's boutique is in Crabapple," he said.

"Got it." I didn't want to rock the boat yet. I planned to say something about his attitude, but his face was still red with anger.

"So," I said, feeling the need to walk on eggshells. "You handled that well."

"Brad's caused a lot of problems for me."

"I can imagine, but I'm sure he's caused even more for his family. Andy may not want his brother around, but he doesn't want anything to happen to him either. It's a pretty common way for relatives of addicts to feel. You should try to be sensitive to that."

He squeezed the steering wheel tighter. "I am sensitive

to that."

I raised my eyebrows. "Whatever you say, partner."

A black lowriding Chevy Malibu hovered on Bishop's tail. I kept my eyes on it through the small mirror on the visor. "You see that?"

He checked his rearview mirror and nodded. "Yup."

"He's a little too close for comfort."

"Just a dumbass kid."

The dumbass kid sped up and rode Bishop's bumper. "A dumbass kid who likes to play pin the tail on the donkey."

"Little shit. Time to teach him a lesson." Bishop pressed down on his gas pedal hard enough for gravity to push me into the seat.

The car sped up, keeping its front end inches from Bishop's bumper.

"Slow down and put out your cherry."

"Not yet," he said. "Let's see how far this kid wants to go." He tapped the brakes and the car behind him slowed too.

"Either that kid took defensive driving or he ain't a kid."

"He's lowriding, and the window tint is dark enough I can barely see him."

I used the reverse camera on my phone to see if I could get a better look. "You're right. I can barely see his head over the steering wheel. Put on the cherry and slow down. I can count at least three misdemeanors so far."

Birmingham Highway is a long, hilly, and winding two-lane road. The speed limit is forty-five for most of it, but it drops down to thirty-five around the curves. When we got to the speed drop, Bishop kicked up to sixty-five and whipped around the curves. I braced myself and kept my neck loose. The car maintained our pace.

"What an asshole," Bishop said.

"I'm on it," I said, and called into dispatch. I gave them

our location and the description of the Malibu. Illinois requires two license plates, one on the front of the vehicle and one on the back, but Georgia only requires one on the back. That only benefited the driver and made law enforcement's job harder.

"Zone three is approximately a mile out. Estimated arrival less than four minutes, copy," the dispatcher said.

"No," Bishop said through gritted teeth. "I've got this."

"We're good," I said to dispatch. "Just ask them to prepare to assist and BOLO for the vehicle."

"Ten-four," she said.

Bishop took a curve at lightning speed, then hit the brakes hard enough for the seatbelt to leave a mark on my neck. The Malibu swerved to the left and passed us, increasing its speed enough to send dust from the other side of the road flying into the air. Bishop sped up and his tires squealed. "Come on, boy, you wanna play? I'll play." He met the back end of the vehicle, keeping what appeared to be less than a foot between us. I removed my spare Glock from my boot and rolled down my window.

"Dispatch, we have eyes on the Malibu tag. Copy."

"Standing by."

"No license plate, er, uh, tag. No dealer stickers. Copy."

"Tracking your location. Zone four is approximately a half mile out, near the roundabout, copy."

"I want him," Bishop said.

"Copy that," I told dispatch.

"He's going to have to slow down at the roundabout," I said. "And so are you."

Bishop didn't respond.

My heart rate increased when the roundabout appeared at the bottom of the hill. Neither the Malibu nor Bishop slowed, and there were several cars rounding the small circle at a turtle's crawl. "Fuck." I set the gun on my lap and tried to relax my body in preparation for the worst. I pulled the seatbelt strap under my arm and secured it as tightly as possible. I'd rather break my shoulders than crush my airway.

We saw the cruiser lights and heard the siren just as we approached the roundabout.

At the last second, the Malibu slowed, switched into the far right lane, and turned off the roundabout. Bishop slammed on his brakes to avoid hitting the minivan heading that direction.

"Look to your right, asshole!" Bishop yelled. There was no way to switch into that lane without hitting the minivan, so he kept his vehicle in the left of the two lanes, requiring him to complete another entire loop to follow the Malibu. The cruiser backed up, flipped around, and maintained pursuit. I grabbed the cherry from his glove compartment and tossed it onto the hood. The cars near us slowed and moved over, and Bishop was able to circle back. He hit the gas hard, but those few seconds were just enough for the Malibu to pick up speed, run through a stop sign, and disappear behind traffic.

The patrolman driving the cruiser apologized over the radio. I politely responded. "Back off. Too many citizens to safely pursue. Copy."

"Copy that, ma'am."

Bishop was breathing hard. Beads of sweat appeared on his forehead. "Son of a bitch!"

I bit my lip. He was pissed, and anything I said could tip him over the edge. The idiot behind the wheel of that car was lucky we backed off. God only knew what Bishop would do to the guy.

He white-knuckled the wheel but slowed to a normal speed. I kept my eye out for the Malibu just in case.

After a few minutes of silence, he finally spoke. "What the fuck was that about?"

The question was probably rhetorical, but I went ahead and answered. "It's what you said. A teenager. Probably compensating for a small dick."

"More like nonexistent."

His body relaxed by the time we arrived at the small area of antique stores and boutiques where Allison worked. As he parked the car, he managed to cool his jets enough to stop sweating like an old man ready to stroke out.

"You okay?" I asked.

"Yes."

"You sure?"

"I said yes."

I smacked my lips together. "Okay then, how about I take lead here?"

"Allison's like my little sister. I know how to handle her."

"Whatever you say, partner."

7

Allison Pruitt reminded me of a mouse. Timid, insecure, but focused on the cheese. In this case, her boutique. "Like I told you on the phone, I...I haven't seen him in a few weeks. Wasn't he at the hotel? Is he okay? Is he in trouble?" She tapped on her iPad screen but wouldn't look at either of us.

"We'd like to question him about an overdose," Bishop said.

Her eyes widened. "Who?"

"A homeless man," I said. "Randall Jeffers."

She scratched her right cheek. "I don't know the name. Why are you looking for my brother if it's an overdose?"

I glanced at Bishop. He nodded, and I took that to mean I could continue. "Your brother's prints were on the syringe we found with the body, ma'am."

She stared at Bishop. He nodded once. She looked back at me. "You're the one who helped Rob with the Troy Light murder, right?"

I turned toward Bishop, expecting him to introduce us. When he didn't, I held out my hand and said, "Yes. Detective Ryder. Your brother Andy is doing some work on my place."

She shook my hand limply and spoke to Bishop. "I haven't seen Brad in a while. I tried calling him the other day, but he never answered. His voicemail was full."

I wasn't surprised that Brad had a cell phone. Most addicts had family desperate enough to stay in touch to give them one. If I had to guess, I'd say Allison forked out the cash for the bill.

"Can we have that number?" I asked. "We may be able to track his location."

"Sure," she said.

Bishop handed her his spiral notepad and a pen.

"What was your brother like the last time you saw him?" I asked.

She finished writing the number on the pad and returned it to Bishop. "What do you mean?"

Bishop spoke. "Was he nervous? Rushed? Did he ask for money?"

"Brad's an addict. He's always nervous and rushed, and he always asks for money."

"I think what he means is did you notice him being more nervous and rushed than before?" I asked.

She crossed her arms over her chest. "What's going on, Rob?"

"That's what we're trying to figure out," he said.

"Has anyone come around asking for Brad? Maybe looking for money?" I asked.

Her eyes shifted to the floor. "Not recently."

According to Andy, she was lying, but I cut her some slack. "Allison, have you ever paid off any of your brother's debts?"

She flicked her eyes up to me, then averted them, looking toward Bishop instead. "I don't have that kind of money, and Andy would kill me if I did."

That meant one of two things. She'd done it before and Andy figured it out, or she'd done it and he hadn't.

"Allison." Bishop stepped closer to her and spoke with a kindness I'd never heard from him. "Andy told us someone came by recently. We need to know what they said. It might help us find your brother."

"You said this was about an overdose." She rubbed her arms and curled her shoulders inward. "Tell me the truth. Is Brad in trouble here or what?"

"We're just trying to get some answers to a few questions, that's all."

"You promise?"

Bishop nodded.

"Someone came by looking for him, but I told him I hadn't seen him."

"Did you know the guy?" I asked.

"I don't exactly hang out with Brad and his buddies."

"Have you seen him before?"

She shook her head. "I don't think so."

"Did he ask for money?"

"No. He just wanted to know where Brad was. I told him I didn't know."

"Can you describe the man?" I asked.

She shrugged. "Mexican. Kind of tall, dark hair."

"What about facial hair? Maybe a beard, mustache?"

She shook her head. "I mean, yeah, he needed to shave, but I wouldn't call it a beard."

"Did he have any tattoos?" Bishop asked.

"He had on a black leather jacket, but nothing on his neck or face, I don't think. I wasn't actually examining him."

"You said he was tall. Was he thin? Muscular?" I asked.

She shrugged. "I don't know. I guess he wasn't really muscular, or I would have noticed, right?"

"Did you tell him Brad stays at the hotel?"

"I love my brother, Rob. I wouldn't throw him to the wolves like that. I said I haven't seen him, and that's the truth."

"If you see your brother, or if anyone comes around looking for him again, let me know, okay?" Bishop asked.

She nodded. "Yeah, sure. Of course." A single tear dropped from her eye.

"We'll find him, Allison," Bishop said. "And I'll let you know when we do, okay?"

She nodded. "Thank you."

Neither of us took the time to smoke, choosing instead to get in the Charger and head back to the department. I started the conversation. "She's keeping something from us."

He kept his eyes on the road and his lips in a thin, straight line.

"Maybe we should keep an eye on her?"

He finally turned to me. "Jeffers used one of Brad's needles and overdosed. We've done our due diligence. We looked for Brad, but we can't find him. It's not unusual for an addict to disappear for weeks at a time. This isn't some big Chicago murder investigation, and it's not something Jimmy's going to want to waste time on. Is it sad? Yeah, but it's nothing more than a simple OD."

"Something doesn't sit right with me."

"What?"

"I don't know yet. I just feel like something bigger's going on here."

"I don't agree."

He was protecting his friends. "I'm not saying Brad shoved the needle into Jeffers's arm."

"Sounds like it to me."

"You're too close to this."

"Says the woman who went after her husband's killer."

My blood pressure rose. "Fuck you, Bishop."

"Fuck you, Ryder."

I crossed my arms over my chest, and neither of us spoke on the drive back to the department. When we got there, I charged out of Bishop's vehicle, slammed the door behind me, and stormed inside. I stopped short when everyone in the pit stared at me. "Screw this," I said, then flipped around and jogged back out the door. I needed a cigarette before I lost my shit on the good old boy network inside. We needed to track Pruitt's phone. Why Bishop didn't push this immediately gave me pause.

"Word is he's keeping his nose clean and his hands out of the pot." Lenny wiped his nose and coughed into his iPhone screen. The cough intensified into a fit that reddened his gray-stubbled face. Once it subsided, he wiped his mouth and spoke again. "Sorry about that."

FaceTime's fun with an old guy. "Have you been to the doctor?"

He shook his head. "It's fine. I got me some Nyquil. It's helping."

"Doesn't seem to be." Lenny Dolatowski was my former captain and a father figure who lived next door to us most of my childhood. His daughter Jenny was my best friend. She was killed by a drunk driver years ago, and since I wasn't close to my parents, Lenny and I developed an even stronger bond. When Tommy was murdered, Lenny was there for me. I didn't think I'd survive, but he made sure I did. In many ways, I owed him my life. As I watched him age quickly over FaceTime, I worried I'd lose him sooner than I could handle. As if I actually believed I could handle losing him at all. "Go to the doctor."

He snarled at me, then set the phone on his kitchen counter, giving me a clear view of his thirty-plus-year-old light fixture.

"When are you going to get a new light? That thing is probably older than me."

I heard him putzing around his kitchen. "Mary bought it a few years before Jenny was born. She loved that thing."

Lenny went to a dark place when his wife passed. It took him a while to come out of it, and since then, he'd refused to change anything in his house. The kitchen wallpaper was peeling, but he didn't care. Mary picked that paper, and he'd die before he changed it. It kept her alive for him. I could understand that. I'd moved from my place because the memories of Tommy overwhelmed me. The ghosts of our relationship lingered. Ghosts that should have soothed me but left me feeling more alone than ever.

Lenny coughed again, off screen.

"What're you doing? The whole point of FaceTime is so we can see each other." I'd gone to visit him in Chicago for a long weekend and bought him a new phone as a late Christmas present. He hated technology, saying the fax machine was the worst thing to happen to the world because he believed it was the beginning of the end of human-to-human interaction. I didn't disagree, but being able to see him on the screen gave me comfort. The apps we installed allowed me to keep track of him in case something happened. He hated that. He was a grown man who could take care of himself, he'd argued. I told him to suck it up and get over it. I also allowed him to see my location and taught him how to check it. That seemed to work, though I had a feeling he'd already forgotten how to do it.

He picked up the phone. "Sorry, I had to take more medicine."

"If this doesn't get better in a day or two, go to the doctor. Please."

He ignored me. "As I was saying, the eyes on Petrowski say he's keeping his nose clean."

"He's buying time. Petrowski's not stupid. He's not going to come for me right away. If he wants his revenge, which everyone knows he does, he'll wait it out. I don't trust him."

Chris Petrowski paid to have my husband, Detective Tommy Mancini, executed. Tommy was days away from bringing the corrupt commissioner in on money laundering and racketeering charges, and Petrowski hired a Chicago gang thug named Miquel Sanchez to do his dirty work.

Sanchez succeeded, but only because I hesitated. I'd walked up on him holding a gun to my husband's head. I prepared to shoot, but Tommy mouthed something, and I hesitated while trying to read his lips. That second changed my life forever, and ended Tommy's. I emptied my magazine on Sanchez, but killing my husband's murderer wasn't enough. I needed to take down the man who hired him, and when I did, Petrowski promised to come for me.

Corruption is deep and wide in politics, and he'd been released just over two months ago. I waited, knowing he or someone who worked for him would show up sooner or later.

I was ready.

"I'm worried about him," I said. "You know how he is. Thinks he's too good to get his hands dirty. He's got people for that."

"We've got eyes on his known associates, but without a formal investigation, that's all we can do."

"I know, and I appreciate it."

"I know you do. If Petrowski or one of his associates as much as jaywalks, I've been assured they'll drag them all in."

It wasn't jaywalking I was worried about. Petrowski was a piece of shit. The kind who used one hand to pat you on the back and the other to stick a knife in it. He played dirty, but he wasn't stupid. He had to know we had eyes on him. As a former politician, his hands were on a piece of every pie, and his conspiracy to commit murder sentence didn't change any of that.

Even before his release, I watched my back. His connections went deeper than I could imagine.

I filled Lenny in on my caseload, the OD, and our search to question Brad Pruitt. Not much to discuss, and not all that exciting either.

He laughed. "That's not a caseload. That's a vacation."

"At least I've progressed from teenagers spray-painting pornographic images on public buildings."

"I don't think I could adjust to that kind of work," he said.

"You're retired. You don't need to adjust to any kind of work."

"Retirement is work, and believe me, I'm still adjusting to it. Been doing a lot of baking and putzing around the house. Beginning to think I need a change."

"What kind of change?"

"Maybe a trip to the South where it's warm and sunny."

I laughed. "Then you're going to have to wait a few months. We're not quite there yet."

"You sound like you like it better now."

"It's hard for a lesbian to weave her way into the web of good old Southern boys, but I'm working on it."

He laughed. "I wondered how long it would take for that one to start."

"Seriously?"

He laughed again. "Come on, you had to know that was coming."

"And yet, I didn't."

"You're a toughie, Rach. Men don't know how to handle toughies like you."

"That's an excuse for being a jerk."

"Maybe, but don't sweat it. They'll come around soon enough."

"I'm not sure about that, but whatever. I know the truth, and that's what matters." I wasn't sure I actually felt that way, but I'd keep saying it until I believed it.

"Speaking of sexual preference, how are the riding lessons going?"

Lenny desperately wanted me to get back on the saddle, and not the one on a horse. He knew about Sean, the trainer from Hamby Equestrian Farm, where I'd gone to find out about riding lessons. "Lessons are on pause at the moment."

"Rach, you moved south for a reason. The least you can do is fulfill that promise."

He was talking about the promise Tommy and I made to each other before his death. Tommy loved horses, and he loved riding. I wasn't experienced enough to have an opinion, but he wanted land for horses in a reasonably warm climate, and all that mattered to me was being with Tommy. He was my home, not Chicago. All I asked was that we lived less than a day's drive from Lenny, so we'd considered Tennessee, Kentucky, and Georgia. But he died, and our plans were ruined.

Everything in Chicago reminded me of my life with Tommy. My house. My job. The bar we'd go to watch sports. The way the snowplows covered our sidewalk with six feet of snow. I needed to get away so I could breathe. I decided to follow through with our plan best I could, and that was exactly why I'd moved to Hamby. I wanted to keep that promise and eventually live the life we were supposed to enjoy together, just alone.

"I know, and I will. It's not that I'm not going to do it. It's still kind of cold here too, you know, and riding a horse with the cold wind on me doesn't sound all that appealing."

"Chicago cold freezes nose hairs, and you walked around in that. I think you can handle a little Southern breeze. What's the temperature there?"

I knew I'd regret saying it. "Forty-seven."

He busted out laughing. "It's twenty-six here. With the windchill, eighteen."

That was pretty cold. "That would kill ninety percent of the people in the South," I said. "They aren't as acclimated to the cold out here, which is why they don't really have a lot of lessons right now." They did, in their indoor arena, but I left that out.

"Guess not." He paused. "But what about that young man from the place? The one you briefly mentioned and have failed to discuss again."

"His name is Sean. And I haven't failed to discuss him again. I just don't have anything about him to discuss."

"You go on an official date yet?"

"It's not like that."

"So make it like that. Consider him practice. It's time to move on. Tommy would want that."

We'd had this conversation dozens of times, and it

always ended the same. "I know, and I am, but I'm not in any rush to forget my husband."

"Honey, you'll never forget Tommy, but it's okay to move on. He'd want that. He'd want you to be happy."

"When was the last time you went on a date?"

He blinked. "This isn't about me."

"You're a widower, Lenny, but I don't see you jumping to hook up with someone new."

He set the phone back on the table. "I'm almost seventy years old. There's a difference."

Not really, but I felt bad for upsetting him. "I'm sorry. I know what Mary meant to you, but you have to understand that I feel the same way. I didn't have almost fifty years with Tommy, but that doesn't mean I don't feel the loss."

"I know that. All I'm saying is the fish won't bite if you don't throw them the bait."

"I don't want the fish to bite." I pursed my lips. "Wait, are you suggesting I'm the bait in this conversation?"

He picked up the phone and smiled into the camera. "If the hook fits."

"Nice."

"I just don't want you to be alone, and I know Tommy wouldn't want that either."

"I'm not alone. I've got Herman."

"Herman is a fish. Up here we call that sushi."

My jaw dropped. "Lenny! He can hear you!"

"What's the lifespan on those things anyway?"

"Three to five years, and he's three, so we don't talk about it."

He snorted. "Whatever floats your boat. My point is, your life's barely begun. Get out and enjoy it a little."

"Yeah, it's a little hard when the entire department I work with thinks I'm gay."

He snorted.

I pursed my lips. "It's not funny."

"You're doing a man's job in a man's world. You knew it would be hard, and you've got to resign yourself to the fact that some of the guys may never accept you as an equal. It's just the way it is."

"That's just another excuse."

"I'm with you on that, sweetheart, but it is what it is. Most of the guys will warm up to the idea that a woman can be tough enough to kick their butts, but some of them can't think on those terms. They're not smart enough to not feel threatened."

"Yeah, I uncover a prostitution ring and half the politicians in town go down, and all I get for it is a rumor."

"Why does that bother you?"

"I don't care about the rumor. I just want them to respect me."

"Then make them."

"Right. What do you want me to do, prance around in stilettos wearing low-cut shirts with my boobs popping out?"

He laughed. "That's not asking for respect."

"I know, but it would be kind of funny."

"And prolong the problem. Listen, God gave you a big mouth for a reason. Use it."

I sighed. "Won't that just fuel the fire?"

He shrugged. "Maybe, but if they're truly intimidated by you, it'll shut them up." He set the phone on his coffee table and fussed with the TV remote. I knew because he held it over the phone and gave me an up-close view. The TV's volume blasted through my speaker. "Oh hell." He clicked it off, and I laughed as the remote flew over the screen and landed somewhere on his wood floor with a thud. "About this OD, you think your handyman's brother had something to do with it?"

"I'm not sure, but after talking to the sister, Bishop seems to want to just sweep it under the rug. That concerns me."

"It's his best friend's brother."

"I know."

"You think Bishop's keeping something from you?"

"More like he's pretending there isn't a problem because he doesn't want there to be."

"It's hard when people you love are involved."

"It caused some serious tension between him and Andy. I can see how he'd want to drop it, but if the medical examiner rules this as more than a simple OD, we'll have to investigate, and if he can't keep a clear head, he'll have to be removed from it."

"What's your homeless population?"

"Next to nothing compared to Chicago, but Hamby doesn't allow shelters in town. That keeps our numbers low, but we're seeing them move this direction, and because of the rise in opioid addiction, some of our own residents are losing their homes."

"Squatters?"

"More every day. It's just crazy to me that the city refuses to put in a shelter. They're worried it will ruin their reputation and invite a bigger problem."

He shrugged. "Sounds like they've already got a problem, and building a shelter isn't going to fix that one. They're right. It just invites more people with the problems to town. You know that." He stared straight into the phone's camera. "But I don't think that's what's bothering you about this. Am I right?"

I sighed heavily. "I think there's more to this, and if he doesn't want to face it, we've got a problem."

"Give him a chance to work through it before you judge."

"I know. A part of me is worried about what he'll do if we have to investigate Pruitt. I don't think he realizes the depth of the rabbit hole he might have to go down."

"Nothing you can do about it. Man's got to work through that one on his own."

"I know."

"Keep moving forward. If something's there, I have no doubt you'll find it."

"I just don't want my partner losing it."

He smiled. "You sound like Garcia."

I shrugged. "I plead the fifth on that."

"I bet you do."

8

I dropped a few pellets into Herman's bowl and apologized for Lenny's harsh words. Herman didn't seem all that put out, and I was relieved. We had a perfect human-fish relationship. He listened when I talked, which wasn't that often, and I fed him and left him to live in peace. It worked for us. I didn't need to baby him, and he didn't require affection.

I admired Andy's handiwork on my new bookcases. He'd taken on every handyman project I'd given him, and I had a feeling his perfectionism wasn't just because his best friend was my partner. He loved what he did, and he was good at it.

I smiled at the photo of me and Tommy at Navy Pier. I examined it carefully, noticing its angle toward the door instead of my couch. I never angled my photos. I wanted to look up from any position in the surrounding area and see Tommy's face, his sparkling smile. Andy must have done another check on his paint job when he was over earlier and moved the photo. I glanced at a photo of me and Lenny he'd given me when I visited, taken at a local bar off Irving Park Road in Chicago. I smiled at the memory. I was happy to be leaving the city then, thinking my fresh start in a smaller town with a focus on the equestrian community was the perfect place to honor my commitment to Tommy. An easy life with no complications. I checked the other photos—two more of Tommy, and another of me and Lenny. Everything exactly where it was supposed to be.

I checked my watch. Before I left the department, I'd texted Jimmy suggesting Bishop and I take an extended break, hoping Barron would have something from the autopsy. I didn't mention Bishop's frustration, but I implied we could use the break. He obliged. I had another hour left, which would hopefully give Bishop enough time to cool off. I gave my teeth another quick brushing, then stared at myself in the mirror. Jeans and a black V-neck shirt. Black work boots with steel toes. Long brown hair pulled into a bun. My usual attire suddenly felt so uncomfortable.

I examined my face. Tommy always said I had my mother's dark eyes, my father's nose, and a porn star's lips. I refused to ask which of my parents I got those from. Tommy was right about my eyes, and as I stared at myself, I realized I looked a lot like my mother when she was my age, just dressed like my father. I stripped down, jumped into the shower for a quick rinse, and then proceeded to dress to impress. I wanted to beat myself with a stick for caving, but if I wanted to squelch the rumor, I had no choice.

I'd just finished slipping into a pair of spandex business pants when my cell phone rang. Unknown caller with a Georgia area code. I declined the call. It immediately rang again. Same unknown number. I declined again. When it rang the fifth time, I accepted the call. "What!" I waited for a telemarketer named Brian to tell me my extended warranty had expired and he could solve all my problems, but all I got was heavy breathing.

"Hell-*o*?" The breathing continued, so I clicked off the call and blocked the number.

I went over and above my normal routine, adding a few curls to my hair and letting it hang loosely on my shoulders. I felt foolish, but still, I put on a fitted black shirt, the one Tommy always said made my figure pop—whatever that meant—then slipped on a black blazer and stuffed my too-wide feet into narrow black leather ankle boots with a slight heel and some cheesy bedazzling—a recent addition Savannah swore would make me instantly Southern. I looked like I was heading to a funeral, but in my defense, my job wasn't the happiest one in town, and I had to admit, I looked more like a female than a dude.

After applying another swipe of mascara and a touch more eyeliner, I decided to up my game even higher and brushed some blush across my cheeks. I stared at myself in the mirror. "You're an idiot. Makeup isn't going to make them think anything different, and what does it matter, anyway?" I shook my head. I'd resorted to talking to myself. Lenny was right, I needed a life. The fact that I felt the need to appease these men surprised me, but if it helped shut them up, the trouble was worth it.

When I returned to the station, I stopped at Bishop's cubby, leaning against the flimsy wall and waiting for him to notice me. When he didn't, I said, "Eh-hem."

He tapped into his laptop. "Brad's phone is either dead or off."

"That can be good or bad."

"I know, damn it." He finally looked up over his readers and smiled. "Wow. What happened to you?"

I tossed my bag on the floor next to the chair and sat. "How do I look?"

He held up his hands, protecting his personal space.

"Oh, hell no. Answering questions like that is why I'm divorced."

"I thought she cheated on you?"

"Apparently, the other guy knew the right answers."

I couldn't help but laugh. "Listen, about earlier. I didn't mean to—"

"I was out of line."

"So was I."

"Move on, then?"

"Already have."

He smiled, shaking his head.

"What?"

"You look...different. Anyone say anything yet?"

"The pit's empty. Can you believe it?"

He chuckled. "They probably heard you coming and ran for cover."

"Trust me, the entire South would hear these heels."

"So, I did a little asking around."

"About?"

"About a new distributor in town."

I crossed my legs, feeling completely awkward. My toes rebelled in the shoes, throbbing their muted screams to get my attention. I slipped off the right boot and stopped myself from groaning in relief. "And?"

"If there is one, he's lying low."

"You think Pruitt made it up?"

"Don't know why it would matter." He handed me a paper with a chain-of-command chart hand-drawn on it. "These are the two main dealers in town." He pointed to the one on the top left. "My guess is this guy thinks he's Prince or something, and the other one, I've had minor dealings with his minions, but never him. He knows how to keep his hands clean."

"Or he's got someone working on the inside."

"If he does, it's not here. I can't imagine we'd have any crooked cops left after the Light investigation."

"We have new blood. Who knows what these guys are doing?"

"Point taken. I still don't think there's anything to this OD."

"I agree, but we need to fill in the holes. Did Barron send anything over yet?"

"Preliminary report says Jeffers had a deadly amount of fentanyl in his blood."

"That doesn't surprise me. It's cheap to make, and the dealers get a bigger bang for their buck."

"Based on what I've seen, it's gaining popularity here. I guess Brad could take that leap."

It wasn't a leap. It was a step on a ladder. Sometimes my partner's naivete surprised me. "You know how it works. Cheaper drug, quicker high. Desperate times call for desperate measures, right?"

He closed his eyes and sighed. "He's not going to make it much longer on this route."

I exhaled. "There's nothing we can do for him. You know that. He has to make that decision himself."

"I know. I just feel bad for his family. Andy's distanced himself, sure, but he's still his brother. And Allison, she loves him. She still believes he can kick this."

"All you can do is be kind."

He shuffled a stack of papers on his desk. "I put out a BOLO on Brad and asked a few of the shift patrol to check around. I'm going through his previous arrests, known associates, that kind of thing. I've got a file on him. It might tell us something we don't already know."

"What would you like me to do?"

"I've been thinking about that Malibu. Something doesn't sit right with that."

"Agreed," I said.

"Maybe you could go through the stolen vehicles, see if it's on the list?"

"It's a long shot, especially with no distinguishable markings. By the way, Georgia's most stolen vehicle is actually the Chevy pickup."

He raised an eyebrow.

I shrugged. "I've had a lot of free time on my hands lately."

"Still worth checking into."

"Agreed. I'm on it." I gathered my things and headed back to my office as quickly as possible, hoping and praying the three guys now in the pit didn't notice me. I turned on my laptop, let it rev up, and glanced out my cubby. I wanted a bottled water, but I'd been in such a hurry to hide, I hadn't stopped at the kitchen to get one. The body count in the pit doubled. Unfortunately, these bodies were still breathing. "Screw it," I whispered. I gathered my nerves, promised my abused toes I'd make it up to them soon, and strutted across the pit to the staff kitchen.

Jaws dropped. Pencils dropped. Someone whispered, "Damn." It was a perfect heart-attack moment for someone from human resources.

I kept my bitch look intact. If I acknowledged their surprise, they'd take away my power, and I refused to let that happen. I removed two water bottles from the fridge, then walked back with my head held high. I caught them staring at me again, but no one was brave enough to say anything when I gave them a not-so-resting-bitch-face glare.

9

Savannah whistled when I walked into Duke's and gave me a lingering once-over. When I sat next to her, she whispered, "Did you take something?"

"What? No!"

She laughed. "I thought maybe you were sick and this new you was a side effect of the medicine."

I groaned. "My feet hate you. In fact, I think I hate you too."

Jimmy laughed. I glared at him, and he immediately stared at his beer bottle.

"So," Savannah said, scooting closer to me. She leaned toward me, and in a voice loud enough for the entire joint to hear, said, "What then, you get all fancied up because the guys think you're gay?"

Jimmy spat out his beer.

I narrowed my eyes at him. "Asshole."

His face lit up like a cherry, and he laughed so hard he couldn't make a sound.

Savannah had no idea how to use her inside voice. "A

few days dressed like this, and the boys will forget your sexual preference."

I eyed Jimmy.

He leaned back and waved his hands in front of his chest. "I'm just here for the beer."

"Will you care if I arrest her?"

"For what?" Savannah asked.

"I'll think of something."

She laughed. "You did good, girl. You've already won half the battle. Now we just have to tackle the other half."

"Yeah?" I nodded toward the bartender. "Coors Light is fine." I turned back toward Savannah. "What half did I win?"

"The chief is scared shitless of you."

I laughed. "That and a dollar will get me nothing. I'm afraid to ask this, but—"

"Don't do it," Jimmy said.

I did it anyway. "What's the other half?"

"Getting one of them to ask you out."

I cringed.

"Told you not to do it," Jimmy said. He took a swig of his beer and ordered another one. "Battle lines have been drawn. Keep 'em coming."

The bartender laughed.

"I'm not desperate enough to go out with a patrol officer."

"Honey, it's not about the date, it's about the possibility of one."

"There is no possibility."

"All they need to do is think there is." She swept a strand of hair from my face. "Oh, sweetie. That eyeshadow. We need to work on that. You're too young for hooded lids."

I had no clue what that meant, but she was right about

my lack of makeup application skills. I preferred the natural look anyway. Makeup and I had a complicated relationship. I didn't like putting it on, and it couldn't apply itself.

Savannah dug in her large cow-print bag and pulled out a smaller—but not small by any means—bag of makeup. "I think I've got some—"

I swung my hands at her. "Stop it! I'm a big girl, Mom."

Jimmy laughed, then saved me with a subject change. "Any news on Brad?"

"Bishop put out a BOLO and tried to track his phone, but nothing. We checked his last known residence, but he left a few days ago. Spoke to Andy and his sister. She said someone came around looking for him, but she doesn't know where her brother is."

"Sounds like a whole lot of nothing."

"You get the preliminary autopsy results?"

He sipped his beer and nodded. "Fentanyl."

"It's going to get worse before it gets better."

"I know. We're already seeing a rise in cases across the northern part of the county, and Forsyth's in deep."

I treaded carefully. "You're going to have to figure out a way to handle these."

He nodded. "We're working with the DEA on a task force."

"Should have been out in front of this already." I shrugged. "Not blaming you, obviously."

"Our previous administration pretended it wasn't a problem."

"Shocker." My tone dripped sarcasm. "I'm happy to help."

He nodded. "Appreciate that."

"Bishop and I think we're beating a dead horse on this OD."

"I think you're right, but Brad might be able to give us some information on his supplier. We should continue to look for him."

"Bishop said he's been using for ten years. You think he can get him to flip?"

"I believe in miracles."

Savannah laughed. "Only because getting me to marry him was one."

I laughed.

"Bishop okay?" Jimmy asked.

"Better now."

"He coming tonight?"

"Not that I'm aware of. I thought it was just us?"

"From the department," Savannah said.

I glanced at Jimmy, who held up his hands. "Like I said, I'm just here for the beer."

I pressed my lips together and glared at Savannah. "You invited Sean, didn't you?"

"I did not invite him."

"Then you told him I'd be here."

Her lips curved upward into a devilish grin. A look I had a feeling made Jimmy do whatever she wanted. "I might have mentioned I'd be meeting a department friend out this evening."

"Great."

"He was going out with his friends anyway. It's not like he's coming just to see you."

"I feel like this is a set-up," I said, looking to Jimmy for a truthful answer.

He sipped his beer again and stared at the shelves of liquor bottles on the bar wall.

Pussy.

Savannah exaggerated her Southern accent. "Oh,

sweetie, it's just a drink or two. What's the big deal? Besides, it'll help with your little problem."

I wouldn't have called it a problem exactly. I turned to Jimmy and shot him an explosion of imaginary daggers from my eyes.

He wiggled his beer in his hands.

Savannah giggled.

"I give up." I downed the beer, then held up the empty bottle for the bartender. It was going to be a long night.

"Two? That's unusual," the bartender said.

I flicked my head toward Savannah. "Blame her."

Officer Michels walked in and sat to my left. Of all patrol, he was one of the few who'd been decent to me when I started. I wouldn't call us friends, but we might end up that way someday. Michels didn't give off the typical good-old-boy vibe bleeding from the pores of most of the men in the department. He spoke without the drawl of those who grew up in town, and his thick, dark hair and deliberate stubble made him appear older than I suspected he actually was. He topped that look off with an even thicker mustache reminiscent of a '70s porn star. Not that I watched '70s porn, but my favorite teacher had the same 'stache, and every guy in high school swore he'd been a porn star.

I smirked when Michels looked past me, clearly not recognizing me. He said hello to Savannah and Jimmy, then ordered himself a beer. A second later, after finally making eye contact, his jaw dropped. "Shit." He leaned back and nodded. "You clean up surprisingly well, Detective."

I punched him in the arm.

He rubbed it. "But you hit like a dude."

I smirked. "No, I hit harder than one."

"I don't want to test that theory."

Savannah nudged my opposite arm. When I glanced at

her, she crooked her head and flung it toward Michels. "Flirt with him," she whispered.

Savannah Abernathy, born and raised in Macon, Georgia, had that *something* most women in the Midwest would kill for. It wasn't easily defined, maybe a mix of sass, confidence, and a big dose of vulnerability that made men want to hold her elbow and open car doors for her everywhere she went. What they didn't get was that vulnerability was total bullshit. Savannah was tough as nails and could bring any man to his knees with a few words and a smile. She once referred to that special skill as "manipulation through pheromones." She swore a true Southern woman could tell a man to fuck off and they'd come back for more.

Most guys I told to fuck off usually ended up behind bars.

I kept my voice low and spoke with a tight smile in case Michels realized I was talking about him. "He's not my type."

"Darlin', if you don't want them thinking you're a lesbian, you need to play the part. Say he smells good or something."

I turned to Michels, covered my nose, and sniffed. I grimaced and told Savannah, "He doesn't smell good. He smells like coffee and mint gum."

"Bless your heart. You have no idea how to work a man, do you?"

"I can get the truth out of them. That's usually all I need from them."

"If that's true, I feel sorry for you. Men like to be complimented. It makes them feel good. What's it going to hurt? Just say something." She peeked past me and whispered, "He's got strong hands. Tell him that."

"What? No! He'll think I'm hitting on him." I caught Jimmy trying not to laugh. "Thanks for the help, Chief."

"Hey," he said, smiling like a kid. "I know how to pick my battles."

"Wimp."

"One hundred percent."

I rolled my eyes, because in the little time I'd known Savannah, I'd learned she was relentless. It was something I usually admired, but not in this case. "Hey," I said to Michels. "You know about the rumor?"

He crooked his head. "Rumor?"

"Come on. Don't pretend you don't."

He glanced at Jimmy. I turned and caught Jimmy using his finger to make a slash across his neck. When he caught me watching, he looked at the bar top. I was about to let him have it, but he got lucky. His cell phone rang. He answered it and walked away.

"Great. Looks like I'm going to be Ubering it home tonight," Savannah said.

"Maybe not," I said.

Michels stayed put, and I suspected he was hoping we'd forget he was there, or at least forget about the conversation Jimmy let him know he didn't want to have.

"It's okay," she said. "I'm adjusting to being married to the chief of police." She winked at me. "And it definitely comes with its perks." She stood. "If y'all will excuse me, I have to use the ladies' room."

I focused on Michels. "Well?"

"Hear y'all can't locate Brad Pruitt."

"You've been decent to me since I started."

He nodded. "No reason not to be."

"I appreciate that, but let's not play this game, okay? You know what I'm talking about, so let's just get to it, okay?"

He stared at my tensed jaw. "I mean, yeah. Some of the guys talk, but I don't think anyone thinks it's true. It's just something they kid about. You know how it goes."

I straightened in my seat. "No, I don't."

He sighed heavily. "Some of the guys don't know why you aren't..." He paused with a look that told me he was searching for the right words.

"Dating?"

He nodded. "Yeah, dating."

"But you all know I was married. You know what happened, right?"

"I've heard some stories, but Chief heard a few guys talking, and he told them to respect your privacy. Said he didn't want to hear talk again or he'd write people up."

"Really?" Jimmy did have my back, except when it came to his wife. He really was afraid of her. "It's a little more than that. And I'm not telling you this because I want you telling anyone the story. If they give a shit, they can Google it themselves." I grabbed my cell phone and did a quick search. I set the phone on the bar and angled it his direction, showing a list of articles on Tommy's murder.

Detective Thomas Mancini Murder Funded by Chicago Commissioner

Rogue Detective Busts Chicago Commissioner for Husband's Death

He examined the list, then looked at me. "Shit. I just thought—"

"You people need to get your gossip straight." Compassion flooded his face. At first, I thought it was pity, and I wanted to headbutt him. "I'm not gay."

"I'm sorry. I didn't know. You want me to say something to the guys?"

"No." Yes. Maybe. "I don't care what they think."

He stared at my hair. "I can tell."

I punched him in the arm again.

He eyed the articles once more, picking up my phone and scrolling through them. "Looks like the asshole's out already."

"Corruption's thriving in Chicago."

"Did they ever catch the guy who pulled the trigger?"

The memory flashed through my head. "They didn't need to. I killed him."

His eyes widened. "Fuck, Ryder. I didn't know."

He didn't need to know I'd walked up as my husband was shot, that Tommy stared at me as the shot fired, that if I'd reacted even a second sooner, I could have saved him. "I don't exactly want everyone knowing my personal business, so I'd appreciate it if you kept it to yourself."

"I understand."

"And for the record, there are a lot of lesbian cops in Chicago, and the guys treat them like equals." That was a bit of an exaggeration, but whatever.

"The guys here think of you as an equal."

"Then why is my sexual preference an issue?"

"It's just talk. Something to pass the time."

I nodded. "Simple minds, I guess."

He laughed. "For sure."

Jimmy returned to the bar. "We've got a hit on Pruitt. Bishop's on his way. I told him you'd meet him there."

I tossed a ten-spot on the bar top. "Where am I going?"

"Texting you the address now."

Poor Savannah. Her fake date setup was ruined yet again.

10

The paramedics and a patrolman I didn't know were already at the location. The patrolman smiled, giving me a once-over that made me want to rush home and take a shower.

"Paramedics inside?" Bishop asked.

"Yes, sir. Looks like the inhabitants had themselves a good time. Maybe a little too much. There's a kid in there too. Young, maybe five? Paramedic's checked her."

"She okay?" I asked.

He nodded. "Scared. Wants to stay with the woman."

Bishop shook his head. "Jesus."

"My partner's with her now."

The house, if you could still call it that, was too far gone to even be considered a money pit. The land might be worth something, but the place was a tear-down, and whoever owned it likely knew that. Blue tarp filled with holes covered holes on the roof. The siding was missing on half the visible area, and even the boards covering the broken windows needed covering. The concrete steps leading to the door were a crumbled mess, and the front door didn't close properly. I hadn't even stepped inside, but I knew it wouldn't be much better.

Bishop stared at my boots. "Why the hell you still wearing those?"

"I was going out. I didn't think we'd get a call."

He smirked. "Very ladylike of you, partner."

"Bite me."

He laughed hard and reached for my elbow as a way of offering to help me up the steps.

"I've got it," I said, shaking him off, the determination in my voice hiding my doubt.

We stood on the front porch, examining the poorly maintained home. "Looks like Brad's living the high life."

"In the literal sense."

I nodded. "Who called this in?"

"No one," the officer said. "Alpharetta picked up a DUI on Highway Nine. Driver said he'd come from here. The officer knew about the BOLO, took a chance and showed him Brad's photo."

"Nice work," I said.

"And the DUI ID'd him?" Bishop asked.

"Said he thought he was the one who gave him the ice."

I couldn't help chuckling. "I love when they bust themselves like that. Makes the job so much easier."

"Probably thought he'd get off by throwing his buddies under the bus," Bishop said.

We moved to the side of the door to make room for two paramedics hauling a woman on a stretcher. The woman's left arm hung loosely off the stretcher, but she had an oxygen mask on her mouth, so she was alive, even if barely. "What about the kid?" I asked as they passed by.

"She's physically okay. Your guys already called Child Services."

"Was the woman her mom?"

He shrugged. "Only one woman inside. Assuming it's her mother."

That wasn't always the case. I sighed. "Thanks."

"Yes, ma'am."

I glanced inside the trashed home. "Looks like the party was pretty intense. Any other ODs?"

"No one else in the house," a third paramedic said as he stepped outside. "Needle marks on the woman's jugular too."

"Damn," I said. Shooting straight into the jugular was a sign of extreme addiction; the next step was usually a fatal overdose. If the woman survived tonight, I doubted she'd make it to the end of the month. Her poor kid.

Bishop dragged his fingers down his short beard. "Shit."

"Naloxone?" I asked.

"Yes, ma'am. She's breathing, but barely, and not responsive."

"Thanks."

"Hope the girl isn't her kid," Bishop said.

"Me too."

We walked inside. The smell—a mix of mold, rotting food, feces, sex, and body odor—smacked me hard in the face. I'd take the smell of death over that concoction any day. I immediately pulled a face mask from my bag, but when I saw the little girl sitting with the fourth paramedic, I walked over to her before putting it on. Face masks scared kids, and I didn't want her to be any more scared than she already was.

I tapped the paramedic on the shoulder. "How's she doing?"

"She's a little dehydrated, so we gave her a juice box, but other than that, physically she appears to be fine."

I nodded. "I've got her."

He stood. "Yes, ma'am."

I crouched next to the little girl, my heart breaking for her. I'd seen too many discarded children lost in their parent's addiction, too young to understand. "Hey, sweetie." I pushed her blonde hair behind her ear. "My name is Rachel. I'm here to help everyone, but mostly you, okay?"

The little girl clutched a doll to her chest as tears streamed down her face.

"I want my mommy."

"I know you do, sweetie. Were you here with her?"

She nodded. "She was sleeping, but the men took her off the bed."

"We're going to take care of everything, okay?"

She nodded.

"What's your name, honey?"

"Emma."

"Emma is a pretty name. How old are you, Emma?"

She held up four fingers. "Five."

My heart hurt. "Emma, were there other people here with you and your mommy?"

She nodded slowly.

I swiped through my phone for Brad Pruitt's mugshot. "Can you tell me if you saw this man here tonight?"

She grabbed my phone with two tiny hands. Her fingernails needed a trim and a good cleaning. "I don't know. Mommy made me stay in here until she woke up."

"Is this where you live?"

She shook her head.

I hated her mother. No kid deserved a life like this. "You're a very smart girl, Emma. Give me just a second, and we'll get you outside and get you a big blanket to keep you warm in one of the cars, okay?"

"Uh-huh." Her little nose was red and swollen from crying. Tears fell down her cheeks. I wiped them with my thumb.

"What do other people call your mommy? Does she have another name? You know, like you're Emma and I'm Rachel? What's your mommy's other name?"

"Cindy."

"Do you have another name? Maybe one that comes after Emma?"

She nodded and said, "Hann-e-gan."

"Hannigan?"

"Uh-huh."

I exhaled. "You are even smarter than I thought, Emma Hannigan. You know that?"

"Uh-huh. Mommy says I'll be a movie star one day and I can take care of her for a change."

Mommy needed an ass-kicking. "We're going to take care of you and your mom, honey. I promise."

She wrapped her thin arms around my neck and squeezed with such strength, it brought tears to my eyes. I hugged her back as I gathered my emotions and carried her to the officer. "I'm never having kids," I muttered. "Take her outside and have your partner sit with her in the back of your cruiser, please. Get her some crackers or something. She's a stick."

"Yes, ma'am."

Bishop walked back into the room. "Poor kid." He tilted his head and stared at my face. "You okay?"

I wiped my cheek and wrapped my hair back in a hair-band. "Where's the father?"

"I'm assuming that's rhetorical?"

I exhaled and asked the patrol if the OD had an ID.

"Not that we found."

"Girl says her name is Emma Hannigan. Said her mom's name is Cindy. Child Services has probably seen the girl before."

He eyed my mask as I fixed it behind my ears. "You carry those around too?"

"Don't you?"

"Thought you used tissue?"

"I don't like tasting the smell of rotting food."

He chuckled. "But you don't mind the taste of dead bodies?"

I rolled my eyes. "I was kidding." Sort of. "I just don't like breathing in black mold. If you've got one, you should probably put it on, especially with how much you smoke."

"Ain't that the pot calling the kettle black," he said, and jogged outside to his vehicle.

I scanned the large living room. The rotting food smell was justified. Garbage almost completely covered the floor. Styrofoam food containers, McDonald's bags, Chick-fil-A bags, beer bottles, gas station coffee cups, and beat-up furniture wasn't my preferred décor, but drug addicts didn't care about that. And they definitely didn't care about mold. I slipped on a pair of gloves, but not because I was concerned about evidence. Crack houses are overwhelmed with insufficient evidence. Ashley could dust for prints indefinitely and we'd get hits on at least eighty percent of them, but they wouldn't do us any good. If Pruitt was here, he was long gone, and like the woman the EMTs carried out, his prints wouldn't tell us anything we needed to know. The best way to find Brad Pruitt was to keep eyes on his regular haunts. If he was still alive and in town, we'd find him. Addicts didn't wander far from their base.

I walked to a back bedroom and cringed at the sight of a ripped and stained mattress lying on the ground and framed by a scattering of used condoms, a sign that women used the mattress to turn tricks for drug money.

Bishop stepped up behind me and sighed heavily. "How can they live like this?"

"The final stage of addiction is pretty morbid."

"You consider this the end stage?"

I nodded. "Even if someone's only been using a short time, once they're hitting the house, it's hard to turn them back."

"You must have seen this a lot in Chicago."

"Routinely. It's hard seeing it through clear eyes, so I guess in a way it's a blessing for those who use the place. There's nothing romantic or comforting about the smells of addicts who'll trick for days on end for their next fix and never once consider finding a shelter for a shower. I've walked into these places and recovered hookers whose johns beat the shit out of them and they were too stoned to notice. When they sober up, they'll drag themselves back for more as long as they get enough cash for their next hit."

"It happens around here too, just not this close to home."

"You've never seen it?"

"Not sorry to admit I haven't."

"You're lucky. At that stage, they're too far gone for that kind of redemption."

"You really think that?"

"It's not just the drugs, it's also the process that gets them to this point. I'd see addicts racing through the streets of Chicago, their car full of users, parachuting to and from every known drug corner in the city just to cop a bag." I carefully picked up a used needle lying on the ground and set it on the table beside the bed. "The rush of adrenaline knowing their next fix is coming as they dodge cops, or better yet, narcon, is part of the fix itself."

"I can't believe Brad's hit this point."

"A lot of addicts get to this point because they can't resist the allure of what we called 'drug corner chaos.' I wouldn't be surprised if Brad fell victim to that." I faced him and spoke softly. "You might want to have a conversation with Andy. He should know his brother is at this level of addiction."

He nodded. "He doesn't like talking about his brother, you saw that."

"Doesn't mean he can't or shouldn't. He needs to know so he can be prepared for what's coming."

Bishop finally agreed. "I'm not getting Ashley on this. There's no point. She could find a thousand prints and all that would do is bog the department down with cases we don't have time to work."

"Agreed."

I pulled off my gloves as we walked outside. The little girl was sitting on the edge of the ambulance. I walked over and checked on her. "How you doing, Emma?"

"Good."

"I'm glad. These men are really nice, aren't they?"

"Uh-huh. They gave me juice boxes and crackers."

"That's awesome. They're going to take you with them, but I'm going to come check on you and make sure you're okay. I promised I'd take care of everything, and I'm going to do that, okay?"

"Yeah."

Bishop and I made arrangements for patrol to take Pruitt's photo door to door in the morning. If someone saw him, they might be able to say which direction he was headed.

11

The next morning, I woke to two texts, one from Sean and the other from Savannah. Sean said he understood duty called and we could all get together another time, which I thought was interesting since I hadn't actually suggested we get together in the first place. Savannah's said Sean looked devastated that he'd missed me. I read the messages at five a.m., and I didn't think they needed or wanted responses before dawn, so I didn't bother.

I tossed on a workout bra, one of Tommy's Chicago PD T-shirts, a pair of black running pants, and my running shoes, and headed over to Anytime Fitness to hit the treadmill for a quick run. I wasn't opposed to running in the cold. I'd done it for years in Chicago. But in Chicago the streets were a well-lit, flat grid. I could easily see vehicles coming from all directions, and usually ran on the sidewalks. Hamby didn't have sidewalks in my area, and the curved, dark roads weren't safe for runners in broad daylight let alone before sunrise. It was a risk I didn't want to take.

The gym was empty except for a diehard lifter, a man doing a ridiculous number of deadlifts with an obscene amount of weight on the bar. He grunted and groaned as he slammed the weights to the ground. I kicked up my pace and stared out the window while upping the volume on my earbuds to distract myself from his caveman grunts.

"The Twilight Zone" by Golden Earring filled my head, my pace regulating naturally to the highs and lows of the beat. A black Chevy Malibu caught my eye as it cruised through the empty lot with nothing but its parking lights on. It slowed to a crawl as it passed the gym's large windows. I removed my earbuds and reduced my running speed to examine it more carefully, taking in every detail I could. The tint on the windows was too dark to see any more than just the frame of someone sitting low in the driver's seat. A few seconds after it slowed, it took off fast enough to leave dust and gravel flying behind it.

I knew the vehicle on first sight. It was the same one that screwed with me and Bishop on Freemanville Road. "Son of a bitch," I said under my breath. I hit the speed button on the treadmill and sprinted at twelve miles per hour for as long as my abused lungs would allow. When they began burning and my throat all but closed, I reduced the speed and walked it out, gasping for air and sweating like a pig. I stepped off the treadmill and bent over with my hands on my knees, then grabbed the bars of the treadmill and stretched as I caught my breath.

"You okay, ma'am?"

I looked up at the man who'd been dropping weights just a few minutes ago. "Yeah, sorry." My breathing labored, I spoke in quick bursts. "Working at increasing my speed."

He nodded. "Don't let that idiot freak you out. It's probably someone compensating for a small di—you know."

I laughed. "I'm with you on that."

"And if he tried to do something, I'd have kicked his ass."

I was surprised he didn't beat his chest and grunt. The guy was all of five feet six inches tall, and even though he had some serious muscle mass, it was unlikely he'd know what to do with it. Fighting is a skill that has very little to do with muscle. "Yeah, I appreciate that, but I'm pretty sure I can handle myself."

He smiled, giving me a once-over in the process. He went to speak, but I stopped him by grabbing my purse on the floor and whipping out my badge. "Promise."

He nodded. "Oh, that's impressive."

Not really, I thought, but I figured it wasn't worth the debate. "Thanks."

As I gathered my things to leave, he suggested we meet up for a drink. "You could bring your handcuffs."

And there it was. Since my first day on the job, when guys found out I was a cop, they were either turned off, or turned on. Rarely was there an in-between. I rolled my eyes. "All those 'roids shrink your dick. I'll pass." I tossed my bag over my shoulder and walked out.

I took the long way home, thinking about the Malibu. Originally, I'd assumed it was some stupid teenager, but maybe I was wrong? Could the vehicle have been taunting me from the start? And if so, why? I hadn't had a big case since the Light murder. Could it be connected to that? Possible, but not likely, I thought. We'd cleaned house with that investigation, and most everyone attached was in jail or pending trial, and those who may have considered dipping their toes in the corrupt water had cleaned up their act.

I'd put a lot of people in jail. Murderers, rapists, drug dealers, money launderers, gang members, bank robbers, corrupt politicians. A few promised revenge, but nothing ever came from them. The only one with the power to push that button was former commissioner, Chris Petrowksi.

His last words to me at his sentencing trial echoed through my head. *Your time will come.* He'd promised retribution. Lenny assured me Petrowski was behaving, but we both knew he was too self-important to do his own dirty work. I took a deep breath and counted to ten. When that didn't help calm my nerves, I grabbed the pack of cigarettes from my bag, rolled down my windows, and lit one. Three long puffs later, I held the cigarette out the window, scolding myself for caving a few months ago and not having the desire or strength to kick the habit once again.

Tommy rested his head in my lap. "I think we're the only people in our precinct who don't smoke."

I smiled down at him while running my hand through his dark, curly hair. "What brought that up?"

"Your smell."

"I smell?"

He laughed. "Lavender and vanilla with a dash of pure Rachel."

"Pure Rachel?"

"You know, that unique-to-you scent. Everyone's got one. It's pheromones."

"You're lucky I smell so good. It's because you're catching me after a shower. Had it been after work, I'd smell like—"

"Secondhand smoke and exhaust fumes."

"And stale coffee."

"That too."

He smiled up at me. "Promise you'll never start."

"Why would I?" I asked. "You've made it clear you won't kiss an ashtray."

"People change."

"Then I promise you I'll never change."

"I'll hold you to that." He sat up and kissed me. "Mmm. Minty fresh." He wrapped his arms around me and kissed me harder.

I shook the memory from my mind.

Andy stood outside my front door with two large Dunkin' coffees in hand.

"Wow! You're early. It's not even seven." Had Bishop updated him on Brad?

He walked into the garage as I pulled my vehicle inside. I closed the garage door and we walked in together. "I'm assuming Bishop called you?"

"No. What's going on?"

I was still sweating from my run, and that, combined with the cold air from smoking, gave me the chills, so I grabbed a sweatshirt from my bedroom and tossed it over my head. Andy waited in my family room.

"We haven't located Brad, but we did get a hit on a location last night." I sipped my coffee, relishing in the warmth it sent rushing through my insides.

"But you didn't find him?"

"Not yet, but we will. These things take time."

"I don't think my brother had anything to do with the dead man."

I breathed in deeply through my nose. "I don't think he did either, and neither does Bishop. Addicts tend to share supplies, and it's highly probable that's why Brad's prints were on the syringe."

"But you're still looking for him."

"We have some questions. It's just procedure. And I think Bishop wants to find him for personal reasons."

"Finding my brother won't do any good for anyone, especially my sister. She thinks she can help him, but he's beyond help. Can't you all just drop it?"

"The place we went to last night is a drug house. It's in pretty bad shape, too. If Brad's hanging there, he's probably not interested in help."

"Anyone there know him?"

"Not by the time we got there. A woman OD'd with her kid sitting right there. I'll follow up this morning to see if she made it, but it didn't look good."

He was obviously more interested than he could admit.

"Damn." He closed his eyes and then slowly opened them. "What happened to the kid?"

"Child Services got her at the hospital. I'm following up in an hour."

"The place was pretty bad, huh?"

"I haven't seen a place like that since I started here, Andy. The woman shot up in her jugular. That's a longtime user. Hard to get more addicted than that."

"Shit. You think my brother's at that level?"

"It's probable."

"I read once they hit a certain place, there's no turning back."

"Sometimes people hit rock bottom, but it's still not enough, and sometimes, they just hover over it until it's too late."

He leaned against the back of my couch. "You've had experience with this in Chicago, right?"

I nodded.

"Tell me the truth, what are the odds of an addict recovering from this kind of heroin addiction?"

"No one recovers from any addiction unless they want to," I said, thinking about my own struggles with smoking. "Long-term heroin use damages the body, but if someone chooses to stop, some of that is reparable, at least to a small degree. What isn't reparable is the damage to the brain. A lot of the time, people have used so much for so long they're unable to stop because their brain needs the drug to function."

"Brad's been an addict for ten years."

"I'm sorry."

"He'll never stop. He's had emotional issues his entire life. Made up this bullshit story about hurting his back and needing painkillers. But I read about it. You can't become addicted to pain meds when you're in pain. The addiction comes if you keep taking the medicine after the pain stops."

"That's correct."

"But he claimed the pain never went away, so he probably wasn't ever in any."

"Maybe he meant the emotional pain."

He nodded. "I guess. I never thought of it that way. I know he had struggles; I just didn't know how bad they were."

"For a lot of people, drug addiction is a disease. Your brother's not a bad person, he's ill."

"And his illness drives him to do bad things."

I couldn't argue with that. "Well yes, but—"

"Disease or not, I'm not sure I can forgive him."

"You're allowed to feel that way."

He finished the last of his coffee. "If I asked y'all to stop looking for him, would you?"

"We still have a few questions, and we have a BOLO out on him. A BOLO is a—"

"Be on the lookout." He smiled. "Best friend's a cop, remember?"

"Right. I can't really say much about the guy who OD'd, but I can say we don't think your brother played a part in his death."

"So why are you still looking for him?"

"Just want our ducks in a row," I lied. "Nothing unusual."

He nodded. "Good. I guess I'd better get to work."

"Right there with you. I'm jumping in the shower."

"No worries. I've got to get some stuff out of my truck. I'll let myself back in."

"Feel free to go through the garage," I said, and closed my bedroom door behind me.

12

I called Child Services on the way to the department.

"Her father is on his way from South Carolina now," the woman said.

I breathed a sigh of relief. "Where is she now?"

"In the playroom here."

"Any news on her mother?"

"She didn't make it."

I exhaled. "May I come by and visit with Emma? I told her I'd take care of her, so I'd like to follow through."

"Of course. Her father should be here soon, so I suggest you come now."

"On my way," I said, making a U-turn and heading to Roswell.

Emma sat in a child-size rocking chair holding a doll wrapped in a blanket. She whispered, "She's sleeping like my mommy."

I crouched next to her. "I hear your daddy's coming to get you. That's exciting." I whispered so I wouldn't wake up the doll.

"Uh-huh."

The Child Services woman tapped me on the shoulder. "Mr. Reynolds, Emma's father, is here now. Would you like to talk to him before he comes in?"

I nodded. "Thank you."

Mr. Reynolds was a heck of a lot more put-together than Cindy Hannigan. He wore a white button-down shirt and a pair of dress pants. "Mr. Reynolds, I'm Detective Ryder. I was part of the call where we found Emma."

"How's my daughter?" The sadness in his voice was obvious.

"She's okay. A little skinny, but okay."

"Cindy didn't make it."

"I'm sorry."

"I expected this to happen someday. I've tried to get custody of Emma, but Cindy never showed up for court. I hired three private investigators to look for her, but they never found her."

I handed him my card. "If there's anything I can do to help, just call me. Do me a favor, take Emma for a checkup."

"You think she's sick?"

"I think better safe than sorry."

"Understood."

I nodded. "Good luck, Mr. Reynolds."

As I moved to leave, he said, "Detective?"

I turned around.

"Thank you."

"You're welcome."

I sat in Jimmy's office with Bishop. "Cindy Hannigan died last night."

"What about her daughter?" Bishop asked.

"Turns out her father's been looking for her. He came in from South Carolina this morning."

"You meet him?" Jimmy asked.

I nodded. "Clean-cut guy. Dressed nice. Ran his license plate in the Child Services parking lot. No record. Not even a speeding ticket."

"That girl deserves a stable home," Bishop said.

"Right," Jimmy said.

"So, I think we all agree we're chasing a wild horse. Brad will show up eventually, but even the preliminary autopsy can't prove he forced the drugs on Jeffers," I said.

"I'm inclined to agree with you," Jimmy said. "But we keep the BOLO on him just in case." He looked at Bishop. "Thoughts?"

"Last night I would have agreed, but now I'm not so sure."

"Why?" I asked.

"Been thinking about it, and things don't add up. The out-of-state dealer, the ice. I feel like we're missing something here, and I think we should dig a little deeper. I'm not saying a full-blown investigation, but if something's happening, we should do our due diligence to find out."

Jimmy tapped a pencil on his desk. "Listen, I understand what you're trying to do. You want to help your best friend's brother, but this isn't the way to go about it. We looked into the vic's death just to verify what we already knew. It's a waste of resources to do anything more than keep the BOLO out."

"Andy doesn't want us looking for his brother," I said.

Bishop eyed me suspiciously. "How do you know?"

"He told me this morning."

"But what if we can get him help?"

"We can't help someone who doesn't want it."

"She's right," Jimmy said. "We're closing the investigation. The coroner already gave his COD. Let's not push back on it." He eyed my partner. "I know you want to help, Rob, but you need to let this go."

Bishop nodded. "I just worry about Allison. She doesn't deserve this."

"Neither does Emma, but we could help her, and we did."

Bishop exhaled, resolved to the fact that our hands were tied. Though for me, having my hands tied was more of a challenge than anything. "That's something."

"You know," I said, trying to alter the air in the room. "I could go for a rabid teenager case right about now."

Jimmy laughed. "Hamby teenagers know they can't get away with that crap on my watch."

Bishop snickered. "Watch what you say. I hear karma's a bitch."

I raised my eyebrows. "Ain't that the truth!"

Bishop and I made a coffee run, and I grabbed three dozen donuts for the pit. He grunted the start of a laugh, but I cut him off. "It's not a bribe."

"Well then, that's awfully kind of you." He smirked, but his tone seemed forced.

I didn't push him to talk about his feelings. If he wanted to, he'd do so on his own. "Okay, fine. I had them sprinkled with fairy dust. The guys will see me differently with the first bite."

"Fairy dust or Ex-Lax?"

I laughed. "Wouldn't that be awesome?"

"Not particularly considering I've already eaten one."

My cell phone rang. I checked the caller ID. "It's Andy," I said, glancing at Bishop.

He exhaled. "Maybe he's heard from his brother?"

I answered. "Hey, what's up?"

"I think you need to come by."

"Everything okay?"

"I'm not sure," he said. "I ran out to get a bagel, and when I came back, something wasn't right. I think someone came in when I was gone."

"Are you in the house now?"

"Yeah, but I checked around, and no one's here. I can't see how anyone got inside. I locked the door when I left, and it doesn't look like anything's been taken."

"What makes you think someone was there?"

"There's a necklace hanging on my ladder."

"A necklace?"

"Yeah. A big gold chain, the real gaudy type, with a skull pendant."

Shit. I eyed Bishop. He furrowed his brow.

"Okay, I need you to go outside, get in your truck, and meet us at the entrance. You understand?"

"Sure," he said. "But whoever was here is long gone."

"Do it anyway, please."

"Yes, ma'am."

"We'll be there in a few," I said, and disconnected the call. "Let's go." I called out on dispatch and requested backup.

Bishop rolled down his window and stuck the cherry on the roof of the car. "You think it's the same kind of pendant as the one we found at Brad's hotel?"

"We'll see." But yes, I did.

"Maybe Brad left it? You know, to let Andy know he was there?"

"Does Brad usually enter homes illegally and leave vague gang symbols as a hello for family?"

He sighed. "Good point."

Bishop slowed and rolled down his window as he pulled up next to Andy's truck. "You okay?"

"Right as rain," Andy said.

"Did you touch anything?" I asked.

"Nope. Went about my business, though. When I saw the necklace, I did a double take, then took a quick look around and gave you a call."

I nodded. "I'll text you with the all-clear."

"Sure thing."

Bishop insisted on entering my place before me. He drew his weapon and called out, "Police."

We ran a check of each room, but Andy was right. The place was empty.

"All clear," I yelled from my bedroom.

"All clear," he replied.

We gave Andy the go-ahead to come back inside so we could ask him a few more questions. I snapped on a pair of latex gloves and examined the pendant necklace. It was the same as the one we'd found at Brad's hotel.

"Like I said, could be his brother," Bishop whispered.

"Don't think so."

"Maybe he owes Andy money, got a hold of a few of the pendants, and, I don't know, figured they were worth something, so he left one as payment?"

"Maybe," I said. But, no.

Andy pointed to the bookcases. "Wasn't there a photo of you and your, uh, husband there?"

I swallowed hard while staring at the spot where the photo of me and Tommy at Navy Pier once sat.

"Did you move it?" Bishop asked.

Andy shook his head. "Pretty sure it was there when I left."

"No." I clenched my jaw and then spat out my next words. "Son of a bitch!"

Bishop eyed me. "Maybe you put it somewhere else?"

"No."

"Maybe you were dusting, and it got moved?"

"I said no." I examined the rest of the room carefully. Nothing else was missing, and I knew.

I knew the wolf was at my door.

13

Bishop took a bottled water from my refrigerator. "Let's just look around, okay? Who knows, maybe the fish knocked it over trying to escape." He walked back to the main living area and searched for the picture inside the trunk, behind the couch pillows, and under the cushions, but no photo. "Maybe the fish ate it?"

He was trying to lighten things up, but his efforts rested on my last nerve. "Real funny, jackass."

He crouched down on one knee, groaning like he'd never be able to move again, and checked under my couch. "Hold on." He stuck his arm as far under as it would go and cursed. "Shit, it's stuck, but there's something here. I can feel it with my fingertips."

I swore under my breath and picked up the side of the couch. "Is it the photo?"

He pulled out the frame and set it on the old trunk I used as a coffee table. The glass was broken, but the photo was still inside. "Guess it got misplaced after all."

"How?" I walked to the shelf and pointed to where the frame belonged. I turned and eyed the couch. No, it didn't.

That much I knew. I grabbed the frame from him, removed the photo from it, and tossed the broken bits into the trash.

"I, uh, I guess it's possible I did that," Andy said.

"Without knowing?" I asked.

He cringed. "I did hit something with the ladder, but I didn't see what it was, so I just figured it was nothing."

Bishop watched me as I studied the ladder, calculating the probability of its swing and where it could potentially send objects flying. Math doesn't lie, and the possibility of the ladder knocking down the photo and sending it flying under the couch were slim to none. Someone had deliberately left the necklace and moved the photo to give me a message.

"There's no sign of entry," Bishop said.

"Fine," I said, planting my hands on my hips. "Let's say Andy did accidentally hit the frame. Did he accidentally leave the skull pendant and chain on the ladder too?"

Bishop and Andy stared at each other. Bishop started to speak, but I stopped him. I needed to listen, to smell, to see if the air in the room felt different. My gut could tell me what to do. I just needed to give it the chance.

I walked back to my combination office and den, where I'd put Tommy's grandfather's oak desk and antique rolling chair. I checked the windows one more time, but Bishop was right. There was no way anyone could get in through any of the second-floor windows without a ladder, and no way they could access the garage, French doors, or even the front door without breaking in.

I walked back into my family room. "Whoever did this knows how to pick a lock." I took out my flashlight and carefully examined my front door's lock. "Scratch marks. It's definitely been picked."

Lenny's words played on a broken record in my head.

We've got eyes on him. Petrowski is behaving. My gut told me something entirely different, and it wasn't usually wrong.

The update on Brad Pruitt weighed heavily on his brother even though he'd tried to pretend otherwise. "Maybe Brad came by while I was gone?"

I shook my head. "Addicts aren't typically lockpickers. And if you haven't talked to him, how would he know where to find you?"

"Good point," Andy said. "But he's disappeared before and then showed up where I was working. He can be gone but still know what's going on with us."

"This isn't your brother, Andy. I'm sorry. But hey, why don't you take the rest of the day off? This stuff can wait, and we've got to get our crime scene techs here to dust for prints."

"I'd rather stay, if that's possible."

"I really want the place checked, and it would be hard for them to do that with you here."

"I understand."

"How long were you gone?" Bishop asked him.

Andy shrugged. "Maybe twenty minutes?"

Bishop glanced at me.

"It's entirely possible if they know what they're doing," I said.

He nodded, then smiled at his best friend. "Go ahead and head out. I'll call you if I hear anything about Brad."

"Appreciate it, buddy."

We walked outside with him and checked the area before letting him leave, just in case.

"Whoever did this was watching," Bishop said. "Looks like Brad's gotten himself tied up with someone bad, and now he's on the run, so they're coming to his family looking for him."

I bit my fingernail. "I don't think so. When Andy left, they picked the lock, went in, left the necklace, and tossed my photo under the couch. They locked the door before leaving. If someone came looking for Brad, they wouldn't take the time to do any of that, especially lock the door when they left."

"Maybe it's a trial run for a robbery. They check the lock, see if they can access the home, do a quick search to determine if it's worth it, accidentally knock over a photo, and then book out."

"This isn't a home casing. This is a message."

"Okay, I can give you a suspicious entry and—"

"The lock was picked. It's not a gimmie. It's a fact. And that pendant has shown up three times now."

"Yes, and each time there's been a connection to Brad Pruitt, not you."

"You can't be serious."

"Follow the facts. The fact is a homeless addict who used one of Brad Pruitt's needles had one on him. The fact is the room Brad Pruitt rented and abandoned had one on the table. The fact is Andy Pruitt, Brad's brother, is working at your house, and a pendant showed up on his ladder. You factor into none of that except for your house."

"The skull pendant is a common Hispanic gang symbol in Chicago with ties to the Mexican cartel."

"And?"

"And I've had very specific dealings with them before."

"I'm sure we'll find they're the same here, then. Those things don't vary much between states."

"You're wrong, Bishop. This isn't about Pruitt. This is about me." I walked over to a small table against the wall and checked underneath. Tommy's Sig Sauer still hung from his self-made shelf. I felt better knowing it was still there.

After two hours of dusting, I let Ashley off the hook.

She wiped her hands on a cloth. "I don't mind doing this."

"Run what you've already found. I'll make sure Andy gets to the department to have his prints taken for reference."

"You sure?"

I nodded. "I'm pretty sure you're not going to find anything."

As she cleaned up her stuff, I took another quick shower and changed outfits. Something about someone being in my house uninvited made me feel gross.

An hour later, Ashley met me just outside the pit. "You were right. There were no prints on the necklace or pendant, and most of the prints on the frame were smudged, but I was able to pull up one of yours and Bishop's. Prints on the door frame and handle weren't clear enough to capture even partials, which is really disappointing, and the ones on the ladder don't come up in AFIS. Mr. Pruitt is coming by, and I'm betting they belong to him. If you'd like, I can go back and dust some more."

I squeezed her shoulder. "You're awesome, and you really need to work for a bigger department. Thank you, but I don't think we'll find anything."

She shrugged. "Let me know what else I can do."

"Sure thing, and thank you, Ash. I really appreciate you."

She blushed and walked away.

I walked into the pit with a feeling of dread hanging over me like a cloud, a stomach sick with weariness, and a fake smile painted on my face. I wouldn't show any fear, not to people I knew or associated with, or strangers. Someone was watching me, and they couldn't see me falter or I'd lose.

All eyes were on me. I didn't go all out with my makeup and clothing today, but I did keep my hair down, swiped some mascara on my lashes, and wore a pair of black spandex dress pants to match my white shirt and black blazer. I owned five black blazers, seven pairs of spandex dress pants, and countless black and white long-sleeve shirts. I'd even worn the same pair of black ankle boots, but my toes weren't screaming as loud as last time. Maybe there was a God after all?

I made eye contact with as many of the guys as possible, laughing a little each time they quickly looked away. Men always gave women so much power without even realizing it. If women dropped their insecurities, they'd realize that power and it would change the world.

Dr. Barron sat in Jimmy's office. He waved me in as I walked by. "Detective, come on in, please."

As I walked in, Jimmy said, "Close the door, please."

I sat beside him. "Hey, Doc. What's up?" When Cochran was the chief, I'd count to ten—if I could make it—every time I had to deal with him. I didn't do that so much these days, but something about that wave and the looks on their faces gave me pause.

"Alpharetta found a body near the recycling plant," Jimmy said.

I breathed in deeply. "Brad Pruitt?"

"There was no ID, but the responding officer knows Pruitt and is pretty sure it's him."

"Pretty sure?"

Barron eyed Jimmy.

I exhaled. "Let me guess. Vic was beaten to death?"

Barron nodded.

"Okay. They can run prints, then."

The chief shook his head, and I knew what that meant. When someone didn't want a body ID'd, they'd clip off the fingers. If they had the time, they'd burn them while the person was still alive, adding that extra torture of the vic knowing their family may never know what happened.

"Shit. Me and Bishop should go. If it's Pruitt, it's ours."

The chief leaned back in his chair. "We're sending Michels with you for this."

I raised an eyebrow. "What about Rob?"

He shook his head. "Bishop's too close. He can't be objective."

"That's not going to stop him from wanting to go."

Bishop walked in just then. "I'm going."

The chief eyed him carefully. "You sure you can handle this?"

Bishop showed no emotion. "Yes."

Jimmy nodded. "If it turns out to be Pruitt, we need to handle it two-hundred percent by the book or the DA will have my ass."

Seeing your best friend's brother virtually unrecognizable would render anyone unobjective, but Bishop was a good detective, and if he could identify the vic as Pruitt, we needed him there.

Barron stood. "I'll head on over. Dispatch requested Alpharetta's medical examiner, who's already on scene, but if the case gets transferred to us, I'll go ahead and perform the autopsy."

Michels knocked on the door and announced himself.

"Come on in," Jimmy said.

Michels stood to the side of Bishop, his hands clasped behind his back.

"We're putting you on as an assist with Detectives Ryder and Bishop," Jimmy said. "Consider it pre-training."

"Yes, sir."

"Let's roll," Bishop said. "I'll drive."

"Where is this place?"

"Just up there on the right," Bishop said. "We'll go in the back entrance, but there's a main entrance near the road."

The light changed to green. Bishop turned on his blinker. "I used to bring cans here when I was a kid."

"Really? Did they pay for them?"

"Yup. If I worked hard enough, I could clear five bucks."

"How many cans?"

"More than my mother wanted to keep stored in the garage. Third time I tried to do it, she tossed them out. Said she needed the space for my dad's lawn equipment."

"Too bad. You could have made millions."

He smiled. "That's a lot of Coke cans."

We arrived a few minutes before Barron. Bishop knew the Alpharetta officers on scene, but neither of us knew the medical examiner. The Fulton County Medical Examiner's main office was in Atlanta, but because of the size of the county, each city had its own medical examiner.

Bishop stared at the badly beaten body propped up against a recycling dumpster. "Damn."

"Looks like he's been dead for at least twelve hours," the medical examiner said.

I slipped on a pair of gloves. "That could put him at the house last night like APD's bust said."

Bishop nodded. "That's what I'm thinking."

Michels's eyes almost popped out of his head. "Fuckin' A, that's disgusting." He covered his mouth and gagged.

Keeping my tone professional, I said, "Walk away until you can get it together." I didn't want him making the department look bad in front of Alpharetta's guys.

I examined the scene carefully, holding my hand over my mouth and nose to block the smell before finally reaching into my bag and putting on my mask.

"Good idea." The Alpharetta officer smiled. "It's pretty bad."

"How bad can plastic and aluminum smell?"

"This is real garbage. People toss a lot of shit in their recycling. I feel bad for the people who have to go through this shit."

"They've got my respect."

For a garbage center, the area surrounding the dumpsters was fairly clean. I looked at the lights off in the distance. "Was probably dark enough for the lights to not do much, and given the location, I don't think anyone from the road would have seen the action."

"There's not a lot of blood on the ground," Michels said. He'd gotten his gag reflex under control.

He was right. The only blood near the vic was on his person, with a few drops staining the ground next to him. Those were likely leftovers from when he'd been killed or his body parts—just his fingers, to the best of my knowledge —had been removed. In most cases, vics didn't bleed postmortem, but a few drops here and there happened all the time. Leftover juice, Garcia used to call it.

"He wasn't beaten here, and he wasn't dragged, so someone dropped him here." I walked behind the two large recycling dumpsters for a look. "Clear back here too."

"We believe he was killed somewhere else too," the Alpharetta officer said.

"When did the plant open?" I asked.

"Employees get here at six, opens at ten to the public."

"We can process the scene, if you'd like," another officer said. "We've got tech coming, but we've been told to give it to you if you think it's your guy."

"It's ours," Bishop said.

I leaned toward him. "You can tell?"

"I'll know for sure in a minute," he whispered back.

I raised an eyebrow.

The medical examiner stood. "Looks like this one's yours, Dr. Barron. Would you like to take him?"

"Let's get him to the main office. We can process faster there."

He was right. Things always moved quicker when done at the larger facilities. We'd also have access to testing right there instead of sending things out. It was a smart move on Barron's part, but we still needed to take a look and put together a theory. "Give us a bit, will you? We need photos."

"Of course," the other medical examiner said.

"Michels, get photos of all the entrances that have a direct path to this area." I glanced up at the two buildings, one in front and one behind the bins, making note of the cameras. "This is a city recycling center, right?" I said to the Alpharetta patrolman.

"Yes, ma'am."

"It's 'detective.'" Then I turned and hollered to Michels as he walked away with his cell phone in hand. "Michels, when you're done, tell the office staff we're going to need to see the videos." I could tell by the bounce in his step he was stoked to be helping.

"On it."

The victim lay on his back, his left arm snapped at the elbow and both of his legs bent in unnatural directions. He was missing a boot. His jacket, a thin Columbia brand zip fleece, was slashed, revealing similar slashes to the torso. The clothing was bloody, telling me the slashes happened premortem.

Bishop crouched down next to the body. His face had been beaten so badly, it was hard to recognize much other than his hair color. The jaw was detached on both sides, his eyes were bloodshot, and his nose and lips were swollen lumps beyond recognition. Bishop stared at the missing digits on his hands. "No blood leakage. Fingers were cut postmortem."

I squatted next to him. "Bishop, let me do this."

"I've got it." He looked at the two doctors for the go-ahead. "May I?"

They both nodded. Bishop gently rolled the vic's right side upward. "No blood as far as I can tell. He was definitely dropped here." He carefully lifted the jacket arm and pointed to the tattoo. "It's him."

"We'll handle the rest," Barron said.

"Ashley's on her way," I said.

"Wait," Bishop said. "Got a bag?"

Barron handed me a small Ziplock bag, and I opened it for Bishop.

"Hairs." He picked three individual hairs from Brad's jacket, examining each one before placing it in the bag. "Too dark to be his."

Michels jogged over. "Only two ways in and out of the entire lot. Back entrance, with a locked gate, and the front. Front's got a gate too, but—"

"It was opened by APD," I said.

"You sure?" Bishop asked.

I nodded. "Already asked."

Bishop held out his hand to Michels. "Show me the locks."

Michels flipped through the photos, stopping at the one of the front entrance. "Standard padlock."

"Easy to pick," I said. Though no lock is exactly difficult. It just takes patience and practice.

Bishop eyed me. "Two locks picked with a Pruitt in the picture sound fishy to you?"

"Sure does," I said.

Michels swiped to another photo. "I also found these fresh tire tracks, and before you ask, I've already done a visual comparison to the treads on all the vehicles here. They don't match."

My eyes widened. "Looks like Michels here's been watching his nighttime crime shows."

Bishop snorted. I was relieved he could still laugh.

"I'm going to make detective," Michels said.

"Baby steps," I said, smiling. "Let's see how you handle the autopsy."

His face turned green.

"I'm not sure he can pass the test," Bishop said.

"The secretary inside is getting us access to the videos," Michels said. "Said to come on in."

We walked the short distance to the no-frills office. I wouldn't expect much from a recycling center, but this place took the concept of lowering expectations too far. The three desks held computers, a printer older than me, and stacks of paper. None of the desks had a chair. Two large folding tables served no purpose other than junk storage—old newspapers and Coke bottles, again older than me. The office person, a full-figured woman, sat in a folding chair at a small fold-out desk with a computer and some basic office supplies. The chair had to be hell on her hips. Her shaking hands and sweaty forehead were clear signs she was nervous, though she tried very hard to stay calm. "The videos are on the computer on that desk in there," she said, pointing to the least crowded of the desks.

We watched last night's video for the back entrance, but it gave us nothing other than a few coyotes.

"Those things scare the hell out of me," Michels said.

I glanced at Bishop, who shrugged. "Have you ever considered a desk job?" I asked.

"Why?"

"No reason," I said, though dead bodies and smells would top the list of reasons he might want to consider it.

The video for the front entrance, the last on the loop, was much better. A black SUV pulled up to the gate, and a man dressed in all black, with his head down and hiding under a plain black baseball cap, jumped out of the back door. He jogged over to the lock, stuck something in it, twisted it a bit, and then popped the lock. The car drove through, and he closed the gate and hopped back in the car without locking the padlock again. The vehicle had no plates.

"Son of a bitch!" Bishop yelled.

I placed my hand on his arm and spoke to Michels. "What about the cameras by the dumpsters? Where are those videos?"

The woman, who had been standing in the doorway, spoke. "Those haven't worked in months. I keep tellin' the boss we need them fixed, but he says it's not in the budget."

Bishop dropped the F-bomb.

Michels couldn't believe we could stop for lunch knowing we'd be viewing an autopsy shortly after. Bishop didn't eat much, which I attributed to nerves, but I scarfed down a tuna salad sandwich like I hadn't eaten in days.

"You always eat that fast?" Michels asked.

"A detective can't live off coffee and donuts, Michels. That's the best lesson I can teach you."

He pushed his turkey club aside. "I can't do it."

I smiled. "Don't want it coming back to haunt you downtown?"

"F you, Ryder." He said it with a smile.

"That's Detective Ryder," I said, my smile just as big as his. "Officer Michels."

Bishop wrapped up his barely eaten sandwich and stood. "Let's go. They're probably halfway through by now."

Doubtful, but I understood his desire to get there ASAP.

The Fulton County Medical Examiner's offices were located in downtown Atlanta, about thirty miles from us. That thirty miles could take two hours depending on the time of day, traffic patterns, and whether some idiot cut someone off and caused an accident. Those traffic times were nothing if the city got a little snow or rain.

We got lucky, hitting post- and pre-rush-hour traffic, but Bishop complained the entire way, and with good reason. From the moment he entered State Route 400 traffic, it was stop and go and a mile of construction here, another there. He explained ad nauseum how Atlanta and the surrounding suburbs burst to life years ago, and the state and coordinating locals failed to create an infrastructure to handle that extended community growth, which just made things worse for everyone. We merged onto Interstate 85 and slowed to a stop.

"Damn it," he said. Thirty minutes later we finally got off the interstate and made a series of turns before arriving at the medical examiner's offices.

Barron and the other medical examiner met us in the reception area and walked us back to the victim's remains. I stayed focused on the surroundings, paying attention to everything I could reasonably soak in with my senses. Detective work is ninety percent gut, five percent law, and five percent clues. My gut hit all of my senses, bouncing from my eyes, ears, and nose before landing in the pit of my stomach. The cop in me never went to sleep. I was always on alert, always paying attention and checking behind myself. It was the way of life.

The head Fulton medical examiner stepped out of a room and introduced himself. Barron already knew him, but I was surprised Bishop did too. As the big guy, I guess it was the ME's job to know his own people and the staff of the departments those people served. It was unusual to me, but I appreciated it. He was older than Barron and carried himself like a pro. Nose up, chin out, back straight. Appearances mattered, and he'd nailed his. "If I can be of assistance," he said, "please feel free to ask." He nodded politely and walked away.

Barron had already done the preliminary work and opened the chest cavity. Michels coughed, and Barron eyed him carefully. "You sure you're up for this?"

"Yes, sir."

"Very well. There are three garbage receptacles in the

lab. If you feel this might be an issue, please bring over the one on the opposite side of the sink. It's specifically for this kind of situation."

I pressed my lips together to hide my smile.

He opened the door to the exam room. "I'll tell you where I am so far."

Brad Pruitt lay on the metal table with his insides exposed.

Bishop stepped back. Michels rushed to the garbage can and tossed his cookies. I've seen a lot of death in my life, but Pruitt's was one of the worst. This was sheer violent anger. Rage. Not a typical drug deal gone bad or even the repercussions of a debt not paid.

The facial damage appeared worse than a few hours ago, and we were now privy to the slashes in the torso, which were jagged and rough, like someone had taken a large, dull knife, shoved it in Pruitt's gut, and pushed up with force.

Michels stepped back. "God." He coughed and gagged. "Who does this kind of shit?"

After closer examination of Brad's face, I said, "Either someone's got a mean hook, or they used a blunt object on his jaw."

"Most likely a baseball bat. If you look at the markings, you'll note the round edges consistent with a bat, though I've yet to find anything to suggest wood or aluminum. I'll pick through the skin and see if any particles remain. If it was a wooden bat, I'll likely find something."

I nudged Bishop in the arm and whispered, "You okay?"

"I'm fine," he said, his voice emotionless.

"In my brief review of the remains, I feel comfortable saying the weapon was all over the victim's torso and legs, but there's more, and we'll get there in a moment." Barron pointed to small welts and contusions under the victim's armpits. "His muscles were badly beaten. Of course, I'll have to run blood tests, but there's a strong possibility his injuries led to his death."

"Are you suggesting rhabdomyolysis?" I asked.

Barron nodded. "At this point, given the condition of his body upon visual examination, the evident advanced deterioration of his internal organs from a simple cursory review, and his known drug addiction, I believe there is a good chance. However, I am only making an estimated assumption, so I will not say for sure until I've done a thorough examination."

"Understood," I said.

"What exactly is rhabdomyolysis?" Michels asked. "Does that mean he was beaten to death, because that's what I'm seeing." He caught Bishop's eyes and looked at the ground.

"More like a heart attack from the beating. When the skeletal muscle is so damaged, it breaks down quickly, causing leakage of various muscle proteins, one being myoglobin, which in this case, led to kidney failure." He added "quickly" again after a breath. "Again, this is a preliminary death evaluation, but I feel comfortable saying he likely wasn't conscious during the stabbings."

"Thank God," Bishop said.

"That doesn't mean the jagged stab wounds are postmortem."

Michels turned around and coughed.

"Did you find evidence of vomit?" I asked.

He eyed me with intent. "You're familiar with this?"

"Yes, sir. Rhabdomyolysis is common with long-term drug use such as Mr. Pruitt's."

He agreed. "As I said, the rapid depletion of myoglobin was likely caused from the severe beating, evidenced from the damage over his entire body. I've only briefly examined his clothing, and I have an assistant doing further examination, but I can safely say there is evidence of vomit."

"And he had no ID in his clothing? Nothing written on the tags, maybe?"

"This isn't kindergarten, Ryder," Bishop said. "And why is it relevant anyway?"

"Homeless shelters tag clothing. If the vic's been to one recently and they washed his clothes, he'd have his name in them. If the ink is dark enough, it could mean he'd had them washed recently. It can help with our timeline of events."

"No ID on his person or clothing, just a necklace in his back pocket."

"Necklace?" I asked. "May I see it?"

He walked over to the metal table a few feet away and returned with a small bag. He removed a gold necklace with a skull pendant. I looked briefly at Bishop, who'd pressed his lips together.

When he spoke, his voice was rough, like he needed to clear his throat. "Does he have any defensive wounds?"

"His hands were bound with electrical tape, which I believe was removed postmortem. There is evidence of the sticky residue on his pants also, but again, it appears to have been removed postmortem."

"That doesn't make sense," Bishop said. "Why would they take the time to do that?"

"To make a statement," I said.

"They beat him to death. Isn't that statement enough?"

Not usually, I thought.

"If it's okay with you, I'd like to continue with the autopsy." Barron glanced at Michels. "Perhaps he should wait outside."

Bishop nodded. "When do you expect a final report?"

"I understand your need for urgency. I'll pull some strings at the lab and see if we can get the bloodwork back in a day or two. Sooner, if possible."

"I'd appreciate that," Bishop said.

"Why didn't we stay?" I asked as we drove back to the station.

Bishop checked his rearview window. "He's too green," he said, referring to Michels in the back seat.

"I'm not green," he replied defensively. "I'm shooting for detective."

"Not that kind of green," Bishop said. "Physically green. Like your face."

"He's right," I said, examining him closely.

Bishop swerved in and out of traffic, slamming on his brakes and speeding up, letting his emotions dictate his aggressiveness. When Michels's eyes widened and he leaned forward, I said, "He's going to be sick! Pull over, now!"

He swerved to the side of the highway and Michels pushed his door open, leaned out, and lost his cookies. I felt for the guy. It's one thing seeing a DOA, but it's another when the DOA is missing appendages and his insides are sitting on top of his stomach.

"Sorry," he said.

"It happens." I handed him a tissue, noting only a few remained in my little package. "This is the best I've got at the moment."

"Thanks," he said, wiping his mouth. "I've just never seen anything like that before. I'm not sure I'll ever stop seeing it."

"It's not easy," I said. "You have to learn to compartmentalize that kind of stuff."

"Is that what you do?"

"Best I can." I shrugged. "At some point you become kind of immune, seeing the remains as the biggest piece of the puzzle, and if you're lucky, you can crack jokes."

"There's nothing funny about the loss of life," Bishop said.

"No, there isn't, but when you've seen as much death as I have, you figure out how to process it."

Bishop had already pulled off the exit and was heading toward the station. We dropped everyone off, gave Chief Abernathy an update, and sat in my partner's cubby brainstorming how to give Andy and Allison the bad news.

"I think they should be together," he said.

Contrary to public opinion, law enforcement doesn't just hop in their cruiser and drop the bad news on the front porch of a deceased's family. We treat every death individually, and each notification selfishly snatches a piece of our souls. I don't like calling myself an expert, but I've given the bad news enough to be considered one. Bishop, on the other hand, wasn't as experienced, and given his personal connection, I bulldozed my way in.

"Andy's still at my place. If we call Allison and ask her to meet us there, she's going to know something's up."

"Andy will think the same if we call him."

I sighed. "I think we should handle this separately but at the same time. If we don't, whoever we go to first will get to the other before we can. No one needs to find this out on the phone, but especially not your friends. I can talk to Allison."

"She barely knows you."

Exactly what I'd hoped he'd say. "Then I'll talk to Andy and you take Allison."

He exhaled. "That's probably best."

"Do you know where she is?"

"I'll call the boutique."

Five minutes later, we were both on our way to deliver the sad news.

15

I pounded my fist onto my Jeep's steering wheel. "Come on, people!" Windward Parkway had the worst traffic load in town. Crowded with rows of storefronts and restaurants framing professional buildings for companies like AT&T, it was the central hub of white-collar businesses for Milton, and a traffic nightmare. Hitting a string of green lights took a miracle, and those kinds of miracles rarely happened any time other than in the middle of the night. I was two minutes behind Bishop already, but we'd both agreed to keep Andy and Allison off the phone until one of us made the call. That way we'd know they both received the bad news.

Savannah called. "Hey, what's up?"

She coughed into the phone. "Excuse me. The crud hit me this morning, and I can't seem to shake it."

"You need anything?"

"A shot of whiskey should do the trick."

I cringed. "Gross. My mother used to take that every time she caught something from one of us. When I was old enough to understand, I figured that was an excuse to get drunk."

"Is your momma a drunk?"

"No, but we were a pain in the ass as kids."

"Aren't all kids pains in the ass?"

I laughed. "According to my mom, we were the worst."

"She was probably lying about that, but she knew her stuff when it came to whiskey as a cure-all."

"I'm more of a chicken soup and saltine crackers kind of girl."

"Carbs for the win."

I laughed.

Her voice turned serious. "You sound down. You okay?"

I wasn't supposed to talk about any investigation, and that line was harder drawn with Savannah since she was the chief's wife. "Just left the medical examiner's office in Atlanta."

"Anyone we know?"

"Savannah."

"I get it. What's on your schedule for the rest of the day?"

"I'm on my way to my place to talk to Andy now."

"Oh no, it was Brad Pruitt, wasn't it?"

"Seriously, are you into some Southern magic or something?"

She laughed. "I'm married to a cop. I know how to listen when he's on the phone."

"Good to know."

"God bless that poor man and his family. Such a wasted life, but don't worry, my lips are zipped tighter than a whore's skirt in church."

I busted out laughing. "Wow."

She chuckled. "Southerners have a way with words. You'll get used to it."

"I'm not sure that's possible. I'm almost to my place. Did you call for a reason?"

"Seems kind of inappropriate to suggest now."

"Trust me, I'm sure I've heard worse."

"I was thinking we could go to that new axe-throwing place in Marietta this weekend."

"Axe throwing?"

"It's the perfect way to release tension after a long week."

"Something happen with Jimmy?"

"Jimmy's the best." She paused. "If you ignore the fact that he can't put anything but his guns where it belongs, and he has no idea where anything in our house is even though none of it's changed since the day we moved in together. Oh, and he leaves his underwear on the floor and he expects me to pick it up!"

My heart sank. Those things used to drive me crazy too. Now I'd give anything to be annoyed with Tommy. I spoke with a poorly executed imitation of her Southern drawl. "Axe throwing in Mare-etta sounds like fun, but it all depends on this investigation. Can I get back to you?"

"Sure thing, hon. Talk soon." The line went dead.

I pulled onto Birmingham Highway at the roundabout and called Andy.

"You on your way home?" he said by way of greeting. "I'm still working, but I can clean up if you need me out."

I checked my watch. It was past five. "Can you stick around? I'm on my way home."

"This about my brother?"

"I'll be there in five. We can talk then."

"It's bad, isn't it?"

"Andy, give me five minutes, okay?"

"Sure thing, ma'am."

"Okay, I'll see you soon."

Andy was around the same age as Bishop, somewhere in his early to mid-fifties. The graying hair framing his face and the slight belly were signs of age, and the baggy pants naturally hanging below his belly, commonly referred to as a plumber's crack, were a telltale sign for me. He was also polite and courteous, rare traits for the younger generations like mine.

He stood outside the garage dipping a paint brush into a small can. I didn't need to open my car to smell the paint thinner. The stuff rivaled exhaust fumes and won. I kept my Jeep in the driveway. He greeted me with a slight nod. I tried to smile but couldn't.

"You found Brad."

I nodded slowly, but before I could say anything, he said, "He's dead."

"I'm sorry."

He set the brush in the can and left it between the shrubs and garage. "Do you know what happened?"

"Not yet, but we're working on it."

"Does Allison know?"

"Bishop is with her now."

He wiped his hands with a blue cloth. "I don't want her identifying the body. She can't handle that."

"Bishop already has."

He sighed. "I'd still like to see him."

I took a deep breath and let it out slowly. "I'm not sure that's a good idea, and I don't know when they'll release his remains."

He stared at the ground and continued to wipe his hands. When he looked at me, tears flooded his eyes. "It's something I need to do. For my parents."

"Understood."

He wiped his eyes with his sleeve. "I expected this. I don't know why I'm upset."

"He was your brother."

He nodded. "I need to go to Allison. Let me get the rest of my things cleaned up." He turned toward the door.

I put my hand on his shoulder. "Leave the stuff. It's not important. Go to your sister. Bishop's with her at the boutique."

"Shit. She doesn't need to hear that there."

I sighed. "We thought it was best to tell you both sooner rather than later."

He nodded. "No, I'm not upset. I understand."

He followed me inside anyway, gathered a few of his things, and placed them in a small pile in the corner of my family room. "I'll be back in the morning."

"No, it's okay. Take some time to..." My words trailed off when I couldn't find the right ones.

"Work keeps me in check."

I couldn't argue with that. When Tommy was killed, I worked night and day just to keep my mind from going where it ultimately went anyway. But that wasn't something advice would change for anyone. Andy would have to come to that on his own.

He grabbed his keys from his pocket, holding them in his hands like a security blanket. "Can you tell me if he overdosed?"

I glanced at the ground and shook my head. I bit my lip as I looked him in the eye. "No, he didn't."

"So he was killed, then?"

"Andy, when they finish the autopsy, we'll—"

He interrupted me. "Tell me, Rachel. Please."

"He was beaten, but we don't know what that means just yet."

He pinched the bridge of his nose. "I knew this would happen. Allison's going to be a mess."

"We'll find the person who did it, Andy. I promise."

"I know."

After he left, I sent Bishop a text telling him Andy was on his way, then I took a picture frame out of the trunk in my family room and used it for the photo of me and Tommy at Navy Pier. I set it back on the shelf. Herman swam over to the glass wall of his bowl and wiggled his back half. "Hey, buddy, you having as rough a day as me?" I dropped a few pellets in the bowl. "Here you are, little guy. Do me a favor, will ya? Keep an eye on Andy for me. He's got a lot on his plate right now. He needs someone fierce like you in his corner."

He snatched a floating pellet and swam to the opposite side of the bowl. Herman liked to dine in private. Herman liked to do everything in private. We shared that trait.

I grabbed a bottled water and sat on the couch, checking my watch. Several hours had already passed since we identified Brad Pruitt's body, and the clock was ticking. We needed answers, and we needed them fast, or we could lose any lead we might find.

Bishop hadn't called yet, which meant Allison was in a bad place, but we both expected that. Still, we had a limited amount of time to find Brad's killer. I gathered my files from the Chris Petrowski investigation and flipped through them until I came to the photos of Miquel Sanchez lying on the autopsy table.

The morning of my first day on patrol, Lenny told me I'd very likely draw my weapon before the end of my first week. "Do everything you can not to exterminate someone," he'd said. He told me I'd carry the death like a barbell across my shoulders for the rest of my life. He said officers were never the same after someone died by their hand, no matter the circumstances, and he wanted me to promise I'd do my best to not fall into that situation, even though he understood I couldn't control it. I made that promise, but he was wrong about it all.

I felt nothing but anger for Miquel Sanchez, and I'd yet to feel any remorse or guilt. I did carry the weight of his death like that barbell Lenny mentioned, but only because I struggled with myself for not shooting him sooner. Maybe Tommy would be alive today if I hadn't hesitated.

I stared at the photo of Sanchez's necklace. A thick gold chain with a skull pendant just like the ones left throughout this spider's web of an investigation.

Bishop finally called. "Where are you?"

"My home office."

"Meet me at the department."

"On my way."

16

Bishop was already in Jimmy's office when I arrived, and he acknowledged me with a slight nod. His rigid posture and clenched jaw told me he wasn't pleased. I eyed the chief.

"You're lead," he said to me.

I stared down at Bishop. He wasn't happy. "What about Rob?"

Jimmy leaned back in his chair. "The DA's already on my ass. The only reason Bishop's even involved is because of you."

"Me?"

"You've handled many murder investigations."

"Yes."

"My guys couldn't catch up with your experience if they tried."

He'd done Bishop a favor. Using my experience was a smart move, but not pulling Bishop entirely and giving me Harry or Sanders was a surprise. "No Harry or Sanders?"

He shook his head. "I can't pull them off their current investigation. They're knee-deep already."

I wasn't aware they were investigating anything. "I'll do my best, sir."

"No, you'll do it, or I'll pull you both off and give it to the Hardy Boys. I owe Alpharetta a favor now, and I don't like owing favors."

We had that in common. "Yes, sir."

"Okay," he said, shuffling a stack of papers on his desk. "What do we have?"

"Shit," Bishop said.

Jimmy nodded. "How about we let Ryder talk?"

I knew if I connected the skull pendants to Petrowski, Jimmy would toss us both off the case, but the pendants had to be mentioned. I hated not being forthcoming with Jimmy, but not enough to wait it out and see where the pendants took us. For all I knew, Bishop was right. They could have nothing to do with me or Chris Petrowski.

And Jimmy Hoffa's buried next to Jim Morrison.

"We have something," I said. "Hold on." I rushed to my office, ignoring the lingering slick sleeves gawking at me as I jogged by. I grabbed the slim file off the top of a stack of case files on my desk and jogged back to the chief's office. I opened it as I sat next to my partner. "Barron found a thick gold chain and skull pendant in Brad Pruitt's pocket. The skull is the same as the one we found on Jeffers, in Brad Pruitt's hotel, and—" I left out finding one in my house. I removed the photo of the skull from the file, set it on Jimmy's desk, and showed him the one on my phone from Brad Pruitt's hotel room. "We find who sells these, we may have ourselves a lead."

Bishop sighed. "Needle in a haystack. Like I said, those things come a dime a dozen." Either Bishop recognized I was holding back the connection to Chicago, or he still wasn't fully on board.

The chief examined the photos. "This one," he said, holding up the photo from the OD in the woods. "Looks handmade."

I zoomed in on the photo from Pruitt's hotel. "So does this one." I flipped the camera toward him and Bishop. "And." I swiped to the other photo of the chain in Pruitt's pocket. "So does this one."

"Check around. See if these are made around here."

"I don't think they are."

"And you know this how?"

I looked to Bishop for a reaction. He shrugged.

"Full disclosure," I said, deciding to lay my cards out on the table. I pulled a photo from the file I'd brought from home and laid it on his desk. "They're identical to this one."

He studied the photo and then glanced up at me. "And you found this one where?"

"Around Miquel Sanchez's neck."

Jimmy leaned back in his seat. "Fuck."

And now he knew.

"Hold up," Jimmy said, eyeing Bishop. "You look like you want to say something."

Bishop scraped his fingers down the sides of his face. "I understand what Ryder thinks, but I'm concerned she's looking at this with too narrow an eye."

My mouth dropped. I crossed my arms over my chest and grimaced. "And he's objective as hell."

I watched the cords on my partner's neck pulse.

Jimmy tapped his fingers on the edge of his desk. "Maybe I should give this to Harry and Sanders."

"Jimmy—"

I cut Bishop off. "We're good. Come on, Bishop. We gotta move."

The chief stopped us. "Ryder?"

I turned at his door. "Yes, Chief?"

"It might just be someone fucking with you."

"I know." It wasn't.

Bishop scowled as he charged out of Jimmy's office, running right into Detective Sanders.

"Watch where you're going, asshole," Sanders said.

I grabbed Bishop's arm. "Let's go."

He shook his arm loose from my grip and went nose to nose with Sanders. "You got a fucking problem?"

Sanders bowed up. "You're my fucking problem." He snorted. "And that lesbo partner of yours."

I knocked Bishop to the side and stuck my face up close to Sanders's. His breath smelled like stale coffee and flavored creamer. "You want to see how big of a problem I can be, asshole? Let's go."

Jimmy walked out and pulled Sanders away from me. He got in his face and screamed, "My office, now!"

Sanders huffed, straightened his suit jacket, and snarled at me and Bishop. I smacked my left bicep with my right hand and lifted my left hand up, flipping him the middle finger. "Sorry about your dick size, asshole."

The few patrol officers in the pit laughed.

"Enough, Ryder," Jimmy said.

Bishop stormed through the pit.

"Hold up," I said, rushing to catch up. I grabbed his arm, and he jerked it away. "What the fuck's your problem?"

He stopped, turned around, and stared at me. His face was red and his nostrils flared. "Don't let this investigation be some conspiracy theory just because the asshole who had your husband killed is out of prison."

My blood pressure rose. "I'm just following the evidence."

"We don't have shit for evidence, Ryder. We've got a few

necklaces and you think your buddies in Chicago are out to kill you."

One. Two. Three.

"The world doesn't fucking revolve around you." He stormed off.

I leaned against the wall just outside the pit, working hard to calm myself and not make even more of a scene. After a minute, I walked over to the patrol secretary and asked for an available vehicle.

She tossed me a set of keys. "Twenty-two. Just serviced, too."

"Thanks."

I slammed through the doors and almost into Bishop smoking on the sidewalk. "Let's go," I said.

"What the fuck is that bullshit, Ryder?"

I headed toward the unmarked SUV. "You want to find Brad's killer, then let's find some fucking evidence."

He walked swiftly behind me and slowed at my side. "You really think the pendants are from Chicago, don't you?"

"I don't believe in coincidences."

"So that's where you're going with this?"

"The only place I'm going is to Brad's hangouts. Now give me something here, and on the way, you can tell me why the hell Sanders hates you so much."

"Start with Good Times."

"On Highway Nine?"

He nodded.

I put the Ford Explorer into drive and pulled out of the department lot. "Well?"

"We've never been friends."

"That was obvious on my first day."

He exhaled. "I haven't mentioned this yet, and I don't want it getting around, so keep it quiet, okay?"

"Damn. I was planning to hang with the guys and gossip tonight while we gave each other pedicures."

He grinned. "Point made."

"Well?"

"I'm taking the sergeant's exam."

I twisted my head toward him. "Really? That's awesome!"

"Sanders is taking it too."

I sucked in a whistle. "Oh boy. The department isn't big enough for two sergeant detectives."

"No, it's not, and Sanders thinks he should get it."

"How does he know you're testing?"

"We got CC'd on an email."

I cringed. "No wonder he's been wearing his ass on his shoulders."

"Listen, about earlier."

"Don't sweat it."

"I really hope this isn't about you."

"Right there with you, partner."

"But if the evidence suggests it is, I'm not going to argue."

I smiled. "Evidence doesn't lie."

"No, it doesn't."

I glanced in my rearview and noticed a car coming in hot behind us. "How's Allison?"

"Bad. Andy's with her." He turned toward the window. "We need to make this right, at least as best we can."

"We will," I said, keeping my eye on the car approaching from behind. My heart raced when it sped up and slowed on my ass. "Shit."

Bishop glanced behind him. "Is that the same fucking Malibu?"

I turned left onto Highway Nine. "Looks like it."

He swore under his breath. "Tap the brakes."

"He's too close."

Bishop got on the radio with dispatch. "Tap the brakes," he said again, louder this time.

Fuck. I hated doing that, but I tapped the brakes.

The Malibu swerved to the left into oncoming traffic, sending a string of cars off the road, horns blaring. The vehicle cut a hard left into a church parking lot. I whipped through oncoming traffic, praising it for stopping and giving us a pathway. The Malibu's tires screeched and lost tread on the parking lot pavement. Smoke spit from the ground as the car sped through the lot and onto the side road.

Bishop gave our location to dispatch.

"Two's en route," she said.

"Suspect heading east off Highway Nine and—" He looked for a street sign, but there wasn't one. "Just south of the Bank of America approximately a half mile north of One-twenty. Request assist from Alpharetta. Copy?"

"Ten-four."

The Malibu weaved in and out of oncoming traffic as two of our cruisers followed behind us.

"We'll get him back at Haynes Bridge," Bishop said.

"He won't go that way. He'll turn right and head toward Old Milton. Less traffic."

I was right. He swung right at the light, riding up on the small median and again darting between vehicles on both sides of the road. Three cruisers came from the opposite direction and crowded the two lanes so he couldn't bust through them. The driver veered to the right, jumped the curb, and sped through a small, undeveloped area. We followed behind, hitting something large and hard under my front left side and blowing the tire. The Explorer deviated to the right. I swung the steering wheel hard, my speed slowed by the damaged tire. "Son of a bitch!"

"Keep moving," Bishop yelled. "I want that asshole!"

The Malibu whipped into the woods as the two cruisers flew ahead of us.

"Ryder! Hit the gas, dammit!"

A loud boom silenced him. Smoke immediately appeared above the small wooded area.

One of the sleeves yelled through the radio. "Male suspect on foot. Hispanic. Five seven, black hair, black leather jacket. Michels is pursuing."

Dispatch confirmed and sent fire. We approached the vehicle cautiously, worried more about a potential explosion than a suspect. Sirens blasted from nearby.

"Son of a bitch!" Bishop yelled.

"That's not a teenager playing around," I said.

He breathed heavily. "What made them come after an unmarked vehicle like this?"

"They're watching me, Bishop. They're coming after me."

"I'm beginning to think you're right."

17

"You didn't see him?"

"No, but I didn't need to. The skulls. The taunting. And the guy's Hispanic. This has Petrowski written all over it." I paced up and down the hall of my townhouse.

Lenny used his commander voice. "Get your emotions in check, Detective."

"I'm not emotional," I lied. "How can you not see what's so obvious?"

"I'm not saying you're wrong. I'm saying stop looking at this from the position of victim and look at it from the position of detective." He paused. "You're pacing right now, aren't you?"

"It helps me think."

"Yeah, I know, when you're emotional. Honey, calm down. Petrowksi hasn't budged. He's barely out of prison. You think he'd come after you this quickly? He's smarter than that."

"Then explain the pendants and the guy in the Malibu." He sighed. "I can't."

"I can. They're messages for me."

They've got a BOLO on the guy, right?"

"For all the good it'll do. Hispanic male in a black jacket isn't much to go on. I realize the patrol around here doesn't do a lot physically, but Michels wants to be detective someday. He needs to be in shape for this kind of position."

"What's your partner think?"

"After getting our ass chased, he thinks I'm right."

"Shit."

"Right. This is a shitstorm, and I'm standing around rocking on my heels in the thick of it. What am I supposed to do?"

Bishop knocked on my French doors. "Bishop's here. I gotta go. Talk soon," I said, and disconnected the call.

He walked in and grabbed a bottled water out of the fridge. "Three hours of bullshit paperwork and you're sitting on your ass doing what? Waiting for Brad Pruitt's killer to turn himself in?"

I stared at him. "Actually, I just got off the phone with Sanders. We planned out your promotion party." I shook my head. "Why is everyone on my ass?" I pointed to my dining room table. "That. That's what I've been doing. Trying to figure out what the hell is going on."

He inhaled and blew it out slowly. "I'm sorry."

I pointed to the white board. "We still need to hit Good Times, and now's probably better than earlier. I spoke to Andy again. He gave me a list of places where he's had to pick Brad up in the past."

"Andy gave you that?"

I nodded. "And Allison told me about a woman Brad used to date. Caroline something or other?"

"Bryant. I'm not even sure she's still alive."

"Unless she's a Jane Doe and no one's looking for her,

she is. Allison said the last she knew Caroline was stripping at the Cheetah."

"Yeah, but that was a few years ago."

"I spoke with the manager. Apparently, she started up again, but she hasn't been there in months. Said he thinks she hit bottom. Said she's either left town or is holed up in some crack house near her parents if she's even still alive."

"I know the place," he said. He chugged the water. "I'll drive."

"What about Good Times?"

"Caroline and Brad were supposed to get married. If anyone knows what he was into, it's her. We'll try her first and go from there."

I checked my weapon, secured it into the holster on my hip, and tossed on my jacket. "Let's go."

We pulled up to the abandoned house off Providence Road. "God, this is a bigger hell hole than the other place."

"Wasn't always. The family lost everything when the market crashed in what, 2007? Bank took back the house, but it never sold. They just left it to die."

"That's common. They're not invested emotionally, and they figure at some point someone will buy the land and tear down the house."

"So they just let it sit and house drug addicts. Nice."

He shrugged. "Doubt they've even been out to check. Whoever does eventually buy the land won't have much of a tear-down to do. This place is barely standing."

"And people sleep here."

Michels arrived in his squad car. "Nothing on the unsub," he said, referring to the runner driving the Malibu.

"You need a running routine," I said. "You should have caught that guy." I was teasing, but the look on his face said he didn't know that. "It's a joke, Michels."

"Oh, yeah. I do run, but joking aside, I need to push myself harder."

I teased him. "You really want that promotion, don't you?"

"Damn straight."

"Any word from Ashley on the vehicle?"

"No prints that match anything in the system," he said. "She did find some grainy cowhide strands. Black, but inconsistent with the leather traditionally used for jackets. Oh, and a hair. She's sending the hair out for DNA analysis, but it'll take a while to find out if it's a match to anything in the system."

I smirked. He'd memorized Ashley's words. "Grainy cowhide is commonly used for leather work gloves. The kind used in construction work and landscape." Both largely Hispanic fields in the metro Atlanta area. Those gloves were also common in Chicago construction jobs. "Anything else in the vehicle? Blood? Duct tape? Anything that could be used as a weapon?"

"No, ma'am."

He'd gone all professional on me with the ma'ams. He really did want the detective position.

"Oh!" He nodded. "And a gold skull pendant. She said you'd want to know."

"Why didn't she call me?"

"Said she tried twice."

I checked my phone. Two missed calls. I checked the volume button on the left. "Damn. I turned off my sound." I flipped it back on.

Bishop stared at me. "You win."

I smiled. "I'll refrain from saying I told you so."

Michels glanced at the home. "You think someone lives here?"

"Lives is an exaggeration," Bishop said.

Michels tilted his head to the side. "Huh?"

"Drug addiction isn't exactly living." I tossed him a face mask. "Put it on."

"You think it's that bad?"

I pointed to a hole in the siding under the front window. "Mold."

He snapped the mask straps over his ears. "I hate these things."

Neil Diamond definitely didn't write "Sweet Caroline" for Caroline Bryant. The skinny blonde woman sat on a ripped and shredded blue plaid cushion on an equally ruined couch. She puffed on a cigarette, taking in a long drag and blowing it out slowly through her nose. I moved to the side. I'd gone several hours without a cigarette, but not because I'd tried. I was too busy to give it any thought. Even though that felt like some kind of sign, the pull of the smoky air fought to take its place.

She leaned back, and her rock-hard breast implants didn't budge. I wondered why anyone would pay to see that skinny, almost lifeless, stringy-haired blonde naked. I had to resist the urge to gawk at her obviously advanced addiction.

"I ain't seen that piece of shit in months." She drew another pull on her smoke.

Bishop kept his emotions in check. "That piece of shit is dead."

She blinked. "Damn." She pushed herself to the edge of the couch and flicked the cigarette ash onto a water-damaged magazine. *Vogue*. As if she had a shot of looking like anyone in the thing. She sighed. "Can't say I didn't see that coming."

If Caroline Bryant felt anything romantic for Brad Pruitt, one of their addictions killed it long ago. "Can't say I couldn't say the same for you."

She stared at me, then looked at Bishop. "Who's the bitch?"

I smirked and flashed her the badge on my pants. "Detective Ryder."

She examined me from head to toe, then retraced the path until she met my eyes. "You don't look like no detective."

"You don't look like a stripper either."

"When was the last time you talked to Brad Pruitt?" Bishop asked.

"Like I said, I ain't seen him in months."

Michels stood to my left. I leaned toward him and whispered, "Check out the rooms."

"Yes, ma'am," he said.

I grabbed his arm as he walked away. "Cut the 'ma'am' crap, will you?"

"Sure thing, Detective."

"What about his known associates. Have you seen them?" Bishop asked.

I placed my hands under my jacket and rested them on my hips, giving her a full view of my weapon. "People like us don't have associates, and we sure as hell don't have friends," she said.

"What about his dealer? You got a name?"

"You think I'm a snitch?" She laughed. "Bitch, I don't need that shit. I got enough problems of my own." She waved her arm to indicate the room. "Keeping up with my castle is a lot of work."

"Especially stoned blind," I mumbled.

She pointed a boney finger at me and shook it as she pushed herself to her feet. She took a step closer to me and breathed into my face. Her breath smelled like rotting flesh. "I don't like you."

I stepped closer, thankful for the added height from the pair of heeled boots I'd yet to change out of. "Feeling's mutual."

"Ladies." Bishop's arm shot between me and the drug addict. "Let's get back to Brad Pruitt. Caroline, I know you two have history. Help us so we can give his sister some closure."

"'Course we have history. The bastard got me hooked on the shit. You think I feel like reliving old times? Shit, man, I ain't barely making it living in the here and now. The past will kill me."

"Jesus Christ," I said. I didn't bother counting to ten. We didn't have time for her BS. "We can do this the easy way or the hard way. Given the choice, I pick the hard way." I detached the handcuffs from my belt. "What about you?"

She sighed. "Heard some talk at Good Times. Word around town is he got himself in some shit with the cartel. Something about not covering his debt. Y'all might could take a drive through The Manor. That's where all the bigwigs from the cartel live." She looked at me like she'd just told me something I didn't already know. "Might could learn something."

"You ever see him with a Hispanic man, under six feet, black jacket? Maybe hanging around Good Times?"

She laughed. "There ain't nothing but a few white men there. Place is full of them Mex-e-cans. We're the minority these days. I don't pay attention to who's who. I get what I need and leave."

"What about your johns? Any of them Hispanic?"

She lit up again, taking her time sucking in the smoke and waiting even longer to blow it out. "I don't fuck for cash."

"I'm sure you fuck for a lot of stuff. There's no such thing as a cigarette fairy."

She glanced at the ground.

"Caroline," Bishop said in a kind tone. He was clearly playing good cop. "Brad's dead. Now, I remember a time when you two were planning to get married, raise a family, and I know you do too. Sure, things got bad, but you know we can get you help if you want it—"

"I don't need help."

"Tell us what you know. Do it for Andy and Allison," I said.

"Andy don't give two shits about his brother."

"Yes, he does," Bishop said.

She nodded. "Always liked Allison. She's got a good heart." She twisted her fake blonde hair around her finger. "They all wear black jackets."

"Like a gang symbol?" I asked.

"No, they're in fashion."

"Your sense of humor is awesome," I lied.

"Raul Morales. He's the supplier. You go to Good Times, make sure you watch out for the falcons—they're the white-ass pussies with their heads shaved." She smiled at me. "They'd love taking on a bitch like you."

"Go on," I said.

"You'll find Raul Morales in a booth in the back. On the left. If he ain't there, stick around, he'll show up eventually." She lit up another cigarette and spoke after a long drag. "You mention I told you, and I'm dead."

"I'll do my best."

"Fuck you," she said.

Michels was already outside when Bishop and I left the house. "Should I get Ashley here?"

"No need," I said. "You find anything of interest?"

"Nothing. No skull pendant either." He smiled. "I figured that's what you sent me to look for."

"You might make a good detective someday after all, Michels."

"Thanks. What else do you need me to do?"

"Go back and check for any late-model black Malibus stolen in the last few days," Bishop said. "Let us know what you find."

"Already searched the VIN on the vehicle, sir. Reported stolen from Atlanta a week ago."

"They left the VIN number on the vehicle?" I asked.

He nodded.

"Means they didn't intend to resell it," I said. "They took it to drive."

"Sounds about right," Michels said.

Bishop agreed. "Search through any recent vehicle theft arrests. Look for anything similar to the unsub and let us know, okay?"

"Got it."

Bishop shot me a death stare as we got into the car. "You're an asshole."

"You're welcome."

He shook his head. "Do me a favor. Be the eyes in Good Times. I'll be the mouth. You got it?"

"I'm lead, Bishop."

"Then fucking act like it."

"Yes, sir."

He sensed the sarcasm in my tone. "Jesus Christ, Ryder. This is my best friend's brother we're talking about."

"I know that. I'm doing what needs to be done."

His eyes shifted between me and the road. "Then do it better, for fuck's sake."

"We have different techniques. That doesn't mean one is better than the other."

"Yeah, pissing off a possible contact is a great technique."

I gave him a few minutes to cool off, then asked, "How was that woman a stripper?"

He laughed. "You've never been to a strip club, have you?"

"I have, but none that hire women that strung out. Is the place desperate or something?"

"The Cheetah's not bad." He glanced at me. "For a strip joint, I mean. The manager probably felt sorry for her and knew she wouldn't be around long. I'm guessing she made her tips in the parking lot."

"I just threw up a little in my mouth."

"There's someone for everyone, Ryder."

"Yeah, I know guys who love the 'rode hard and put away wet' look."

"Nice."

18

The Good Times parking lot needed a makeover about as much as the bar itself. The gravel wasn't the kind you brought in with a truck, dumped, then raked flat, it was just broken concrete crushed and smashed by weather and tires until it resembled the real stuff. The Good Times sign hung lopsided on the front of the building, flashing only *od Tim* in neon yellow. "Who's Tim?" I asked. "And why are they advertising his overdose?"

He rolled his eyes. "Remember. I talk, you watch."

"I didn't agree to that."

He glared at me. "I'd like to walk out of here alive."

"And you think your kind heart can guarantee that? You can't be that naïve."

"Ryder."

"Fine. You talk. I'll add my thoughts when necessary."

He shook his head and climbed out of the vehicle. We walked in with imaginary neon signs flashing *cop* across our foreheads. Thankfully, popularity wasn't my thing. I kept my hand on my weapon, making eye contact with each and every person possible. I swallowed back a curse word when some guy licked his lips and mouthed *let's fuck* to me.

The world is full of gentlemen.

We stood to the right of the bar and examined the room. Good Times was a no-frills place. The décor was limited to a few flat-screen TVs, one hanging on each wall, some neon tequila and beer lights, and those old pin-up girl posters popular eighty years ago. The round tables set out in two straight lines down the length of the bar created a pathway, allowing the bar patrons and those in the booths to move freely. The painted cement floor offered nothing for the already lacking décor, but the bar clearly wasn't meant to impress. The space was small enough to see the back wall as well as the small crowd of guards manning Raul Morales's booth. Bishop finally placed his hand on his weapon as we walked over.

Two steroid-loving, Shrek-like humans showed us their muscles along with two very large Glocks.

"We're not here for any trouble," Bishop said. "We just want to talk to Mr. Morales."

"Let them by, amigos," someone said from the table.

I smiled at the bigger of the Shreks. "Nice chatting with you."

A short Hispanic man with dark hair shaved close to his head with inch-long spikes on top was admiring a plate full of meat and Mexican rice. He offered us a seat at the booth.

I moved my jacket to show my badge. "We prefer to stand, thank you."

"You are here about Mr. Pruitt."

"Word travels fast," Bishop said.

Morales sipped a drink I couldn't identify. "In my world, yes. In yours it takes a bit longer, no?"

"I understand he hadn't made good on some debt."

"Ah, but you see, you are wrong. Mr. Pruitt paid his debt. At the time of his death, he was free and clear with me. Therefore, we had no reason to take action." He eyed me up and down slowly.

"How much did Pruitt owe you?" I asked.

"You got a hearing problem, senorita?" He smirked. "I said he paid his debt. Perhaps you would like something to help with your hearing?"

"I'll pass."

"Did you continue selling to him after he paid his debt?" Bishop asked.

"I do not work with customers with poor credit, Officer." He held up his hands. "I am just a small business owner struggling to survive. I give someone product. I expect payment. Pruitt fulfilled his financial obligations, and we parted ways."

"Any idea where he got the money?" I asked.

"Perhaps he pulled it out of his *culo*?"

I knew enough Spanish to know that meant ass. "That had to hurt."

Morales smiled. "You are funny." He gave me a once-over again, settling his eyes on my chest. "I could have fun with you. Perhaps you would like to stay awhile and...?"

"I'd rather burn in hell."

"That can be arranged." He wiggled a finger at one of the Shreks, and I felt the pressure of a gun on my back.

I gripped my weapon tighter. Morales smirked and flicked his finger, and the brute backed off.

"It is not easy for a user to come up with the kind of cash Pruitt owed. His *culo* was not big enough for a wad like that. And trust me, I know. But he made arrangements to pay, and we accepted them." He eyed me again. "Now your *culo*, pretty lady, I would like to give a try."

I dropped my hands onto the table. "I'd prefer sticking my gun up your *culo* and watching the shit show."

His lips formed a thin, straight line. He nodded once, and one of the Shreks strong-armed me, yanking me backward by my collar. I placed one hand on my weapon and jabbed my other elbow into the person's gut. As he bent over, I raised my opposite elbow and smacked it into the side of his head.

He swore in Spanish.

"Leave her," Morales said.

The man stepped back and grunted. "*Puta!*"

I turned toward him and smirked. "Like I haven't heard that before."

Bishop's face heated to a fiery red. I guess keeping quiet meant keeping still too. Whoops.

"Officers, I made a promise to no longer sell product to Mr. Pruitt. While I may deal in a business you do not approve of, I am a man of my word. Though I am sure you are aware there is another gentleman supplying this community. Perhaps you should consider a discussion with him." He picked up his fork. "Now, my dinner is getting cold."

"Just a few more questions. Please, feel free to eat," Bishop said.

He smiled but didn't reach for his fork.

"When was the last time you saw Mr. Pruitt?"

"It has been some time. I do not engage with my customers socially, Detective."

Bishop nodded. "And you work from this space? This is your office?"

He nodded.

"Do you recycle, Mr. Morales?" I asked.

He squinted, and small age lines sprang from the sides of his eyes. "I do not understand."

Morales didn't flinch, didn't look down and to the right, or away at all. He kept his eyes focused on me, and that, along with the general confusion on his face, told me he didn't know what the hell I was talking about.

Bishop said, "Can anyone attest to your whereabouts the past three days?"

He smiled. "Many people, yes." He eyed the bartender. "Julio will tell you I have been here, in this booth."

My partner nodded. "We'll be talking to you again, Mr. Morales."

We turned around and walked toward the door. A flash of dark moving quickly near the front of the bar caught my eye. A Hispanic man, under six feet and wearing a black leather jacket, shoved the bartender out of the way and rushed through the door into the kitchen. He glanced back just as the door opened, and we made eye contact. He smiled.

"Son of a bitch!" I grabbed my partner's arm. "Bishop! That's him!" I bolted to the bar, climbed on top of a chair, and jumped over, sending drinks and who the hell knows what else crashing to the ground.

I pushed through cooks and metal carts. "Which way?" I screamed.

No one answered, but I caught a glimpse of the far right side of the kitchen. A short, chunky guy the size of a small bull stood in front of the door with his hands on his hips. My gun was already out. I dropped my hand to my side and gut-kicked him. He curled over and went down like a grade-school bully. "Consider yourself lucky it wasn't lower," I said as I jumped over him and shoved myself through the door.

I stopped and examined the parking lot carefully, my

heart racing, my heavy breathing clouding my ability to think clearly. "Fuck!"

Bishop ran up beside me. "Son of a bitch!"

"I saw his face, Bishop!" I skirted between cars, using my flashlight for a clear view, but it was pointless. "I saw his face!" I leaned against a car, trying hard to catch my breath. My blood raced through my veins. "Damn it!"

"Okay," he said, staring at me like I'd lost my mind.

"No. You don't understand. I saw his face!"

He stepped back as I gathered my emotions. "You saw his face. That's good, Ryder. Real good."

One, two, three...get it together, Ryder. "I know the guy."

Bishop and the chief stood behind me as I searched NCIC, the National Crime Information Center, for the right file. I clicked on Arturo Perez and pushed back from the desk. "Him. This is the guy in the black leather jacket."

"Was he part of the Petrowski investigation?"

I shook my head. Technically, he wasn't, but he was related to Miquel Sanchez. I waited until I knew which direction they'd go before I offered that little gift as further evidence my past was now my present. I printed his information and walked over to grab it. After ten pages, the printer stopped. I gathered them, stuck them in a file, and brought them to Jimmy's office.

"I'll get the coffee," Bishop said, walking through the pit to the kitchen.

I threw the file on Jimmy's desk. "I knew it. I fucking knew it." I pulled my hair from its tie and let it fall down my back, then ran my hand through the loose strands at the top of my head. A quick glance at the clock on the wall told me the night had moved quickly into the next morning. "We need a BOLO. Now."

Jimmy sat behind his desk and took a deep breath. "I know I'm going to regret this, but are you sure it's Perez?"

I steadied my eyes on him. "Yes."

Bishop returned with the coffee. He'd added cream to mine but only enough to turn it mucky brown. I sipped it anyway. He opened the file and spread the papers out on the chief's desk. "You really think you got a good enough look at the guy to say for sure?"

How many times would I have to answer the same question? "The asshole smiled at me. He fucking smiled."

Jimmy examined the mugshot carefully. "Call Michels."

"Yes, sir," Bishop said. He removed his cell from his pocket.

"We don't need Michels," I said. "It's Perez, one hundred percent."

"He pursued the driver of the Malibu on foot. He might recognize him from the photo."

"Why can't you just put out the damn BOLO?"

He pointed to the chair. "Sit."

I reluctantly sat.

"I need you to look at this from an unemotional stance, Ryder."

I dropped my hands and clenched my fists out of Jimmy's view. "I am not emotional."

"Listen, I believe it's possible this is the guy you think it is, but do you really want to put a BOLO out for Perez?" He leaned forward. "And let the entire Chicago Police Department know you think Perez is here?"

I closed my eyes and swallowed hard, taking a deep breath and releasing it with a sigh. "Shit."

He leaned back and relaxed. "First rule of a good detective: don't put all your cards on the table."

"Then we do the BOLO based on appearance."

He smiled. "We can do that, but half the patrol in the state will be pulling guys over. Not a wise move in this political environment."

"I don't give a fuck about politics, Jimmy." I grabbed my jacket and bag from Jimmy's conference table and charged out, the adrenaline pumping through my veins taking over. Four patrol officers in the pit followed me with their eyes. Once I passed them, I stopped, turned around, and yelled, "I'm fucking straight, you assholes!" I let the door slam behind me and walked past five other officers before making it to the back entrance of the department. Stopping at the edge of the parking lot, I found the pack of cigarettes in my bag and lit one up. I breathed in the smooth mix of vanilla and licorice and felt the hint of relaxation come quickly. I hated that cigarettes gave me that release, but in the moment, I just needed to chill.

Sanders pulled up, got out of his car with a bag of Chick-fil-A in his hand, and smiled. "Ryder," he said as he approached.

"Shouldn't you be studying for that sergeant exam, Sanders?"

He narrowed his brow. "You got a problem, Detective?"

Chief Abernathy walked out and shook his head. He nodded toward Sanders, said, "I got this," and then glared at me. "Inside. Now."

Each of the four officers still in the pit made eye contact as I walked by. I pointed two fingers at my own eyes and then flicked them back at the men.

Jimmy slammed his door behind him. "Let's try this again, and how about we make it professional this time?"

I leaned against the back wall and crossed my arms over my chest. Bishop raised his brows and shook his head. He mouthed, "Relax."

I inhaled and counted to five while I released the breath. Telling a pissed-off woman to relax is like telling a toddler they can't have a candy bar in the checkout line at the grocery store. I recounted, finally making it to ten without telling my partner to shove his advice where the sun don't shine.

Jimmy didn't look at me, but he didn't tell me to sit again, either, so there was that. He handed Michels the mugshot of Arturo Perez. "This the guy you chased off Deerfield?"

Michels examined the photo long enough for me to know he couldn't tell. I'd worked with enough people, civilians and law enforcement combined, to know that when someone had any kind of heightened emotional engagement with another person, if they saw the person's face, they rarely forgot it. Michels didn't see Perez's face, so there was no way for him to recognize him. He didn't need to. I knew. That's what mattered.

"Sir, I can't say for sure. I didn't see his face."

I pressed my lips together so I wouldn't blurt out something I might regret.

Jimmy handed him the profile shot. "What about his profile?"

Michels shook his head again. "Sir, I didn't see any facial features I can compare to these photos. He was running, and I lost him." His tone didn't hide his frustration and embarrassment.

I felt bad for him.

"Can you give me a description of what you did see?"

Michels nodded. "Hispanic male—"

"How do you know he's Hispanic if you didn't see his face?" Jimmy asked.

He pursed his lips. Michels was about to make a judgment call, which, in our field, is called profiling, and not well received by the public. We all waited for him to figure it out. "I don't, sir. I just made an assumption and that was wrong."

The chief nodded. "Go on."

"Approximately five foot seven, maybe 140 pounds. Dark hair, though he was wearing a cap, so I can't determine much more than that. Jeans, black leather jacket."

Jimmy nodded. "Okay. Do me a favor." He scratched something on a piece of paper, ripped the paper off the pad, and handed it to Michels. "Look up this guy, but don't put out a BOLO. Get with patrol and the next shift's captain and let them know to be on the lookout for him. I do not want a BOLO, do you understand? Just eyes out for him. If they see him, bring him in."

"Yes, sir," Michels said.

"Thanks."

Michels rushed out of the room, and Jimmy looked at me. "Is that acceptable?"

"It has to be." I stood up straight, forcing myself to stifle my emotions. It wasn't easy.

"Look." Jimmy's expression softened. "I get it. You see someone who looks like someone from your past, and you react. But even you said the guy you think this is wasn't part of the Petrowski case. What am I missing here? What aren't you telling me?"

"Perez is Miquel Sanchez's cousin."

"Sanchez. The guy you killed?"

I nodded. "Don't you see? Petrowski sent him. He knew I'd recognize him."

Jimmy dragged his fingers down the sides of his face. "Go on."

"Bishop and I have had several incidents involving the Malibu, but to the best of my knowledge, my partner hasn't seen it without me present."

"Have you seen it without him present?"

"Yes. It was in the parking lot of my gym. Pulled up to the window and then sped off. There was a witness."

"Any known direct association with Chris Petrowski?"

Shit. "Not that I'm aware of, but I can find out."

He examined Perez's mugshot carefully. "No defining features easily recognizable to the eye."

"No, sir, but having arrested Perez several times, I—"

He folded the file closed. "I understand." He leaned back in his chair. "Let's do this. Call your ex-partner in Chicago and see if he can locate Perez. Tell him to keep it under the radar. If this is the guy, we don't want it getting out we know he's here."

"Thank you, Jimmy."

"And let's give them a few days to do their due diligence. In the meantime, we'll keep patrol on the lookout unofficially. That work for you?"

"Yes, sir."

"Ryder, tread lightly. You make this too personal and you're out. You understand? It's bad enough I've got Bishop pissing himself from anger. You go postal, and the DA will kick us all in the balls."

"With all due respect, Jimmy, that wasn't postal."

He flicked his head toward the door. "And do me a favor. Stay away from Sanders."

I smiled.

"You really are a pain in my ass, you know that?"

"Sure do."

19

I stayed in my cubby until the early morning hours scanning through NCIC arrest records for Miquel Sanchez and Arturo Perez, looking for anything to connect them other than distant DNA. Both were part of a large Hispanic gang in Chicago. My gut told me Perez was connected to Petrowski, just like his cousin. I was able to physically map out a link of connections that put Perez right in the middle of the action, but only on a surface level and, to the best of my knowledge, not in any direct contact with Petrowski himself. I dialed a number and paused before hitting the little green icon on my cell. I took a deep breath, then hit it.

A groggy, rough voice answered. "Garcia." A moment of silence and then, "Ryder? You okay?"

Hearing my former partner's voice both invigorated and calmed me. "I'm good."

"What the hell, then? It's the middle of the night."

"More like the early morning."

"Earlier here, you ass. This better be important."

"I think Arturo Perez is in Hamby."

"Fuck. Seriously? You think Petrowski sent him?"

I filled Garcia in on what I knew.

"The vehicle?"

"Stolen from Atlanta."

"They left the VIN?"

"Yup."

"Shit. Any prints?"

"Nope. They had the vehicle wiped, and he wore gloves."

"Then how do you know it's Sanchez?"

"I saw him."

"You get a BOLO out?"

"No. Chief doesn't want to."

"Why the hell not?"

"He doesn't want to lay all our cards on the table like that, and I see his point."

"Right. Okay, so you want me to ask around, see what I can find out?"

"Please."

"You know everyone's watching Petrowski."

"And you know he's going to keep his hands clean, but that doesn't mean he's innocent."

"Let me talk to my guy. If Perez is in town, he'll know."

"Thanks."

"You doin' okay otherwise?"

I coughed, and before I could respond, he said, "Jesus Christ, Ryder. You're smoking again?"

"Yeah, and I already feel like shit, so you don't have to add to that."

Anthony Garcia knew me almost as well as Tommy had. That's how partners work. You learn everything about the person you entrust your life with, and good or bad, you still protect them. When it's a matter of life or death, partners require that kind of connection.

"Go for a run. Hit the bag. There are other ways to deal with this."

"I know."

"What does your new partner say?"

"Not much."

"He's scared of you. You're pretty damn intimidating when you're balls to the wall."

"So I'm told."

"Let me get on this. I'll call you when I have something."

"Thanks, Garcia."

"You bet."

The morning shift began rolling in. I rubbed my bloodshot eyes and guzzled multiple cups of horrible burnt coffee to keep my brain functional. A few of the patrol acknowledged me with strange smiles, and I assumed word got out about my minor outburst, but I didn't care. I made copies of my notes and the map connecting the gang activity between Perez and Sanchez, then put them in two separate files and left them on Jimmy's and Bishop's desks. Then, feeling bad, I made another copy and left it for Michels too. He wasn't a detective yet, but he'd worked hard on this, and he should have all the pieces to solve the puzzle.

I drove by the gym, checking to see if the guy who'd been there to witness the Malibu was around, but the place was empty. The sun peeked over the trees, casting a shimmering purple and gold haze over them. I ran through Dunkin's drive-thru and, too wired from the bad coffee to go home, headed to Hamby Equestrian Farm, knowing Sean would be there.

The horses grazing in the pasture at sunrise gave me a feeling of comfort. Regular citizens would drive by this without a care in the world, oblivious to the growing destruction of their cushy life by factors they neither knew nor understood. Peace and happiness weren't guarantees. Life could change on a dime.

The entrance gate was closed and locked, but since the horses were out, I knew Sean was there. I sent him a text telling him I had a delicious coffee waiting at the gate.

Less than two minutes later, a black pickup drove down the entrance road. He climbed out and smiled as he removed the lock and pushed the gate open. I opened my Jeep's window and held out his large coffee.

"Thanks. Come on up," he said.

"You sure?"

"Wouldn't say it if I wasn't."

I smiled. He waited for me to enter, and I thought he was going to close and lock the gate, but he didn't.

I parked my vehicle next to his. He smiled and held up the coffee as I climbed out of my Jeep. "Thanks. This is a nice way to start my morning."

"I'm calling it my late-night pick-me-up."

"Another case?"

I nodded. "Big one, too."

"Want to talk about it?"

"Thanks, but I'm good."

"Understood." He flashed his straight white teeth. "For what it's worth, you don't look the worse for wear."

I gave him a tired smile. "Thanks."

"Feel like taking a walk with me?"

"May I pet the horses?"

"They would be disappointed if you didn't."

I wasn't entirely comfortable with the horses yet, but petting them no longer scared me. Their peaceful beauty had an almost calming effect on me. Tommy said they'd always done that for him, and I was beginning to understand how.

We walked toward the stables. Sean patted the head of a beautiful black horse named Cadet. The horse snorted, and he shoved a pitchfork of hay into the stall. "There you go, buddy. Calm yourself."

I smiled as the horse chomped on his breakfast. "You really have a connection with them, don't you?"

"I've been doing this a long time."

"I have a fish."

He tried not to hide his smile. "Fish are good."

"I know, for dinner."

His smile appeared in full force. "Your life doesn't exactly allow for a bigger commitment to a mammal. A fish probably keeps you a little grounded, though."

Was I that easily readable for him or was he just compassionate?

He turned toward me and tilted his head. "You okay?"

I sipped my coffee. "Yeah. Yeah, I'm fine." Cadet wandered to the front of the stall, flicked his head at me, and snorted.

"He wants you to pet him." He handed me a carrot from his pocket. "Remember how to do this?"

"Flat hand." I held out my hand and smiled. "Here you go, Cadet." His whiskers tickled my palm when he took the carrot. I slowly moved my hand to pat the space between his eyes after he finished chewing the small treat. "Good boy, Cadet. Good boy."

"He likes you," Sean said.

"The feeling's mutual."

Sean stuck the pitchfork into the hay and tossed some in another stall. "So, what's on your mind?"

"What do you mean?"

"You've come around a few times, and you've always had something on your mind. I may not know you that well, but

I'm smart enough to know when you're trying to process something and need someplace comfortable to do it."

We both knew the horses in the stables weren't the only large animals in the room. Sean just told the elephant to take a seat and fed it a peanut. It took a lot to render me speechless, but he succeeded. "I, uh, I..."

His eyes sparkled when he smiled. "Don't sweat it." He held up his coffee. "I just appreciate the caffeine."

I checked my watch. I was back on official duty in a little over two hours and desperately in need of a cigarette and a shower, and maybe another cigarette. "Well, I have to be at work in a bit, and I'm sure my partner would appreciate me showering." I turned to leave, and he followed me out. We didn't say anything as we walked toward my vehicle.

When I opened the door, he finally said, "Rachel?"

I faced him, and he held up the cup again. "Next one's on me."

I smiled and nodded, then climbed into my Jeep and left. I drove the entire way home wondering why I felt drawn to someone I barely knew. I could rationalize it all I wanted, pretend it was the horses, but deep down, I knew otherwise.

Once home, I fed Herman and gave him an update on the case while he feasted on his pellets. Since he had no input, I went outside and stood on my patio, chain-smoking through two cigarettes. When I walked back inside, my eyes went right to the picture frame and Tommy's face. I stared down at the pack of cigarettes in my hand, then tossed them into the kitchen garbage can. I hung my head, shamed by the photo of a man who didn't judge me in life and wouldn't in death, either.

Bishop leaned against the department's kitchen counter sipping the burnt stuff. "You look like shit."

"Good morning to you too." I poured a cup of thick, syrupy goo. "Who made this?"

He shrugged. "Wasn't me. Saw the file. You get any sleep?"

"Some of us don't watch the clock when we're working an investigation."

"And others know being alert is half the job."

I walked to my cubby. Bishop followed, file in hand. He sat in the chair in front of my desk. "You want to know what I think?"

I set my bag down and took off my jacket. "If I say no, will you shut up?"

"I don't think you're completely off the mark here."

"But?"

"But even a little off the mark can kill an investigation."

"I never forget a face, Bishop."

"I'm not questioning your capabilities."

"Then what're you questioning, my objectivity?"

"I think I should take lead."

"Your best friend's brother was murdered. You think you're impartial enough to take lead?" I laughed. "I call bullshit."

"You can call whatever you want, but this is different. Abernathy shouldn't let you work the investigation if there's even a possibility of it being connected to your husband."

"You and me both."

"Right, which is why we both have to take our emotions out of this. He's right. One screw-up and the DA will be on our asses."

"You don't think he'll pull us, do you? Harry and that asshole Sanders don't have a clue."

He dragged his fingers down his five-o'clock shadow. "Doesn't matter. If we don't get our shit together and stop acting like assholes, we're done, and I don't want to drop something this big in Sanders's lap. He's not smart enough, and I don't need to give him any ammunition for the sergeant position."

"Good." I dropped an F-bomb. "I spent the entire night organizing that information! It shows a possible connection, and we need to move with it."

Jimmy walked into the cubby and leaned against the partial wall. "Harry and Sanders have a confidential informant who might know something about Pruitt. They're working him now. I'll keep you posted."

My jaw dropped. "Those two have a confidential informant?"

Jimmy smirked. "They're good detectives, Ryder."

Twice in a few hours, I'd been speechless. What the hell was happening?

"Come on," Bishop said. "Let's get out of here and have some real coffee. You look like you need it."

———————

I tapped my fingers on my thighs as we drove through town. As he passed the Dunkin' Donuts, I pointed and said, "Wait. I wanted real coffee."

"Keep your pants on, we're going for real coffee."

"But it's Dunkin'."

"There's other real coffee in this town, partner."

Not in my opinion. "Where?"

"Community Cup."

"Ah, I got it. It's a cinnamon roll kind of day."

"It's always a cinnamon roll kind of day."

"Those things will kill you."

"Not if the cigarettes do first."

That hit me in the ego. "Ouch."

"Truth hurts."

The shop was in the middle of a remodel, but that didn't stop them from tempting people with the smell of coffee and baked goods. The line was already out the door, but the staff was quick and efficient, and it wouldn't take long. I grabbed a seat while Bishop ordered his cinnamon roll, our coffees, and a banana for me.

A tall man dressed in a black suit and white button-down walked in our direction.

Bishop's eyes widened. "Whoa. Didn't expect to see him out in public."

The man was very attractive. "Damn, he's easy on the eyes."

The man walked over to our table and extended his hand to my partner. "Rob, long time."

"Nice to see you," Bishop said.

He stared at me for a moment. "Detective Ryder. Scott Blackberry."

Shit! I stood and offered my hand. "Mr. Blackberry."

An awkward silence filled the air. And not just at our small table. The entire place shut up and watched us. Scott Blackberry was unpopular in town in a hated-celebrity sort of way.

"I, uh, I...oh, hell. I don't know what I'm trying to say."

I smiled. "No need to say anything." I felt for the guy. It was a bold move, going out in public. His marriage to Kathi Blackberry ended before the Light investigation, but Hamby's a small town, and people like to dig up old dirt and toss it around for fun.

"Yes, well, the looks I'm getting around town aren't all

that pleasant, but I have a child and I need to honor her wishes."

Blackberry's ex-wife was awaiting trial for her part in my first official case in Hamby. It wasn't pretty, nearly reaching Chicago-level crime, and I respected the guy for having the balls to come back and live with his wife's decisions. I respected their daughter more for wanting to stay and put up with the guaranteed BS she had to be getting from her elitist friends. I'm not sure I'd have the guts.

"It'll pass," Bishop said. "Something else will happen, and people will move on. Just give it some time."

"I'm not sure having an ex-wife working a prostitution ring with the former mayor's wife will disappear anytime soon, but I appreciate the encouragement, and I wanted to thank you. My daughter could have easily ended up a victim."

I didn't have the heart to tell him she was already a victim. "We just did our job, sir."

"And I appreciate it." He smiled and nodded once at me. "Detective."

I nodded back. After he left, the rest of the café hummed along, already gossiping amongst themselves, their phones in hand, ready to spread the gossip. I sipped my coffee. "Community Cup, where people come to shit on their neighbors." I eyed Bishop. "I know what you did there."

"What?" His smile gave him away. "Fine. He called me this morning and asked if we could meet. I thought it might give us both some perspective."

"He didn't stay long."

"Would you?"

"Good point, and while I appreciate the effort, I don't need thanks for doing my job."

"Maybe not, but it's good to know you did the right thing."

"And here we go. I am doing the right thing. I'm not wrong about this."

"I'm not saying you're wrong. You talk to Garcia?"

I nodded. "He's on it. If Perez is in Chicago, he'll find him and let me know."

He picked up his phone and tapped on the screen. It rang a few seconds later. He answered it right away. "Anything?" He paused. "What? You're sure?" More silence, and then, "Okay, appreciate you keeping us in the loop. Any word on the hair?" He nodded. "Thanks." He ended the call. "Ashley went through the vehicle again."

"Did she find anything else?"

He nodded. "She's not happy about missing it, but she did find a partial set of prints inside the trunk door."

"And?"

"They don't match anything in the system."

"Shit."

"No word on the hair, but that could take weeks, she said."

"I know. Fulton County lab is backed up and it's not a priority."

My cell phone rang. I checked the ID. "It's my part—former partner." I hit the green icon. "What'd you find?"

"Perez was picked up on probation violation around five this morning. He's in County now."

I swore under my breath. "That doesn't mean he's not our guy. He could have gotten back home already."

Bishop glanced at his watch.

"I'll let you know if I hear anything. In the meantime, keep me posted," Garcia said.

"I will. Thanks."

Bishop shook his head before I had a chance to say anything. "It takes half a day to drive to Chicago from here." He glanced at his watch again. "It's been a little over twelve hours since you chased the guy out of the bar. It wasn't him, Ryder."

I shook my head, but I wasn't sure I believed it myself anymore. "Shit."

"There's a first for everything."

"Screw you, Bishop." I stood.

"We've lost a lot of time on this already." He stuffed the partially eaten roll into the little baggie beside his plate. "I might know someone who can help us. Let me make a call."

20

Twenty minutes later we were sitting at a Starbucks on Haynes Bridge Road with Captain Jack Bradwell of the Alpharetta Police Department. After Bishop's quick introduction, Bradwell offered to buy coffee.

"I'm good," Bishop said as he held up his bottled water.

"If I have any more, I won't sleep for days," I said.

Bradwell smiled. "I'm told sleep's overrated."

We all laughed.

I watched Captain Bradwell walk away. He had the lean physique of an athlete. Trim but strong, slim waist, and broad shoulders. He kept his hair short, and his caramel-colored face showed no sign of stubble. I whispered to Bishop, "That's a big dude. Got to be close to seven feet."

He nodded. "Six-nine. Had a full basketball scholarship to Vanderbilt."

"Holy shit. Why didn't he go pro?"

"Once told me he felt better suited for the law than for sports. He was an Army reservist first. Served two years in Afghanistan after college, then went reserves. He's been with APD for I think about five years now? Good man. Knows the law."

Captain Bradwell sat across from me and smiled. He placed a manila file folder on the table. "I read about your case. I'm sorry for your loss."

"Thank you."

"I've spoken with my informant. I can get you a meeting, but he needs a guarantee this won't come back to bite him in the ass."

"We can do that," I said. Bishop shot me a look, but I ignored it.

"I need to attend."

I eyed the file. Confidential informant files were always red, not the standard manila kind. Always. The red separated them from other case files so internal investigations or other officers recognized them quickly and could access the confidential information. Why wasn't the file red? Was it his CI's file or did it belong to another case? "I'm good with that."

"Who's the CI?" Bishop asked.

He examined the room, then pulled a pen from his shirt pocket and wrote a name on a napkin. He turned it toward us and slid it into the middle of the small table.

My eyes widened. "Damn. That's an oxymoron if I've ever seen one."

"You can't see oxymorons," Bradwell said, smiling.

"We can't make any promises related to any current or future investigations other than this one," Bishop said.

"Understood." He took a drink from his paper cup. "Okay, then. Los Senoritas in the supermercado off Route 20 and Pilgrim Mill, Cumming. Twenty-two hundred hours." He stood. "I'll meet you there."

"Why not the department?"

"My CI can't be seen at the department, not unless he's brought in wearing cuffs."

I nodded. "Got it."

When he walked out the door, I tapped Bishop's shoulder. "The file wasn't red."

"What file?"

"The file Bradwell had with him."

"Probably was something else he's working on. Bradwell's good people."

"If you say so." I sat staring at Perez's mugshot. How could I have been wrong? I closed my eyes and flashed back to the man in the black leather jacket. Same build. Same facial structure. Both traits Perez shared with his cousin.

Bishop glanced at my phone. "We need to follow where the facts take us." He checked his watch. "I have an appointment."

I grabbed my coat. "Let's go."

"Actually, it'll be a few hours. How about I take you back to the department. You should follow up with Ashley and call Barron. See if he's finished the report on Brad's autopsy yet."

"What's the appointment? Online hookup?"

"Over my dead body."

"Some chicks dig that."

Ashley examined several photos spread out on a lab table, a magnifying glass in hand, loving every minute of it. She glanced up and smiled when I coughed. "Did you know a body can still bruise after death? I find that fascinating."

I walked toward the metal table. "Is that Brad Pruitt?"

She nodded. "Dr. Barron dropped off the autopsy report.

It's online too, but he knows how much I like this stuff, so he gave me a copy." She handed me a file folder. "Left me yours too."

I opened to the final results and read them. "Damn."

"I've read it's common."

"Very, but that doesn't mean it'll be easier for his family to hear."

"The beating itself was awful. The photos tell a story, but Mr. Pruitt was in bad shape before he died. Many of his internal organs were already in complete failure. The beating may have precipitated his death, but he was going to die soon anyway." She held a photo up to the light and stared into the magnifying glass. "Still ruled a homicide, though, so that's good, right?"

"I'm not sure there's anything good about any of this."

She studied another photo of Brad's chest. "This wasn't planned. Look at those marks. That's pure rage right there."

I tilted my head. "You ever consider going to medical school?"

"That's a little out of my budget."

"There's loans for that."

"I'm good for now." She opened my file to the report. "Breadknife. That had to hurt."

"Yes." I considered the photo. "And those aren't just lying around in the middle of drug houses."

"We don't know where he was killed."

"No, but the type of knife helps narrow down possible locations." I flipped through the photos. "Can you do me a favor?"

"Sure."

"See if you can find a knife that matches that pattern. Start with restaurant supply sites. If you find one, or even something close, find out if they deliver to Good Times."

"Can't I just call Good Times and ask about their knives?"

"No. The place is a front for drugs. They'll toss everything they've got if they know we're looking at them."

"I'm on it."

"Hey, Ash?"

"Yeah?"

"Any word on that hair from the Malibu?"

She shook her head. "I'll see if I can get a rush on it."

"Thanks." I took the report to my desk and read through it twice. My initial thoughts were right, and so was Ashley. The knife wounds were rage wounds. Whoever did this was pissed off, their anger at peak levels. They wanted him dead, but they wanted him to suffer first. I leaned back in my chair and dropped my head over the seat, covered my face with my hands, and sighed. "Shit."

"Is that Brad's autopsy?"

I dropped my hands and nodded to Bishop. "It's ugly."

He held out his hands as he sat. "Let me see."

"Wait. Before you do, there's something you need to know."

"Just give me the file, Ryder."

I tossed the autopsy file across my desk. "The pictures are rough, but the cause of death makes sense."

He scanned the report, then dragged his hand down his facial stubble. "Son of a bitch.

Acquired Immune Deficiency Syndrome? He was beaten and stabbed to death. He didn't die of AIDS."

"No, complications related to AIDS and septic shock. It's not uncommon with addicts."

"I know." He flipped through the pages in the file, then sighed and set it back on my desk. "This is going to kill Allison."

"It's still ruled a homicide, and finding his killer will help both her and Andy heal."

"I'm not sure they'll ever recover from the damage Brad's done."

"Maybe not, but they'll move on. Knowing it's over is much better than the constant struggle when he was alive."

"Tell that to a grieving sibling."

"Ashley's looking into the knife. If we can match it to Good Times, we narrow our suspect list tremendously."

"Right." He stared at my wall.

"In the meantime," I continued, "I did an extensive search on NCIC." I opened my Perez file and spread out seven sets of rap sheets and mugshots. "Seven possible suspects, three in Georgia and four in Illinois."

He glanced at the photos. "What are these?"

"Perez lookalikes from Chicago and here."

He examined them further. "Shit, they do look like him. You think it's possible Petrowski sent someone who resembled Sanchez on purpose?"

I nodded, then pointed to the first three mugshots, leaving the other four to prove a point. "Maybe he didn't send anyone. Maybe he found them here."

His eyes widened.

"These three are from Georgia. All known associates of Morales. The other four are known associates of Miquel Sanchez."

He exhaled. "Were you involved with any of their arrests?"

I shook my head. "Tommy was. His info on Petrowski brought down an entire drug ring."

"Any of them these guys?"

I put one photo on top of another. "These two. The other

two are MIA. Best guess is they went into hiding and are using other names now."

He rubbed his chin. "And behaving."

"Or just haven't been caught, or better, in town to see me."

"You asking Garcia to keep an eye out?"

"Already have, and Joey's already on it."

"Your tech guy."

"Yes. If these two are using new identities, he'll be able to find out."

He nodded. "That's a start."

I stuffed the photos into my file just as the chief walked in.

"DEA just busted a meth conversion lab off Mountain Road. They've asked for an assist. I'm giving it to you two."

"Us? What about Harry and Sanders?"

"They're working their CI for Pruitt's murder."

Bishop stood. "Maybe we should push them along, help them work faster?"

"It's their confidential informant. You show up, and they'll lose him." Jimmy looked at me. "This is an assist only. Go, make nice, offer help, then leave. That's all."

Jimmy didn't do things without a reason, so I trusted he had one. "Got it," I said. I stacked all my files into a pile and stuffed them in my bag.

"Yes, sir." Bishop stood and walked quickly to his cubby.

I slipped into my shoulder holster and secured my weapons. "Why weren't we informed before the bust?"

"Task force isn't local. They got the intel and moved quickly."

I nodded. "Got it."

We walked out of my cubby and met Bishop as he left his.

Jimmy filled us in on what he knew, which wasn't much. "Looks like they got a few Mexican nationals, but not sure how many just yet."

"Damn. Anything other than liquid?"

"Over five hundred pounds."

"Jesus," Bishop said.

Bishop checked out a department cruiser, and with our lights and sirens on, we made it to the location in ten minutes. We showed our IDs to the DEA agent at the front of the driveway. "Detectives Bishop and Ryder, Hamby PD," he said.

Special Agent Olsen filled us in. "Five hundred pounds and over three dozen barrels of liquid."

"That's a big bust for our town," Bishop said.

"It's a big bust for any town," Olsen said. "There are six counties involved, but this location is the base. We've got a team on a barn in DeKalb County used to store approximately 150 pounds of meth. We'll check legal status on the arrests, but we know what that'll show."

"Any legal names?" I asked.

"On the two nationals, yes, but the others are sketchy."

"Can we have a look?"

"Sure, but if you've got an active investigation on any of them, it'll turn over to us."

"Understood."

He looked to Bishop for a response.

"No active drug cases for the department, Agent."

I liked Agent Olsen. His strong jaw and confident posture told me he knew what he was doing, and believed he was good at it. He didn't come off as cocky, which I appreciated, and judging by the way his beige pants and green shirt fit, he clearly used his gym membership.

Olsen pointed toward three black vans halfway up the

long driveway. "Have a look. Let me know if you recognize anyone."

"Will do," I said.

They'd separated the men, sticking the two nationals in black sedans and the four unsubs in the two vans, each man separated by a steel wall. An agent dressed in all black opened the first van's side door. Bishop and I examined the two men, whose hands and feet were cuffed to bars attached to the steel wall. I checked for any similarities to our Malibu driver, but they weren't close. When I glanced at Bishop, he shook his head.

We both recognized one of the next two, making sure to acknowledge that nonverbally so the agent wouldn't notice. Bishop knew the two nationals from photos, but not a case connection. We walked back over to Agent Olsen and let him know we weren't familiar with the unsubs or nationals pertaining to any prior investigations.

"One of the men in the second van is a known associate of Raul Morales," I said. "Local dealer in town."

"We know him," he said.

"Full disclosure, we're working a murder investigation where our victim was a previous client of Morales, but at this time, we have no evidence to show Morales's involvement."

He nodded once. "Detective Ryder, correct?"

I nodded.

"You ever see a conversion lab?"

"I'm from Chicago PD. I've seen them multiple times."

He nodded. "I bet you have." He eyed Bishop.

"I could always use a refresher," Bishop said.

He handed us pairs of booties and gloves and walked us inside. The drywall in the main area had been removed, leaving just the wood frames to hold up the ceiling.

"Looks like a five-star operation," I said sarcastically.

"The portable burners are top of the line. Those things run close to two hundred a pop."

"I have one of those propane tanks," Bishop said.

"Easy to get anywhere, unfortunately," Olsen said. He pointed to a row of blue barrels sitting in front of the back wall. "These guys don't scrimp on their supplies. Tells me they're making a pretty penny on their stuff."

"It's easier to produce this kind of volume with quality tools," I said.

He laughed. "Right. Too bad it's going to sit in an evidence locker now." He finished showing us around and walked us out. Like Jimmy said, he hadn't asked for any assistance.

"Agent Olsen, is there anything we can do for you?" I asked.

"Not at this time, Detective. We just needed to know about the men."

"Understood," I said. "We may be in contact about the Shrek-looking one."

He smirked. "Shrek? Isn't that a cartoon character?"

"Yes, sir."

A smile stretched across his face. "Very well." He handed us his card. "If you learn anything, please call, and I'll update you if I learn anything on your guy."

"Thanks," I said, but I knew the drill. This wasn't a provisional task force that used local police as temporary agents, so DEA would only update us if they needed something. The only way we'd get our hands on any information was if Jimmy pressured them for it. It didn't matter. What mattered was we had something to use with Morales, and I was champing at the bit to do that.

"Looks like one of the Shreks got himself in a bind," I said as we got into the car.

Bishop chuckled.

"You're calling Captain Bradwell, right?"

Bishop pulled back onto the road. "Yes." He made the call while driving.

"No phone in hands while driving," I sniped. "It's the law."

He ignored me but placed the phone in a compartment on the cruiser's dashboard.

"Bradwell."

"Bishop here. We need to see Morales now."

"Not sure I can make that work."

"We were just at the DEA bust on Mountain Road. One of the guys was at Good Times with your informant the other night."

"Shit." He breathed hard into the phone. "Let me call you back."

We drove across town toward State Route 400, expecting to head either to Cumming or somewhere in Alpharetta. I called Jimmy and gave him an update.

Bradwell called back ten minutes later and gave us a new meetup location. "You've got thirty minutes to get there or he's gone."

"We're fifteen out." Bishop ended the call and said to me, "Same hotel Brad was staying in."

"Coincidence?"

"I'm going with no."

"Right there with you."

21

Captain Bradwell met us in the back of the building. We walked over to the side and took the stairs to the second floor, and Bradwell knocked on room 201. The other Shrek answered the door. I stopped myself from congratulating him on his freedom.

Raul Morales sat at a small table near the window. The curtains were drawn, and only a desk lamp provided dim light in the room. Shrek stayed by the door while two other men, far less Shrek-like than the first, stood on each side of Morales. He puffed on a cigar and nodded at us.

"I will not speak of the lab," he said.

I stayed still, my eyes glued to him. "Your guy from the other night, the one who held the gun to the back of my head?"

"An unfortunate mistake on his part," Morales said.

"Is his connection to the meth lab unfortunate also?"

He stayed quiet.

"He's going down for it. Let's hope you're not connected, because they'll offer him a deal to nab you."

"As I mentioned," Captain Bradwell said to Morales, "it's a DEA bust. Locals have no authority."

Morales stared at me and Bishop, then glanced at Shrek and nodded. Shrek opened the door and the three thugs exited, leaving us alone with Morales. He stood and walked over to the kitchenette, opening the small refrigerator and taking out a Modelo beer bottle before popping it open.

"Your buddy's hanging in the back of a black SUV awaiting what will likely be a cold jail cell with a hard metal john," I said.

"As I said, I will not speak of the incident."

"You do you," I said. "Just making sure you understand we have no control over any of that."

"It is understood. Now, Mr. Pruitt's death is unfortunate, yes, but I cannot claim involvement."

"Cannot or will not?" I asked. "Words matter."

"Your Brad Pruitt was in over his head. Any death is a tragedy, but business is business, and as I said before, I am a man of my word."

I glanced at Bishop, noting the redness blooming on his cheeks. He kept his posture straight and his expression blank, but I knew it took a lot of effort.

"Whose business?" I asked.

"Not mine," Morales said. "Let me be clear once again. I cut off Pruitt weeks ago. If I had wanted him dead, he would be dead. He made promises he could not keep, but I made an agreement with his debt payer, and I have honored that."

"What debt payer?" Bishop asked.

"A gracious family member paid his debt in full. He was bad for business, but I was assured he would not come to my men any longer. As long as he stayed away, I promised to do the same."

Bishop stayed perfectly still while speaking calmly. "You're saying his family paid his debt?"

Morales nodded. "That is exactly what I am saying."

"Who specifically?"

Morales smirked. "His sister."

I rolled my eyes and shook my head. Allison's intentions might have been good, but she'd put herself in serious danger, playing a game she knew nothing about.

"Then what? He didn't stay away, so you took him out?" Bishop asked.

The tension in the room was palpable. Bishop considered the Pruitts family, and if Allison was in any kind of risk, I couldn't predict his actions. I stepped closer to my partner.

"Again, I did not kill him, but I do believe I know who did."

Morales set his beer on the table and placed his hands where we could see them. It was a calculated move, and one I took to show cooperation. "We made an agreement. I have honored that agreement."

"An agreement, my ass. You just bought his sister," Bishop said.

"It was a simple business agreement. I did not purchase anything from the woman. That is not the way I work." He stared at Bradwell. "Again, business is business, and I only make promises I can keep."

I wanted to call bullshit, but out of respect for Bradwell, I kept my mouth shut.

"But," Morales said, "I speak only for my business. As you know, there are many other distributors across the city, and if Mr. Pruitt owed someone else, I cannot guarantee he or his family would remain safe."

"Just cut the crap, Morales. Who do you think killed Pruitt?"

"I need guarantees." He eyed Bradwell.

I watched the two, carefully checking for nonverbal communication and noting their trust. When Bradwell caught my eye, he nodded once. He knew something, but he wasn't going to say it in front of his informant.

"Was it the man I chased out of Good Times the other night?" I asked.

Morales held up his palms. "He is not part of my organization, and I am not aware of his identity."

"Yet he was in the club you use to make your business transactions."

"It is a great country, this United States. A truly free world."

"Who does he work for?" Bishop asked.

"I have never seen the man before."

I raised my eyebrows. "You sure about that?"

He nodded. "It is my business to know everyone in my line of work. He is not a known associate, and I had not seen him before that evening."

I had to take him at his word, but I knew he wasn't telling us everything. I'd brought the file of mugshots with me. I held it up and then set it on the table, pulling out each photograph one by one, starting with the two men from Chicago.

"I do not recognize him," he said to the first.

"This one?" I asked of the second.

"No."

The test would be if he acknowledged the three from Georgia, his own men. If he was smart, he'd know we already knew the answer, but criminals are surprisingly stupid, and usually the ones who played smart were the dumbest. I dropped each photo onto the table one by one, not giving him a chance to speak, then met his eyes.

He nodded. "I can assume you know I am associated with these men."

"They all look a lot like the man in the black jacket."

"Similar features, I will give you that."

Bishop's patience was deteriorating quickly. "Enough of the bullshit. Who killed Pruitt?"

Bradwell touched his shoulder. "Bishop."

"Perhaps it would be in your best interests to speak with El Uno." Morales looked straight at Bishop. "However." He walked toward the nightstand and directed his next comments to me. "It is 'detective,' yes?"

"Yes."

He opened the drawer, removed a small cigar case, and walked back to the table. He opened the case and set it down facing the door.

"You are like me, si?"

"I don't prey on weak people. I help them."

He smiled. "I fill a need, meet a growing demand. I did not create the problem, Detective. I simply benefit from it." He paused, removed a cigar, and snipped off the end. "But that is not my point."

"Okay, I'll play. What's your point?"

"Like me, people do not want you involved in their business."

"I wouldn't say that's unique to just us."

He nodded once. "Tell me, why is this man after you?"

"What makes you think he's after me?"

"As I've said, it is my business to know things."

"What is it you know?"

He lit the cigar, took a puff, and blew it out. "The word is you are looking for someone from your past."

My heart raced. "What do you know about that?"

"I know nothing."

"Bullshit." I stepped closer to him. "You know something, you'd better tell me."

Bradwell took a step closer and Morales took two steps toward me. I tilted my chin up.

"Not everyone is trustworthy, Detective. You should be careful with whom you place your trust."

I turned toward Captain Bradwell. "Is this guy fucking serious?" I snapped my cuffs from my belt. "He's coming in."

Bradwell grabbed my arm. "Detective Ryder, no."

I stared at his hand on my arm. "Hand off, Captain, or this is going to get ugly quick."

He removed his hand. "Morales and I have what you might call an arrangement. He's working with me on several cases at the moment. You take him in, it could blow everything."

I re-attached my cuffs and pointed at Morales. "You make one wrong move, asshole, and you can kiss your CI agreement goodbye. Do you understand?"

He smiled.

Bishop tapped my forearm. "Come on." He glared at Morales. "Your information turns out wrong, we'll bring you in for obstruction of justice, you understand?"

He smiled again.

Asshole. I jabbed my finger toward him. "You're a piece of shit," I said, then pointed at Bradwell. "And so are you." As I headed out of the room, I glanced back at the cigar case, my heart racing when I saw the skull printed on the inside.

Bishop put out a BOLO for Jose Parra, or, as he liked to be called, El Uno.

22

Allison slammed her hands onto the boutique's counter. "What did you think I'd do, just let them kill my brother?"

"You should have come to me," Bishop said. "You don't know what these people are capable of."

"They're capable of robbing my parents blind, beating the shit out of Brad multiple times, threatening to rape me, threatening to kill my parents, God rest their souls. I'm not afraid of them, Bishop. They can't hurt me any more than they already have."

Bishop's jaw dropped in shock.

"And there wasn't time to consider other options. It's not like Brad told me upfront. He tried to work it out himself. He did, but it was too late, and by the time he told me about it, he made it very clear if his debt wasn't paid, they wouldn't just come after him. What was I supposed to do?"

"Allison." I stayed calm compared to Bishop's heated emotions. "Who was there when you paid Morales? Where did you do it?"

"Here. They came here. We'd closed for the night. Brad was in back. The guy, I guess the, I don't know, the main guy or something? He came in. I gave him the money. He promised he wouldn't hurt me, and he gave his word he'd stop selling to Brad. That's all that mattered to me."

She was so upset, she hadn't answered my question. "Was anyone else with him?"

"Yeah, I mean, they stayed outside. Two men, I think?"

"When was this?" Bishop asked.

"I don't know, five or six months ago, maybe?"

"You should have come to me."

"There wasn't any time."

I handed her the mugshots from Georgia. "Any of these guys outside that night?"

She held up the second of the three. "Him, I think." She tipped her head back and sighed. "I don't know for sure."

"Look again," Bishop said, struggling to stay calm.

She did as he asked. "I don't recognize the others, Rob. I swear. What does it matter anyway? Brad's dead, and the guy I paid promised he would stay away."

"These guys are killers, Allison. They don't give a shit about promises!"

I took the photos and put them back in the file while Bishop lectured her on the stupidity of her actions. I couldn't argue with his statements, but his approach left something to be desired. Allison was on the verge of hyperventilating. I stepped in front of my partner and walked around the counter, placing my hand on Allison's shoulder. "It's okay." I then used my phone and opened up a text message from Michels, who I'd called en route to the boutique. I showed her a photo of Jose Parra. "Have you ever seen this man?"

She nodded. "He came looking for Brad a few weeks ago. I...I told him I hadn't seen him in months, and that wasn't a lie."

"Did he threaten you, touch you?"

She shook her head. "He told me to tell my brother he was looking for him, that's all." She stared at Bishop. "I should have told you, but it happened so often, and I hated always bothering you." She wrapped her arms around me and sobbed. "I just wanted to protect him."

She soaked my shoulder with her tears. I can handle blood. I can handle severed and mutilated body parts. But the emotions of the people left with those body parts rip my soul apart. I patted her back and felt her relax a little. "Allison, did the man come alone? The second one?"

She shook her head. "He had two other guys with him."

"Can you describe them?"

"Both Mexicans, average height, but one worked out, you know? He was built like the one talking to me. Shaved heads. The big one had a tattoo of a cross on his neck."

"Okay. That helps."

"He's dead because of me, isn't he?"

"No," Bishop said. "You couldn't control what your brother did. He made his own choices, Allison. That's on him."

"How much did you pay?" I asked.

She pressed her lips together, then stared at her feet. "Ten thousand."

"Jesus," Rob said. He paced the length of the counter, cussing up a storm.

"Please, Rob. Please find his killer. I won't feel safe until you do."

Bishop made a promise that might be impossible to keep.

I hated to give her even worse news, but it would come out sooner or later. "Allison, Brad's autopsy report came back."

She wiped her nose, and her eyes, bloodshot and swollen, begged for hope. "Did he feel any pain?"

Sometimes lying was best for the living. "We don't think so, but, honey"—I held her hands—"Brad had AIDS."

She blinked. "He what? No. He said he got tested all the time. He even had a relationship with a pharmacy. They gave him clean needles."

I doubted that. That practice wasn't as common as addicts pretended. "It's an unfortunate situation for many addicts, Allison. I'm sorry."

"But he was murdered. The AIDS didn't kill him. He was beaten to death, right?" Her eyes begged for something good. "It's still a murder investigation, right?"

"Yes, but it's complicated."

"I don't understand."

"His organs were failing. They were already in septic shock. His heart stopped." I left out the gory details, and even though what I said wasn't entirely accurate, it gave her some peace she desperately needed.

She cried some more, then wiped her nose and said, "Can we have his body?"

"Soon," I said. "Soon."

As we left, Bishop slammed the boutique door behind him. "Piece of shit killed her brother and knows where she works. Once he finds out she paid Morales, he'll come back for the money."

"We'll get protection on her."

"I'm sending her away."

"They could have people watching her already," I said.

"I don't give a shit. I'll get Michels to pick her up, bring her in, and we'll transport her with another vehicle. She can wear a uniform. They won't watch for that."

"You'd be surprised," I said.

He turned and glared at me. "She's like family to me."

"I know, but we have to be careful, calculated, so she's safe. Okay?"

He nodded.

"I don't think Andy knows she paid the debt, but that doesn't matter. If they want the money, they'll come looking for him too."

He nodded. "He wouldn't have let her pay it."

"That doesn't matter anymore."

Michels called. "We got a hit on this El Uno."

"Where is he?"

"You ready for this?"

"Shoot," I said.

"In our interrogation room."

"Damn, nice work."

"Don't thank me. He was already here with Harry and Sanders."

"No shit? That's their informant?"

Michels chuckled. "Yup."

23

Jimmy sat behind his desk and closed his eyes slowly, then opened them and called the front desk. "Call Harry and Sanders in, please."

I kept my lips zipped for a change.

"Captain Bradwell?"

Bishop nodded.

"He should have come to me."

"As I said, I contacted him," Bishop said.

"I don't give a fuck who made the call. I've worked with him. If his guy knows something about one of my men—" He glanced at me. "You know what I mean."

I smiled.

"Then he should have called me."

I watched the second hand on the clock above the chief's head, the rhythm of my heartbeat almost matching its tick.

He pointed to me. "You should have called me."

"We called Michels and got the BOLO out. It's not procedure to call you for that."

"I don't give a damn about procedure. You have a viable suspect from a CI, you bring me in. You got it?"

I bit my lip. Jimmy wasn't stupid, and he hadn't jumped the ranks of the department as fast as he had because of his looks. He was a good cop, and a good cop knows some cases require drawing outside the lines. But he was the chief, and his job was to keep his team inside the lines. "We followed the path of the investigation, Chief."

He glared at me. I shifted in my seat. And with perfect timing, our two fellow detectives knocked on Jimmy's door.

Bishop stood and spoke before anyone else had the chance. "Your informant killed our vic."

Sanders bowed up and went nose to nose with him, which seemed to be happening a lot lately. "Fuck you, Bishop."

"Bullshit," I said. "Brad's sister ID'd him at her store. He was looking for Pruitt. You do the math."

"Enough," Jimmy said. He checked the BOLO in the system. "Which room is Parra in?"

"Two." Sanders glared at Bishop. "And based on the information our CI provided, we took the liberty to bring in Raul Morales as a possible connection to the DEA meth lab bust, as well as a viable suspect in the Pruitt murder investigation."

Sanders and Harry just crossed a case line no good detective would ever cross. You don't go rogue on another detective's case, not without at least giving them a heads-up.

"Shit," Bishop said. "We need to get Bradwell here. We promised him we'd keep Morales out of jail."

"Get him on the phone," Jimmy said. He directed his frustration at Sanders and Harry. "What the fuck were you thinking? All of you! Jesus Christ! I feel like I'm dealing with a room full of amateurs."

Sanders's lips formed a thin, straight line. "Sir, we aren't aware of any agreement between the department and Captain Bradwell."

Jimmy looked to me and Bishop.

I cringed. "We haven't had a chance to put it all into the system." I stared at Sanders. "We've been a little busy investigating a murder."

Jimmy rubbed his head and sighed. "Fuck."

I explained the situation.

Harry covered his ass. "Our informant assured us his information is correct."

I reminded my boss of the unintended consequences of the situation. "Chief, I know Morales personally. He has men with him twenty-four-seven, and I guarantee they're nearby as we speak. I can safely say this El Uno dude, or Parra, or whatever the hell he goes by, works the same way. Right now, we've probably got at least ten sets of eyes on the department. We have to tread carefully."

"Damn, we can't bring Allison in yet," Bishop said. He made a call to patrol and got three on her boutique.

"Son of a bitch," Jimmy said. "This is a fucking train wreck."

"Our CI claims Brad Pruitt owed Morales money, something to the tune of ten grand. Word was he went into hiding because he couldn't pay it."

"His sister paid it. Confirmed by both Morales and Allison," I said.

I caught Sanders rolling his eyes before he asked, "You trust the cartel?"

"About as much as I trust you."

Jimmy didn't give Sanders a chance to respond. "Ladies."

His landline buzzed and a woman's voice came over the line. "A Captain Bradwell to see you, sir."

"That was quick," I said.

Bishop mumbled, "He was already on his way."

"Please have someone escort him back," Jimmy said over the speaker.

"Yes, sir."

Bradwell looked pissed, and I didn't blame him. I glanced at Bishop, who was directing glares between Harry and Sanders.

Jimmy stood and shook Bradwell's hand. "Captain."

"I understand you brought my informant in for questioning on the Pruitt murder?" He spoke to the chief, but it felt obvious he was talking to me and Bishop.

"Detectives Harry and Sanders have information that points to your informant as the killer."

"Witnesses?"

Harry spoke. "Our informant is a business associate of Morales."

Captain Bradwell scowled at Detective Harry. "A business associate? Do you have anything that puts my informant at the scene? Any evidence other than a verified paid debt connecting him to Pruitt's murder?"

"We believe our informant is telling the truth."

"Who is the informant?"

I offered that one up. "Jose Parra."

He turned to me. "El Uno? Are you serious?" He turned back to the chief. "I'd like to talk to Mr. Morales."

Jimmy nodded. "Bishop, Ryder, escort Captain Bradwell to the interrogation room."

Sanders stepped toward the door.

"Not you," Jimmy said. "You two stick around for a moment."

My eyes shifted toward Bishop, who acknowledged me with a raised brow.

As we walked to the interrogation room, we gave Bradwell a brief explanation of the situation.

"I understand. Let's hope Morales will too."

I didn't see Morales as the killer, but that didn't mean I trusted him. He'd tried to manipulate me earlier, and even though I knew he wasn't telling me something, I had to play things carefully. If I wanted him to give me what I needed, I had to appear to be on his side, show him I believed he didn't kill Pruitt, and let him think that's all that mattered to me. It wouldn't be easy, but nothing I did was.

Morales sat staring at the one-way mirror, his lips pursed so tightly they lost color. He wasn't pleased, and if we didn't recover quickly, we could lose not only a relationship with Captain Bradwell but with a credible source for Brad Pruitt's investigation as well.

"I did not have Pruitt eliminated. We have already discussed this," Morales said. "Why am I here?"

"Raul, I had no idea this was going to happen," Captain Bradwell said.

"Neither did we," I said. "Two other detectives have been working their CI for the case, and we didn't communicate with them because we—"

Bishop helped me save face. "We wanted to keep your involvement private."

He didn't flinch.

"It was a mistake, and we apologize," I said. I hated eating crow someone else cooked, but we needed the guy.

"You are not being charged," Bishop said.

"They have no evidence, then?" he asked.

Should they?

"They have an informant who they claim provided them the information."

"Who?" he asked.

Bradwell tilted his head. "That's not how it works, Morales."

"What evidence do they claim to have?"

"Just that Brad Pruitt owed you about 10K and didn't clear his debt, so you had him eliminated."

"As I have mentioned, that is incorrect. I assume you have verified this, yes?"

"Yes," I said.

"So, I may leave?"

"I'd like you to stick around a bit," I said.

He looked to Bradwell, who said, "I'll keep him with me. You have any questions, give me a call."

I nodded. "Give us a few minutes to get an escort, okay?"

"An escort?" He eyed Bradwell. "What is the reason?"

"A moment?" I walked toward the door, and Morales followed. "We've got Parra in another interrogation room, but I suspect that, like you, he's got eyes on the department. I don't want a gang war outside the building."

"Got it."

"We'll have you out of here in a few minutes," Bishop said. "But we'd appreciate it if you didn't leave town."

"I have no plans to leave anytime soon, amigo." Morales leaned back in his chair and smiled. "Please give El Uno my regards."

When Hamby built their city buildings, they used a well-known architect who specialized in bunker rooms for politicians' homes. The community's tax dollars paid a pretty penny for a bunker room at City Hall and a tunnel to and from the PD. I hated giving that kind of information to Morales, but we didn't have a choice. Michels and Bradwell escorted him through the tunnel, where he was picked up in the back lot of City Hall, near the garbage dumpster, and driven down the street and across Windward Parkway, where he'd told his men to wait.

In the meantime, Bishop arranged the safe house for Allison and Andy while I had a little chat with Parra.

I smiled and said, "My name is Detective Ryder," as I flipped a chair around. I sat with the back propped up against my front. "We have ourselves a little problem."

Jose Parra smiled, and it sent chills up my spine. He wasn't the average-looking Hispanic immigrant here for the cartel. He looked to be a level above Morales on the cartel's family tree, or else he just wanted to make the impression of tough guy to whoever crossed his path. His muscles were the too-large and too-ugly kind only steroids could create. I wondered where he found the time for that kind of workout, let alone that strict of a diet plan.

"And I have provided my contact with information to solve your problem."

"Yes, I understand, but I need some holes filled."

He nodded.

"It must be tough, working a large territory like this."

"I do not have any problems."

I smiled, stood, and flipped the chair around to sit casually with my legs crossed. "I'm new to this department. Came from Chicago. You ever been?"

He shook his head.

"Great city. Fantastic food. Fantastic!" I shook my head. "I miss the food more than anything." I sighed for effect. "It's been a big life change, coming here. Different lifestyle entirely, and there's a lot of competition here in the department. You probably understand that competition thing?"

"I have done well."

I nodded. "Mr. Parra, I'm not here to bust you for making a living. You do you, right? I'm here because I have a dead addict, and you're pointing the finger at a distributor, but I have someone else pointing the finger at you. Can you explain why someone would want you going down for this?"

"I did not kill Mr. Pruitt, and I have provided information regarding the man who did."

I sat back, relaxing my shoulders to make Parra feel as comfortable as possible. His smirk told me he thought he was smarter than me, and his eyes constantly traveling to my breasts said he didn't have a whole lot of respect for women. His kind came a dime a dozen, and I could play with his head all day, but I didn't have that kind of time, and I really didn't have the patience.

"Yes, and I appreciate that. Can you tell me what you told Detectives Sanders and Harry? What led you to this conclusion?"

"Our business works off of verbal commitments. Mr. Pruitt did not live up to his commitment, and he paid with his life. It is a simple business transaction."

I pressed my lips together and nodded. "So, let me make sure I understand. According to you, Brad Pruitt made a verbal agreement with Raul Morales for a purchase. Morales decided Pruitt, a known drug addict, was good for it —probably several times for this kind of debt—and when it came time to pay, he couldn't, so Morales killed him."

He nodded. "A simple business transaction."

"Sounds like it, but there's a problem with that."

"And what is that?"

"Pruitt's debt was cleared some time ago."

He smiled. "That does not mean his death was not an end result."

"What about your relationship with Mr. Pruitt? Did you provide product?"

He blinked. "Promises have been made." He ran his

hand through his hair. I watched as a piece fell to the ground and another floated down and landed on the tabletop.

"I understand. Tell me this, when was the last time you saw Brad Pruitt?"

His face lacked all expression, and I knew I'd lost him. "I would like to see Detectives Harry and Sanders, please."

"Just one more question. Can anyone attest to your whereabouts over the past few days?"

"Detectives Harry and Sanders, please."

Bishop walked in, held the auto-lock door open. "A minute?"

I nodded. "Be right out." I smiled at Parra. "Thank you for talking with me. I'll get the information I need, Mr. Parra."

He stood.

I headed toward the door and then turned around. "I'm sure we'll run into each other again very soon."

I tapped on the door once, and Bishop opened it. I let it close behind me.

"You learn anything?"

"More like accomplished something."

"Being?"

"He knows I know he's full of shit, and I put him on gentle warning."

He smiled. "Good. We've got our first drug cartel war in town. Should get interesting."

"It'll be a slow build. If one of them ends up dead, it makes the killer look guilty, and they know we'll come right for them. They'll both sit on this, give it time to die off, and then the violence will start."

"So much for our low crime numbers."

I laughed. "You got Allison and Andy?"

"Allison's already en route to the safe house, but Andy's not answering his cell. He at your place?"

"He was, but I haven't heard from him in a while. Did you send a patrol over?"

He nodded. "His truck's not there."

"He said he planned to finish building my gun shelf in the kitchen today. He probably just went to get materials and left his phone at my place. He's done that a few times."

He flicked his head toward the interrogation room. "You need me in there?"

I shook my head. "He's asked for Sanders and Harry. He won't talk anymore, and if we push him, he'll lawyer up. I get the feeling he's higher up on the cartel's management chart. I don't want to deal with his attorney yet if we don't have to."

"He still throw Morales under the bus?"

"Yup, and he shut up when I asked if he's seen Pruitt recently."

"Shit. You think he's good for it?"

I pursed my lips. "I'm leaning toward him. He was pretty passive-aggressive about Brad's death, and Allison identified him from the photo. I couldn't place him with Brad, but I didn't blatantly try either." I chewed on my nail. "Let me try one more thing. Do me a favor. In five minutes, go get Sanders and Harry and send them here."

"Will do, then I'm going to find Andy."

"Got it."

I walked back into the interrogation room. "Sorry about that," I said. "Your detectives will be here shortly."

He nodded once.

I sat in the chair again. "While we're waiting, tell me how you became an informant for two small-town detectives. I'm from a big city, and it just seems so odd to me that you'd want an in in this podunk town."

"Businessmen establish relationships based on need."

"And you needed two detectives?"

He shrugged. "It is good to make connections."

"I can relate to that. I've got CIs back home who still give me information." I sent myself a text message, then set the phone on my lap and waited until the right moment to hit send. "As a matter of fact, my best CI is a tech god. You know the kind, right? He can find anything about anyone or any situation with a few taps of his fingers. Pure magic." I hit send and the phone immediately beeped. I removed it from my lap and read my message to myself, then nodded. "Hmm. Looks like one of your guys was busted earlier today. Meth conversion lab."

His jaw clenched as I pretended to continue reading, then responded without hitting send. "Damn, and one of Morales's guys too." I looked up at him as I carefully hit send, then set the phone face down as it dinged with my message. "You know you had a guy working with Morales?"

He narrowed his eyes and scowled at me.

I read my message, looked at Parra, then set the phone face down on the table again. "Mr. Parra, it seems your minion is throwing you under the bus." I leaned forward. "He says you did business with our vic, and when he owed you money, you went looking for him and took him out."

"You are lying."

I leaned back and crossed my arms over my chest. "Of course, we don't know your guy's name. He told them it's Julio Iglesias." I laughed. "But I'm pretty sure the singer is a little older, a little less buff, if you will, and he definitely doesn't have a shaved head or cross tat on his neck." I let that sink in, watching him closely.

He turned his body slightly to the right. It was a bold, calculated move of dismissal. I needed more to make him nervous. Parra's neck was similar to a football player's. Thick, short, almost the same width as his head. The cords on the sides protruded and pulsed, and I knew he was agitated but trying hard not to show it. He wore a thick rope chain around his neck, but it lacked something I could use. The skull pendant.

"And he said you're good for the kill." It was a long shot, but I took the gamble. "Said you even paid someone from Good Times to get you a knife just to throw off your scent and blame Morales."

"I would like an attorney now."

"You can talk to Sanders and Harry about that." I smiled.

24

Harry and Sanders charged into my cubby. Sanders let out a string of cuss words so loud I had to fight back a smile. His puffy cheeks turned varying shades of red the more pissed off he got, and watching his nostrils flare as he swore was entertaining.

I stayed in my seat, letting them think they could intimidate me by standing and yelling down at me. I crossed my arms and smirked.

Jimmy walked in. "My office. Now!"

I lagged behind the two grumps, giving them a few extra seconds to control their shit.

It didn't work, and they sounded like two-year-olds. "She all but told our informant she thinks he killed Pruitt."

"Dang, I thought I made it pretty clear I thought that."

If looks could kill, Sanders would go down for first-degree murder.

Jimmy dragged his hands down his face and sighed. "Ryder, you got evidence?"

I nodded. "Ashley made some calls. Found out the knife

came from a restaurant supply company online. They tracked a recent sale to—"

"Let me guess, Good Times."

"Yup."

"But that's Morales's turf."

"Everyone's got a price. I made a few calls, got Michels over there, and boom! Got their newest bus boy to admit Parra dropped five bills for a bread knife. Kid said that was the best he could get. Swears he didn't know what Parra needed it for."

"Good work," he said.

Sanders eyed me suspiciously. "You didn't have any of that when you talked to our informant."

He was right. I'd gotten the information from Ashley shortly after I left Parra. "I worked a hunch, and I asked Ashley to check restaurant sales companies for similar knives." I smiled. "The girl is good. She found the company and figured out who they sold it to." I pointed my finger at Jimmy. "You need to pay her more or you're going to lose her to a bigger city. Trust me on that."

"I appreciate the advice," he said, and then added, "So, let me get this straight. You didn't actually work a hunch, you took a risk and it paid off."

I nodded. "But it gets better. One of the guys at the conversion lab bust works for Parra."

"Really? Along with one of Morales's thugs?"

"Small world, I guess. I recognized him from Allison's description, so I might have used that to my advantage too."

"Can you place Parra at the recycling plant?"

"Bishop found three hairs on Brad Pruitt's jacket."

"So we need a DNA sample from Parra."

"Parra likes to run his hand through his hair when he gets nervous. Unfortunately for him, he's losing it, and he left one on the table. Ashley compared it to images of the one found on Brad's clothing."

"Root?"

I shook my head. "I know comparisons aren't absolute, but there's precedent for this. Rarely do hairs from different people show the same microscopic characteristics. She'll have it tested, but I'm guessing it's a match."

"Why would he do the killing himself? That doesn't make sense."

"I'm going with competition. He knew Morales was Brad's original supplier. I'd bet Morales does more business than Parra, and it pissed Parra off. Take out the competition and give yourself a raise."

Jimmy looked at the other detectives and shrugged. "Sounds like enough to hold him."

Sanders inhaled and released the breath. "Fuck."

"Get to it, Detectives."

"You two did great," Jimmy said, patting Bishop on the back. "First one's on me."

Bishop sat at the end of Duke's bar. "Just a water."

I raised my hand toward the bartender. "Make that two."

"Y'all are getting old," Michels said. "Maybe it's time for some new blood?"

"New blood is one thing, but redneck blood, that's a whole different story." Bishop smiled. "I'm just joking with ya. You did good, Michels. You'll make a good detective someday."

Michels blushed.

Savannah, sitting on my right, leaned in and whispered,

"You could practice getting back in the swing of things with that one, honey."

I cringed. "We're not going through this again. Besides, even if he was remotely my type, which he's not, the stache just kills it for me."

She giggled. "You're right. Jimmy's mustache tickles. I don't like it."

"Ew." I stared at her. "Wait. Jimmy doesn't have a mustache."

"Exactly."

I laughed.

"County assured me we'll have the hair analysis back in twenty-four hours. Just in time for his bail hearing," Jimmy said.

"Bastard better not get bail," Bishop said.

I chugged my ice water, not realizing how thirsty I was, then yawned.

"Hey," Bishop said. "How much sleep have you had this week?"

"Not enough. I'm exhausted."

"Go home. Get some rest."

I pushed back on the bar, sliding my chair out. "I think I'll take you up on that."

"Damn, I think that's the first time you've listened to me."

"Probably."

Joey, my tech guru and confidential informant from Chicago, called as I walked to my vehicle. He'd helped me with hundreds of cases back in the day in exchange for immunity to most everything he did. Sometimes a cop needs help getting information in ways they can't get it themselves. "Your guy's got cell phones with monthly plans. Can you believe it? Pinged them both about thirty minutes ago near Tinley Park. Cell records show calls from the area for the past few days."

"It's okay. We got our guy tonight."

"Petrowski send him?"

"No."

"Seriously? Dayum. That means he's still a threat. Sucks balls, babe."

He was right. "I gotta go. Thanks for helping me."

"I got your back. You know that. Listen, I'll let you know if I hear anything, K?"

"I appreciate it."

After I disconnected the call, I drove home with an ominous cloud of dread hanging over me. The knife connected Parra to the guy running out of Good Times, and Morales had confirmed he didn't know him, so it was plausible. But something didn't feel right. That guy had smiled at me. Sure, it could have been because he knew he was getting away, but what if it wasn't?

What if it was because he knew me, and he'd just played his best card?

25

The lake's waves slammed against the rocks, sending splashes of cold water toward us. Tommy wrapped his arm around my shoulder and pulled me close. "Look at that moon."

I admired its brightness, the way it illuminated the night sky, casting shadows onto Lake Michigan. I shivered from the cool night breeze.

"Here." Tommy moved behind me and pulled me close, bending his legs and pressing them onto my sides for added warmth. "Better?"

I leaned back against his chest. "I'd prefer if we were naked."

His warm breath tickled my neck. "That's easily done."

I laughed. "We don't need an audience, baby."

He whispered in my ear. "They're already watching you, Rachel."

I bolted up, my eyes wide and searching the dark room. For a second I didn't know where I was, didn't recognize my own townhouse. I expected to see Tommy next to me. I grabbed my gun on the trunk in front of the couch and listened. My family room was empty. I exhaled. "It was a dream, dumbass." I turned on the light next to the couch, and my eyes went straight to the photo of me and Tommy. His smile stretched across the room and wrapped itself around me. "It was just a dream." I glanced at my watch. Almost five a.m. I set my gun down, stretched, then walked over to Herman's condo and dropped in some pellets. "Bon appetite, little dude."

I shuffled to the kitchen, feeling the warmth of Tommy's Blackhawks sweatshirt down to my knees as I prepared my coffee and examined the gun shelf on the wall while it brewed. Andy wasn't finished, and according to Bishop, he would be back because he had no intention of going to any safe house, especially now that we had his brother's killer.

Allison, on the other hand, was tucked away at the safe house. At least she agreed with better safe than sorry.

The gun shelf looked great, though that wasn't a good name for it. It was a shelf, yes, but with a fake base that opened to conceal a weapon. I'd shown Andy a photo and asked if he could install it if I decided to order one. He told me he'd rather make it. He thought it would be better quality, and I agreed. The shelf and compartment were complete other than staining, but he decided to do that after he determined the design was right. It was. I grabbed my spare gun, a small Ruger I didn't love, but it shot well, and set it inside the compartment. The gun fit perfectly, which was the plan. Andy had designed the small shelf and built a bottom to it that looked like a decoration but easily opened if one knew where to push. He could make a killing selling them to gun lovers and cops.

I finished my coffee, tossed on a pair of sweats and a T-shirt, then headed to the gym for a workout. I fought myself about having a cigarette first, but Garcia's face popped into my head, and the good side won.

I loved working out in an empty gym. The silence

appealed to me. I knew how to tune out the overhead music, and I wasn't bothered by grunting or talking or, dear God, bad singing, and the sound of weights dropping didn't send me reaching for my gun.

It was peaceful, and I needed peaceful.

I did six sets of squats, starting at the highest weight I could manage, then adding two and a half pounds to each side for the next three sets and leaving it there for the rest. If my quads could talk, they'd tell me to fuck off, for sure. I walked off the burn, doing a circle around the free weight area. I added a few sets of bench presses, then pull-ups and some ab work before hitting the treadmill for a three-mile run. I used my earbuds for that, playing a running mix I'd put together from Spotify, starting with "Radioactive" by Imagine Dragons.

I finished my three miles in just over twenty-four minutes. Not a record time, but considering the garbage fighting my lungs, good enough. I made it outside just in time to watch a red Malibu leave the parking lot. The lights in the lot were dim, but still bright enough to see there wasn't a plate. I jogged to my car, cussing myself out for wasting time digging for my keys. By the time I'd pulled out of the lot, the car was gone. I pounded my fist on the steering wheel. "Damn it!" I took a deep breath, opened my window, and lit up a cigarette. My hand shook as I smoked, and it pissed me off, so I tossed the thing out, then berated myself for littering.

Get your shit together, I thought. It was just a car. Or was it?

Jimmy insisted we take the day off after closing an intense investigation, but I laughed at the thought. Days off gave me too much time to think, and besides, I wouldn't exactly call that an investigation, not compared to my cases in Chicago.

I drove to Dunkin' and picked up an assortment of bagels, even more cream cheese, and a tumbler of coffee, and while waiting for my order, texted Andy to let him know he didn't need to eat before coming over. It wasn't biscuits and gravy, his favorite, but it wouldn't send him into cardiac arrest as quickly.

I turned on my shower to heat the water, dropped a few extra pellets into Herman's bowl, and as I walked past my office, I backed up and opened Tommy's cabinet. Removing all of his Petrowski files, I set them on the trunk in my family room.

The hot water soothed my nerves but did nothing to revive me. Once I rinsed the conditioner out of my hair, I switched the water to cooler, then cold, holding my breath as the cold water soaked my skin. I stood in it until I felt somewhat revived and couldn't stand it anymore.

In the kitchen, I poured myself a cup of coffee, topped it off with too much cream, then toasted the top half of a sesame bagel. Chicago didn't make bagels like New York, but they still dunked them completely in their topping, coating the entire thing. In Georgia, best I could guess was they just brushed the seasoning over the top part, leaving the bottom with a plain, bready, and completely boring taste. I tossed the bottom half back into the bag and loaded the top with extra cream cheese. Maybe I should reconsider the heart attack thing for myself? Clicking on my smart TV, I set it to the NBC Chicago early morning news, then dug my files out of my bag and spread them out with Tommy's as I sipped the coffee. I took one of my yellow legal pads and got to work.

Andy knocked on the door. "It's me."

I'd waited to lecture him until he arrived. "Choose your bagel poison."

"Got an everything?"

I nodded and walked into the kitchen. "Toasted?"

"Wow, you buy me breakfast and then make it? I feel like I should marry you."

I laughed. "I am in the market for a sugar daddy, and one who's handy is definitely a bonus."

"You lost me at sugar daddy. Try barely-making-a-living daddy."

I smiled. "Let's just stick to incredibly talented handyman."

"Works for me."

"Not going to lie, I'm worried about you." I poured his coffee while the bagel toasted.

"I haven't run from these people before, and I'm not now, and y'all got the guy, so I don't need to hide."

"I understand." And I did. I respected his stance, but I didn't think it was a smart one. I was trained to handle what might come his way. He wasn't. I handed him a paper plate with his bagel. "Look at this, I'm using my best china for you too."

"I must be special."

Smiling, I leaned against my kitchen counter. "I appreciate everything you're doing for me, and I'm really sorry about Brad."

He sighed. "I've been sorry about Brad for a long time. I knew this day was coming. I'm just glad it happened after my parents died."

I nodded.

"How long will they protect Allison?"

"I'm not sure. Parra's lawyered up, but I'd be surprised if the judge gives him bail."

"But it's possible?"

"Unfortunately. He's a known drug dealer linked to the Mexican cartel. I suspect his papers are fake, but I don't know the judges well enough to say what they'll do. And there's always the chance that the cartel's got a judge on their payroll."

"I never imagined this area would get like this."

"Drugs are like a cancer. The cartel supplies the addiction, but it also feeds off it. Once the cancer appears, it travels so fast through the body of a town, it's hard to stop. And it's immune to community demographics. These days the entire Atlanta area is worse off than Miami."

"Damn." He dropped his head and removed his Braves cap, then ran his fingers through his hair and replaced the cap. "What happens if this Parra guy makes bail?"

"If he's released, I strongly suggest you go with Allison."

"We can't afford to stay locked up, especially her. She makes less money than I do."

Better to live and struggle to make ends meet than be dead, I thought. "There's no easy solution to this."

"I hate my brother for what he's done to us."

I doubted that was true. "I understand."

"Anyway, I'm taking down the gun compartment to stain it. Can I do this in the garage?"

I nodded. "Keys are on the table. Go ahead and park my Jeep in the driveway. I'm working from home today."

"Gotcha." He headed toward the table and then turned around. "Does it ever go away?"

"What?"

"The anger of losing someone like this."

"I'll let you know."

He nodded, then grabbed the keys and walked to my garage.

The background noise of Chicago's news soothed my brain. City people needed that noise to survive. I'd grown up with horns and sirens and screaming neighbors in a house in crowded Irving Park, and adjusting to the quiet of the Atlanta suburbs had been rough. I still didn't sleep well, but more than anything, I blamed that on sleeping alone. I missed Tommy all the time, but mostly in the dead of night, and my dream had left me with a lingering feeling of sadness and trepidation.

I believed Jose Parra killed Brad Pruitt and ineffectively tried to frame his competition. I'd been wrong that his death and Jeffers's overdose were attached to my past. I let my emotions, be they anger, paranoia, or revenge, cloud my judgment. Had I given up the useless rhetoric playing on repeat in my head, Brad might still be alive. His death was on me, and at some point, Bishop or Andy would recognize that and blame me too.

But still, knowing that didn't stop my head from messing with me. Morales's words flashed in my brain. *Why is this man after you?*

I logged into the system on my laptop and ran a complete search on Jose Parra. I printed out anything I could find on the guy, then scanned photos of him, photos of known associates, you name it.

Something wasn't right.

Nothing connected him to the Malibus or the skull pendants. I hadn't asked him about those on purpose, especially the pendants. We needed a hard line connecting them to him, and if I showed that card, I could forget about that hard line. Only now I was beginning to think that hard line didn't exist. And unless I could connect the guy in Good Times to the black or even the red Malibu, that line would disappear completely.

I pushed the computer to the side and searched through Tommy's files next. I'd memorized most of his notes, but every time I read them, I learned something new. I removed the photos of the gang members on Petrowski's payroll and stared at them.

Why is this man after you?

Morales and I shared that question in common, and more importantly, we shared the fact that we both believed the man was after me, but neither of us could—or would—explain why. I hoped the answer was in Tommy's files. If there was a connection, Tommy would be the one to make it, or at least lead me down the right path.

I brought his files to my dining room table and stared at my white board. "Screw it," I said, and ripped everything off the board. I tossed it all on the table and started over. When in doubt, Tommy always said, begin at the beginning.

Three hours later, it still made no sense. If not for the skull pendants and Morales's statement, I had nothing to connect Brad and possibly his dealers to Petrowski. But that didn't mean there wasn't a connection. What was I missing? I needed a true connection, something small. A fingerprint, anything.

Bishop knocked on my door, and Andy let him in. The two spoke privately in the garage for a bit. I poured Bishop a cup of lukewarm, hours-old coffee, and when he came in, I invited him to sugar it up himself. He refused a bagel, saying he'd prefer to eat a chicken finger salad from a fast food joint for lunch. The thought of that hurt my stomach.

He stared at my white board. "We got the guy, remember?"

I bit my lip. "I know."

"Then why is this still up?" He walked closer to the board, studied it, then turned and stared at my messy dining room table. "Shit. You're kidding, right?"

"She's been working on it since I got here," Andy said.

Bishop checked his watch. "So, what? Three hours?"

"About that," I said.

He didn't give me a chance to defend myself. "We should be more worried about gathering evidence to secure a conviction, not wasting our time chasing a cow down the road."

I crooked my head to the left. "Is that a Southern expression?"

Andy laughed. "No. It's a real thing, and your partner's got personal experience."

I shook my head. "I don't even want to know."

"Probably smart," Bishop said. "Get your stuff. I want to go have another chat with Caroline Bryant. She knows more than she's saying, and we might be able to work a deal with her."

I smiled. "Ya think?" I closed my laptop and stuffed it in my bag. "Give me five to get my gear ready."

While I did, Andy bragged on his gun shelf to his best friend. I smiled when Bishop asked what he'd charge to make him one.

26

I removed my SIG from my left boot, ensured it was ready to shoot, then set it on the floor near my feet.

Bishop raised an eyebrow. "Why'd you bother putting it in your boot to just take it out?"

I shrugged. "Habit, I guess." I checked my department-issued weapon one more time, then secured it back in the holster.

"Let's stop at the RaceTrac or something first," I said.

"You can't need more coffee."

"Not for me. You think Bryant's going to be chipper and awake at this hour?"

"Good point."

He stopped at the RaceTrac. I jogged in, then returned with a few bottles of water and two large coffees, one black and one with sugar and cream. I held them up for Bishop to see. "Got her a variety of choices just in case."

We pulled onto Bryant's street, but unlike the other homes, hers was dark inside. From what we could tell through the blocked windows.

"Does she actually own this place? If so, that's some strange kind of miracle."

"Her parents do, and I only know that because I checked the other day. I would have said it was in foreclosure, but nope. They let their daughter live like this."

"They're providing her shelter, and it's not under their roof, so it's probably the only option they had. It's a form of enabling, but I understand their desire to keep her as safe as possible."

He nodded. "Andy's mom once told me she'd rather Brad get high at home, where she felt she could protect him. I never understood that."

"That's because your kid isn't an addict."

His eyes shifted toward me. "Don't even put that out there, Ryder."

I pretended to lock my lips.

We knocked on the door, but as expected, no one answered.

"Did you hear that?" I asked.

"Someone whispering for help? I think so."

I smiled and set down the drinks, then Bishop and I removed our weapons. "You ready?" I asked.

He nodded.

I smiled, said, "Police," and kicked the door open with my right leg.

The door flew open, detaching from the top hinge.

Bishop stared at me with his jaw hanging open. "Damn."

"I live for that shit."

He laughed.

The place was quiet, but that didn't stop us from checking each room.

I used the empty side of my shoulder holster for the SIG, then changed my mind and stuffed it into my waistband instead. Tommy was a cowboys and Indians fan, and he'd taught me the remove-and-twirl move from the old-school movies. I never planned to use it, but stuffing my weapon into my waistband brought back the memory. "Not now," I mumbled under my breath. I didn't need emotions creeping in and fogging my mind.

Three men sat on the living room floor with their backs against the tattered couch. A half-dressed girl who couldn't have been much older than twenty lay on the couch, a thin jacket pulled over her upper and very naked half. None of them moved. If kicking in the door didn't wake them, our footsteps on the nasty carpet wouldn't either.

"Back bedroom," Bishop said.

I followed him.

The room's curtains were drawn, and based on the direction of the windows, it wouldn't get much sunlight this early in the day.

Caroline lay on the bed, a bearded man with his pants down to his knees pounding the last nail into her soul through her crotch. She didn't move. I wasn't even sure she was awake.

I flicked on my flashlight and shined it on the bastard. "Party's over."

He glanced at me, his mouth hanging open. "Fuck!" He stood, tried to pull up his pants, but tripped over himself three times.

I glanced at Bishop, who was actually chuckling as he watched the guy fearing for his life.

I rolled my eyes. "Really?"

"What? It's funny."

"Fine. I'll handle it, then."

"Be my guest," he said, still laughing.

I played bad cop. "Get them on and get out. This is your

free spin. I see you anywhere near here again and you're done. Got it?"

He grabbed a jacket on the floor and bolted out the bedroom door with a, "Yes, ma'am."

Seeing that kind of fear in someone's eyes was one of the fun parts of my job. Hopefully, he'd learned a lesson, but I doubted it.

Caroline Bryant pushed herself up onto her elbows. "What the fuck?"

"Jesus," Bishop said. He'd stopped laughing, his smile turning into a scowl. "She wasn't even awake."

"Probably because he sucked at the job."

"What the fuck, Bishop?" She groaned. "It's the middle of the damn night."

"It's almost noon," I said. It was only a slight exaggeration. I picked her clothes off the floor and tossed them to her. "Get dressed."

She stared at the twenty-spot sitting on the small box next to the bed. I quickly grabbed the cash and stuffed it into my jacket pocket.

She wiped her face. "That's mine."

"And you can have it back after you answer our questions." I set the tray of coffees on the box. "Left side is black. Right has cream and sugar. Take your pick."

"Talk to me after I wake up." She rolled herself into a ball, so I opened one of the bottled waters and flung the liquid at her face.

It took her a moment to realize what was happening. She curled in her shoulders and covered her head with her bony hands. "What the fuck's your problem?"

"We need you reasonably coherent, Sweet Caroline. Drink the coffee."

"You arresting me?"

"We haven't decided yet."

She stared at Bishop. "She's still a bitch."

"Tell me something new," he said, smirking.

"I didn't do nothing," Bryant said.

"Newsflash, sex for money is a crime," I said.

"It's twenty bucks. I'm worth more than that."

"Awake maybe," I said.

"That's a twenty issued by the Treasury Department," Bishop said. "You might be a cheap whore, but you're still a whore."

Damn. Bishop was good.

She took the coffee with sugar and cream. "What do you want from me?"

I removed my phone from my other pocket and pulled up Jose Parra's photo. "You know this guy?"

"Shit, woman, you know I'm dead if I say anything."

"Honey, you ain't far from dead now. Take the risk."

"Fuck you."

"You're not my type."

She looked up at me again, her bloodshot eyes so swollen she could barely open them.

"Come on, I brought you coffee." I used my sweet voice.

Bishop coughed.

"Give me back the cash, and I'll talk."

"That's not how this works."

She sighed and ran her hand through her stringy hair. "Fine. It's El Uno. What about him?"

"He killed Brad Pruitt."

She stared up at me, then at Bishop. "He's dead?"

Bishop nodded.

"And for what it's worth, you might want to get an HIV test. Pruitt had full-blown AIDS," I said.

"Fuck."

"Got a list of your johns?" My question was sarcastic.

"Fuck you. They use protection."

I shrugged. Condoms weren't perfect, but I wasn't there to debate statistics.

"Where do you get your drugs?" Bishop asked. "Morales or Parra?"

"I don't know. Just a guy."

Bishop did his research. He pulled out his cell and flipped through photos, asking Bryant if any of them was her dealer.

"That one," she said, pointing to the last photo.

Bishop checked it and made eye contact with me before saying, "He's with Parra."

"Bingo," I said. The more of Parra's men we got, the better chance we had of rolling one of them. Dealers were just that, prone to making deals, especially ones that kept them out of jail. Deportation, however, was another issue.

She shook her head. "I mean, El Uno's the distributor, but he don't physically give me my shit, that guy does."

"You good with him?"

She sipped her coffee, then finally pulled on her shirt. "Huh?"

I spoke clearly and slowly. "Do you owe him any money?"

Her upper lip twitched. "I might be an addict, but I ain't stupid."

For some, acknowledgement is the first step to recovery, but Bryant was long past wanting to recover. I placed my hands on my hips, which pushed my jacket aside, revealing both weapons. I smiled. "Do you owe Morales any money?"

She flung her hand in the air, spilling some of her coffee. "I pay my debts."

Bishop spoke calmly. "We have a turf war starting here,

Caroline. Parra's in lockup, but you know that doesn't mean he'll stay there."

"And his people still work for him," I said.

"What're you trying to say?" she asked.

"If you know anything about Brad's murder, you need to tell us," Bishop said.

"I don't know anything."

"We can protect you," Bishop said.

She laughed. "Like you did Brad?" She stared at Bishop. "He liked you, you know. Said he looked up to you as a kid. I know he came to you for help, but you didn't help him, did you? You're a piece of shit, just like the rest of his family. Don't tell me you can protect me when you let your best friend's brother die." She threw her cup across the room, splattering coffee on the already ruined rug. "Now give me my money and get the hell out."

I dropped the twenty on the bed. "Watch yourself, Bryant." I tossed my business card next to the money. "You call me if you grow a set and want to do the right thing."

We turned around and walked out just as she ripped my card to shreds. It was worth a shot.

Bishop pushed past me and rushed to his car. He leaned against it and took out a cigarette, lighting it up and taking three long puffs. I kept my mouth shut and waited.

"She's wrong," I finally said.

"I know." He took another puff. "I spent years trying to help Brad. I had him set up for rehab four separate times. You know how many he went?" He didn't give me time to answer. "Two. Left the first one after a week, and the second, he didn't even make it twenty-four hours. His addiction cost his parents their life savings, and me a portion of mine." He flicked the cigarette butt to the ground and smashed it under his boot. "Fuck her."

"Did you see the guy running out with his pants down? I don't need his sloppy seconds."

Bishop laughed. "I don't pay for sex, but damn if I did, it wouldn't be with an addict."

"He's probably got low self-esteem." I paused for effect. "Or a small dick."

"Get in," he said. "We're going on a field trip."

"Oh, goodie. Did you bring a bagged lunch?"

A few minutes later, we arrived at Rest Haven Cemetery in Alpharetta.

"Are we going ghost hunting?"

"If so, this would be the place." He opened his door. "Before Hamby became its own city, we were part of Alpharetta, did you know that?"

"I've done my research."

"This place has been here since the 1860s." He walked over to a plot. "Mary Camp Manning. She donated the land that became Alpharetta and part of it eventually Hamby." He crouched down and wiped dirt from the ground next to her stone. "Andy's parents wanted to be buried here."

I glanced across the large cemetery. "Looks like there are plots available. Too expensive?"

He shook his head and dusted off his hands. "There's open space, but no one can figure out where it is. The city records are limited, and no one wants to disturb the final resting places of those who might be buried without markers."

As we walked around the cemetery, he told me the rest of the story.

"The cemetery was designed for something like fourteen hundred grave sites, but back when it was first opened, many of the families of people buried here couldn't afford markers. Years later many of the records were lost, so instead of attempting to mark graves, Alpharetta decided to just leave it as is, and stopped allowing anyone who hadn't already purchased a plot to buy one."

I nodded. "Which explains why there are some recent burials." I pointed to a 2007 tombstone.

"Yes, some of these families are from Mary Manning's days and their plots were purchased back when the records were still available."

"I never thought of you as a history buff," I said.

"Just find some things interesting."

"Why are we here?"

He stopped. "Andy's parents were devasted when they couldn't be buried here. I went to the city to see if there was any way to make an exception. That's when I learned about the burials."

"That must have been hard news to deliver, but you did what you could."

He lit up a cigarette. "The day I told Andy's parents, his mom pulled me aside. She said if anything ever happened to Brad, to make sure I found out and brought his killer to justice."

"And we're doing that."

He nodded as he blew out the smoke. "Doesn't seem like enough. I should have been able to stop it before it happened."

"You couldn't have known."

"I know."

"And like you said, you did everything you could to help Brad. He made his choices. That's on him, not you."

"He looked up to me like a brother as a kid. I could have done more back then."

"You were a kid."

He turned and faced me, then walked behind me and

stopped at another burial site. "Dr. Oliver P. Skelton." He stared down at the ground. "During the Civil War, he helped save Milton County records by carrying them to Elberton, Georgia. He became the first postmaster in town."

"I didn't realize this was a different county before it merged with Fulton."

"Happened in the early 1930s. People are still pretty ticked about it too."

"Hence the constant talk of becoming North Fulton County."

He nodded.

I stared off into the distance, imagining the people buried under the grass, those who were remembered, those we'd never know, those left alone without the acknowledgment of a marker.

The last time I visited a cemetery was about six months after Miquel Sanchez's funeral. I'd wanted to attend, but Lenny threatened to cuff me to his radiator if I tried. Sanchez's mother must have spent her life savings on her killer son's stone. Multiple strands of rosary beads hung from the sides, sat in piles on top of the stone, and lay on the ground next to it. I didn't count, but if I had to guess, I'd say there was at least a buck's worth of pennies on the dirt.

My mother used to take us to the cemetery in Crete, Illinois, when I was a kid. You need to know your family history, she'd said. Find peace in the dead. I hated the place. It just seemed so sad. Sanchez's grave was different. It gave me joy to know that son of a bitch was in the ground where he belonged. If there's a hell, I hope he's burning in it.

"You in there, Ryder?" Bishop nudged my arm.

I shook myself out of my memories. "Just thinking."

"We all carry demons on our shoulders, don't we?"

"My demon's dead and buried in Chicago, right where he belongs."

He shrugged. "One of them anyway."

"Right. We're missing something, Bishop."

"You still think your Petrowski's involved somehow?"

"The skull pendants. Morales's vague comment. The Malibu. They're not random, but I can't link them to Parra."

He exhaled. "And we can't play that hand with Parra or we could screw ourselves."

"Exactly, but I checked everything I could find related to Parra. Nothing tells me this stuff is linked to him."

"Maybe the pendants are just what I thought. Crap jewelry addicts thought they could trade for drugs or cash?"

"And the Malibus? Morales's vague comment? What about the guy in Good Times who Morales swears he's never seen before?"

"Could be one of Parra's guys, maybe new to town?"

I shook my head and bit my bottom lip. "No."

"We need a hell of a lot more than some popular charm necklace and a comment from a low-level Mexican cartel for a case against Chris Petrowski to stick."

I kicked a wet brown leaf on the ground, but it didn't budge. "That's not going to be easy. Petrowski's smart. He doesn't get dirt on his hands."

"If he wanted you dead, why string you along like this?"

"To watch me suffer. I put him away for life. That's got to sting."

"But he's out."

"Irrelevant."

"You really think he'd risk being put back in prison?"

"He won't go back to prison. I guarantee he's got every judge in Cook County in his back pocket by now. He's a politician, he won't make the mistake of getting caught again." I picked a stick off a random plot and set it beside the stone. "Tommy was this close to busting him, and the bastard killed him to stop him."

"And then you came along."

"There's only one way this ends with Petrowski, and that's with him in a grave. Where I should have put him two years ago. I won't make that mistake a second time. He'll underestimate me."

He exhaled. "I did that."

"What?"

"Underestimated you."

"It's a common thing in my life."

"You know what it taught me?"

I looked him in the eyes, waiting for his answer.

"That when your gut tells you something, I need to listen."

"My gut isn't telling me a whole lot right now."

"It's probably said more than you think. You just need to listen more closely."

"So what are you saying?"

"I'm saying we've got some free time. Let's use it wisely."

27

Jimmy caught us as we walked into the pit. "What're you two doing here?"

"We got a conviction to secure," Bishop said.

"And some hunches to look into," I added.

"Got anything for either of those?" he asked.

"We're working on it," I said.

"Good, then you've got five minutes." He waved his fingers in a follow-me motion. "You can be the first to use the new official crime investigation room."

"Can you give me five?" I asked. "I need to make a quick call."

"Sure thing," he said. "Meet us there. I'll take Bishop now."

Bishop smiled and wiggled his eyebrows like he was the teacher's pet.

I made a call to Special Agent Olsen with the DEA. "Detective Ryder, Hamby PD. We met at the conversion lab bust?"

"Yes, I remember. Got something for me?"

"I was hoping you could give me something."

"Parra's guy."

I blinked. "Yes, sir. How'd you know?"

He chuckled. "I'm smarter than I look."

I hadn't related his looks to his brain, but whatever. "I need him to roll on Parra."

"But you already got Parra."

"Yes, but I might have led Parra to believe his guy rolled."

"That's a bold move."

"Can you help?"

"It's already in motion. He'll testify against Parra, and your confidential informant Morales's guy too."

"Morales isn't my CI."

"I stand corrected. Bradwell's CI."

I was impressed. Olsen knew his stuff, and he knew his turf. "You *are* smarter than you look," I joked.

"Just means you owe me one."

"Deal. Oh, one more thing."

"Shoot."

"I'm sending you a photo. It's a pendant we've found at several locations pertaining to our investigation. Our vic and a recent OD had them on their person when their bodies were discovered. It's also a popular gang symbol in Chicago. Used by the cartel."

"I'll take a look, let you know if it's used out here, but I don't recall any skulls for the cartel here."

"Thanks."

"Give me ten, and I'll text you."

"I appreciate it." I ended the call and walked to the new investigation room.

The day Jimmy took over as chief, he put a rush on one of Cochran's pet projects that never quite got started. I knocked on the new investigation room's door, waiting with slightly elevated breath in anticipation of what filled the small room. Chicago's dissatisfied taxpayers' checks kept that department's technology ahead of most, and I struggled with the behind-the-times Hamby equipment. It would be nice to see what Jimmy put together.

We'd been allowed to peek in once or twice, but lately, not at all. "Awesome," I said as the chief opened the door.

And it was awesome. Several computer display screens lined the walls, and three plexiglass standing boards stood between two large conference tables. There were several computers on those tables and some equipment old enough I didn't know its purpose.

Bishop looked at me. "Anything I need to know?"

I nodded. "Special Agent Olsen assured us Parra's guy will testify."

Bishop pumped his fist. "Yes!"

Jimmy smiled. "Nice job."

"It's far from finished, and I'm pretty sure I owe that guy now."

"I'm going with a yes on that," Bishop said.

"Me too," the chief replied. "Okay, so we've got IACIS, NCIC, two search screens for whatever records our tech team can dig up via other searches, and then this." He pointed to a separate computer. "This one's specific to CODIS, and it's my favorite."

We already had access to the Combined DNA Index System as well as the others through our laptops, but having it all in one room was golden.

"Oh," Jimmy said. He pointed to a table along the back wall filled with equipment I used in high school biology.

I played with the microscope. "Why isn't this in the lab?"

"Cochran had it in his budget. I just left it there."

"Probably wanted to cover his ass before anything got to Ashley," I said.

"Seems likely," Bishop added. "You know, I saw my first larvae through one of these things." He stuck his eye up to the lens. "Thought I wanted to be a doctor, but that changed the trajectory of my life."

"And sent you straight to the bathroom," Jimmy said.

I laughed. "Seriously?"

Jimmy nodded. "Bishop recycles his stories."

"I do not."

I cringed and shrugged. "Actually, you kind of do."

"Bite me, Ryder."

"Do we need sensitivity training? Because that can be arranged," Jimmy said.

"That was sensitive for me."

Jimmy rolled his eyes. I walked over to the microscope and nudged my partner out of the way. "The first time I looked in one of these, I was in seventh grade. We were supposed to be dissecting frog feces."

"Supposed to?" Jimmy asked.

"I don't think I want to hear the rest of this story," Bishop said.

"I do," Jimmy said.

"Turned out Frankie Angelini stuck his finger up his butt and swiped it on the slide. When he announced it to the room, Sister Maria Bianchi tossed her cookies on her desk."

Bishop gagged.

Jimmy laughed, then asked, "You went to a Catholic school?"

"I lived in a very Italian neighborhood. Everyone went to the Catholic school."

"But you don't believe in God," Bishop said.

"You say that many Hail Marys and you'd stop believing too."

Someone knocked on the door. Bishop answered.

"Hey—wow!" Ashley's eyes popped. "This is amazing!" She gave the room a slow once-over. "We're big-time now!"

"Close," I said.

"I got the hair analysis back," she said. "I put a rush on it."

"Which one?"

"Oh, right. Well, the ones found on Brad Pruitt aren't back, but the one you gave me, I still think it's a possible match. I sent it out already, so we'll just have to wait and see. I'm talking about the one in the Malibu."

"And?" I asked.

She spread the papers on the table. "Do you know anything about pulling DNA from hair?"

I nodded. "As we've discussed, I know it's not as good of a match if you don't have the hair follicle."

She nodded. "But it's not a deal breaker, either." She handed me and Bishop a photo of the hair from the Malibu. Jimmy looked over my shoulder.

"Basically, there are three ways to check for DNA in hair. One links the Y chromosome, showing a link from father to son and grandson." She removed a chart from the file. "Another one tests from other chromosomes, except X and Y. It's commonly used to check for heritage lines like cousins."

Ashley liked her forensics, and she was good at her job. "Which one is this?"

"Neither. No follicle, so we could only run an mtDNA test."

"Mitochondrial. For the maternal side, then," Bishop said.

We all stared at him.

"What? I took biology back in the day."

"He's right," Ashley said. "This DNA is passed from the mother." She looked up at me. "The person this hair belongs to shares the same mother as Miquel Sanchez."

28

I dropped into a chair. Everything I'd thought, everything I felt deep in the pit of my stomach, was on point. I was right. Petrowski had come for me. "How is that possible? I know all of Sanchez's brothers. They're all doing time in Menard."

Bishop raised a brow.

"Maximum security prison in Illinois."

"DNA doesn't lie," Ashley said.

She was right. That meant Sanchez had at least a half-brother, possibly a full brother, I wasn't aware of.

"Where's the name," Bishop asked.

"I thought I'd let Detective Ryder pull it up herself." She looked at me. "I should have—"

"No, I want to do this." I typed the DNA information into CODIS and waited while it ran through billions of possible matches. When it stopped, I said, "Son of a bitch. They're related?"

Garcia picked up on the first ring. "Eyes and ears still working for you, partner."

"You're on speaker," I said. "I just hit send on a text. Let me know when you get it."

"It just came." Silence for a moment, and then, "You know the kid. That's Benny Hernandez."

"Right. He's also at least a half-brother of Sanchez's."

"No shit?"

"DNA doesn't lie," Ashley said. "Oh, sorry," she said when I looked at her.

I smiled. "She's right."

"Where'd you get his DNA?"

"Hold on," I said, sending him two other photos via text. "Wait for it."

"Son of a bitch! How'd we miss this?"

I showed Bishop and crew the photos of Sanchez and Perez. "He looks a hell of a lot like Perez, doesn't he?"

"This the guy you thought was Perez?"

"The vehicle was clean except for the hair. Ashley rushed it through the lab and just showed it to us."

"I had a hunch," she said.

I owed her dinner for a week.

"Nice hunch there, babe," Garcia said, his slight accent more prominent than usual.

Ashley beamed.

"Can you put out a BOLO?" I asked. "I'll do the same here."

"If he's there for you, he hasn't come back."

"I know, but we need to cover all the bases," I said. "I want Petrowski in for questioning." I slammed my fist on the table. "And I want to be there via video. Can you make that happen?"

"He'll lawyer up before I can get to him."

"Not if you don't tell him you're coming."

"He won't talk, Ryder. You know that."

"Just try."

"I'll do my best," he said. "You keep me in the loop, okay?"

"Always, partner." I glanced up at Bishop, who shrugged.

"I'll handle the BOLO," Bishop said. He sat at the table and henpecked on a keyboard.

Jimmy pulled me aside. "You okay?"

I nodded. "I'm good."

He examined me closely. "I'm keeping someone on you. I don't want any eyes off you, you understand?"

"I don't need a babysitter, Jimmy. I've got this. Plus, I've got Bishop. He won't leave my side."

"It's not a babysitter, it's extra eyes."

"Fine," I said, knowing there was no point in arguing. "I need some time. Couple hours, maybe?"

"You're not going to do that rogue cop thing again, are you?"

I crossed my heart. "No. I just need to let out some aggression."

"Do that. We'll get back with Parra and Morales. See what they know."

"If they know anything, they're not going to say."

"We'll see about that."

As I straightened up my desk, something I always did when I needed to process information, Michels walked over. "You okay?"

"Wow, who told you?"

He dropped his head.

"It wasn't the chief, that much I—"

"Holy shit! Are you sleeping with Ashley?"

He glanced out of my cubby into the pit. "Can't you whisper? We don't want anyone to know we're dating."

"So, it's not just booty calls at the end of shift?"

"Jesus, Ryder. You're such a dude."

"Don't say that to anyone else." I smiled. Ashley and Michels. Not at all expected.

He laughed. "What can I do?"

I grabbed my extra gun from the locked drawer at the bottom of my desk. I kept it there for emergencies, and my life suddenly felt like one big emergency. "Keep your eyes out for Hernandez. I want him breathing."

"I'm sorry I didn't catch him before," he said. "I'll train harder."

"You're a good cop, Michels. You'll be an even better dick someday."

He walked me to my car, where Bishop and Jimmy stood. "I'll get my cruiser," he said, and walked away.

"What?" I asked.

"Savannah's asked to meet you at Taco Mac at seven." Jimmy checked his watch. "That gives you just enough time to forget whatever it is you were going to do without our help, get ready, and get over there."

"You're babysitting me?"

"Go get ready."

"Get ready?" I stared down at my clothes. "It's Taco Mac. I am ready."

"She asked that you not wear your work outfit."

"She wants me to change for wings and beer?" I hitched my hip to the side and set my hand on it. "What's your wife up to now, Chief?"

He shrugged. "All I know is she called your cell twice, but you didn't answer. I told her I'd let you know." Jimmy smirked. "You don't want to stand up my wife, do you?" He rotated on his heel and walked away, with what I assumed was a smile on his face.

"Taco Mac?" I said to Bishop. "We don't have time for that. We need to find Hernandez." Michels pulled up, leaving his cruiser idling. He was my bodyguard. I couldn't help but laugh.

"Didn't sound like you had a choice in the matter. I'll order in and do what I can to make some headway. Go on."

"Seriously?"

"What?"

"You're just going to leave me with Michels?"

"You're going home. I didn't think you'd want me hanging out while you shower, and like you said, you don't need a babysitter."

"I'm making a stop first."

"Where?"

"The range."

He raised his brows and tilted his head. "Then I'll tag along."

Bishop and I have shot together at the range two times. He considered his weapon to be a last resort, and though he was a good shot, I was better. I'd spent hours at the Chicago PD Training Academy after Tommy's death, taking out my anger on Sanchez over and over. Rules only allowed for retired police to use the range, but the manager knew and loved Tommy, and let me shoot any time I showed up. No matter how much anger I shot into that target, it never went away.

Hamby PD had an arrangement with SharpShooters in Roswell, even going as far as giving officers a private area.

Rarely had I shot with anyone there, but this time there was an Alpharetta officer shooting when we arrived.

He popped the barrel to check for bullets, removed the magazine, and set them both on the stand. He greeted us with a nod while he packed up his things and left.

Michels held the door open from outside. "What'd you say to him?" He looked straight at me.

I held up my palms. "Nothing. He just got his shit and left."

"Em."

I stared at Bishop, who said, "You didn't have to say anything. Your expression was pretty obvious."

"What expression?"

Michels laughed.

"The one that says get the fuck out."

"I wasn't aware I had that expression." I smiled. "I thought I had one standard bitch look."

"Right," Bishop said.

Michels laughed and closed the door behind him.

I readied my three weapons, adjusted my AXIL earplugs, then moved the target to just before the back wall.

Bishop tapped on my shoulder. "Why so far?"

I removed an earplug. "What?"

"Why so far?"

"Twenty-one-foot rule, remember?" The rule, which was more of a training theory, stated that, among other things, officers weren't presumed safe from a suspect outside of twenty-one feet.

"Got it."

"I'll bring it in."

I started with my Sig Sauer because it was my favorite. After I emptied the magazine, I went to my department-issued weapon, then the personal one I kept in my desk. I should have stopped home for the Ruger, but it was unlikely I'd use that.

Bishop hit the button to bring in the target, ripping it off and replacing it as I reloaded. The door opened behind us and Michels stepped in.

"Damn," he said, checking out my shots on the target. "Girl can shoot."

I shook my head. "Woman, and duh."

Bishop chuckled. Michels waited around for me to finish reloading, then stayed to watch.

Every time I shot, I pictured Sanchez's face. And Tommy's. Saw the hate in his eyes, saw him mouth something to me. Something I couldn't understand, and it was that second, that pause I took to figure out what he'd said, that gave Sanchez enough time to kill my husband.

I'd never know what Tommy said, and that would haunt me the rest of my life.

I pulled the trigger, time after time, nailing the bullseye and the four smaller bodies surrounding it. With my final bullet, I shot the target straight in the forehead. I could go back in time and kill Sanchez all over again, always without that hesitation during the only time that mattered.

29

Andy sat on my couch stuffing his face with Baked Lays and onion dip. "You're still here?"

He blushed as he tossed the bag on my coffee trunk and stood. "Just taking a break."

"You can stay as long as you want," I said, laughing. "Everything okay?"

He nodded. "I'm taking a break."

"Break from what?"

"I removed the shower faucet in your bathroom and fixed it, so you've got better water pressure and hotter water. I'm doing the guest bath next. I noticed the tile's settled in the guest bath too, so I picked up some grout, and I'll touch that up."

He was trying to keep busy. I understood. "Just let me know what it costs."

"You didn't ask, so I don't feel comfortable charging you."

"Hey, Andy, can you fix my shower faucets and the tile in the guest bath, oh, and anything else that'll keep you busy? Thanks."

"Smartass."

"You sound like Bishop."

"I'll take that as a compliment." He smiled. "You home for the night?"

"Unfortunately, no. I've been summoned by the police chief's wife to eat wings at Taco Mac."

He laughed. "Savannah's a good girl. I like her."

"I wouldn't exactly call her a girl. She's my age."

"Anyone younger than me is a kid. It's proven science."

I laughed. "Does that mean anyone older than me is ancient?"

"Damn, you're rough."

"So I'm told." I removed my gear and locked it up. "Bishop was going to come by, but I made sure he knew I had to shower, and he got all kinds of awkward when I said that. Had he known you were still here, he would have come."

"He's struggling around me. Doesn't know what to say."

I sighed. "He feels like he's failed your family."

"He hasn't."

"Give him some time. He'll work through it."

"Maybe you could push him along? Tell him we're good."

"He knows that. He just wants to do the right thing. "Once we have a better handle on the case, he'll feel better."

"You mean he might not pay for killing my brother?"

I placed my hand on his shoulder. "He's going down for it, Andy. We just want everything we can find to make sure nothing gets in the way of that."

He nodded. When the concern left his face, he smiled. "Hey, how do you like the gun compartment?"

I walked into the kitchen. "It's great. You going to make one for Bishop?"

"Thinking about it. Maybe when I'm done with your place."

I nodded. "So next year?"

"Sounds about right."

"I've been asked to wear normal clothes and shower, so I'm off to do that."

"Never make a Southern girl mad, that's what my momma taught me."

"That's only because your momma didn't know any Chicago Italian women." I winked and closed my bedroom door behind me.

After my shower, and a careful critique of my limited wardrobe, I finally settled on Tommy's favorite sweater, a fitted royal-blue V-neck. I squeezed into a pair of dark Silver jeans, again, his favorite, and matched them with heeled black leather boots hitting just under my kneecaps. I knew I'd get the makeup lecture, so I swiped on a little more than normal, then crunched my hair dry with a diffuser and added a little mousse.

"Wow!" Andy was visibly surprised when I walked out of my room. He whistled. "You clean up real good. I bet your father kept you under lock and key."

"Most of the time my father didn't know I was around."

"Oh, I'm sorry."

"Don't be. My real dad, the man I feel did the real work, lived next door."

"He still around?"

I walked over and showed him the photo of me and Lenny. "Yup."

He smiled. "Looks like a nice guy."

"One of the best."

He stuffed his hands into his pockets. "I'll be here a while."

"I appreciate what you're doing. If you don't want to go home, you're welcome to stay here." I flicked my head toward the front door. "I've got a patrol on me. I can leave him here if that helps."

"I'm not worried. You got the guy, and I know I'm safe. I just like keeping busy."

"I understand," I said, then stepped out of my comfort zone and hugged him. "You couldn't help your brother, Andy. Don't carry that guilt."

"I know," he said, hugging me back. "Now go on and have some fun."

I grabbed my department gun and clipped it onto my waist. I preferred the Sig because it was small, but I couldn't carry it in my boot.

"You're packing for wings?"

"I'll keep it in my car. Just used to having one with me." After giving it some thought, I walked over to one of the shelves Andy built, opened a box, and removed a small switchblade. I clipped it onto the waist of my thong, adjusting it until the waist of my pants camouflaged it from view.

Andy raised an eyebrow.

I shrugged. "Pretend you didn't see that."

"I think it's smart."

"Better safe than sorry."

I knocked on Michels's window. "You need to eat. Do me a favor, get something, then come back and keep an eye on Andy, will you?"

"I'm supposed to be on you."

I pursed my lips. "Do I need to call HR for that?"

He blushed. "You know what I mean."

"I know. I'm going to dinner with Savannah. I'm sure the chief will be there too. I'll tell him I threatened you. Now go.

Get something and come back. You can even go inside if you want."

"That's okay. I don't know Andy."

"Guess this town isn't as small as it seems."

Taco Mac sounds like a Mexican restaurant, but it's not. It's more of a Tex/Mex sports bar with a wall full of specialty beers from various microbreweries. I'd been there twice. I liked the sweet Asian heat roasted wings, but I'd yet to try any of the microbrews. If I was forced to drink beer, I usually went with something light.

I texted Savannah as I left my place. She said to meet her in the bar, but surprise, surprise! I sat down in a chair next to Sean. "Hey."

He looked surprised and then not so much. "Hey! Oh."

"Ouch."

He smiled. "I think we've been set up."

"I think you're right."

A short blonde bartender with fake eyelashes at least two inches long tossed a coaster in front of me. "What can I get you?"

"Whatever's on the light menu, please."

"You got it."

Sean laughed. "She really wants this, doesn't she?"

"I'm sorry?"

"Savannah. Us. She really wants it."

"Oh." I bit my lip. I wasn't used to being that upfront with someone about my private life, especially someone who seemed to want to be more involved in it than I could handle. "Savannah's a character." I picked through my bag to keep my hands busy, fiddling with the pack of cigarettes, wishing I could light one up and relax.

"For the record, I didn't ask her to do this."

"Understood."

"But since we're here..."

I zipped up my bag after getting the piece of gum. "I have a serious investigation I've got to work on, but I'll—"

"Wow, she said you'd say that."

I fake-smiled. "Did she now? I thought you didn't know I was coming?"

"Not about this. I got a random text from her asking if you'd committed to lessons yet. I told her that you would probably start soon, and she said you'd say that." He laughed. "Damn, she's good."

I hadn't forgotten how his eyes sparkled when he laughed. "Nice hat," I said. "I think the guy working on my house has the same one."

"I'd say nine out of ten men have a Braves hat like this."

"Guess I should remember that in case it comes up in a future investigation."

He smiled. "So, still pushing back your lessons?"

"I'm working on my calendar this weekend. Maybe I can pencil them in."

"I heard about Brad Pruitt. Is that the big case?"

I nodded. "Bishop's close to his family."

"If I recall, he's buddies with Andy Pruitt, right?"

"Yes. He's the one doing the work on my house."

"That's got to be tough. Heroin is brutal."

"Yes."

The bartender set a glass of beer in front of me. "You want anything to eat?"

Sean ordered ten medium roasted wings. I decided

eating finger food and trying to have a conversation wasn't worth the effort, though I'd begun to crave those sweet Asian heat wings. "Just a Caesar salad, please. No protein added."

"Yes, ma'am. I'll put that in for you two now."

"Uh, separate checks, please," I said.

"Done," she replied.

"So," Sean said.

"So," I replied.

"Wow."

"What?"

He pressed his lips together, then blew out a breath. "It's much easier to talk with you at the stables. I feel unusually awkward right now."

"You and me both." I used the bar's edge as a drum, tapping a made-up beat with my index fingers. "Listen, about my random visits."

Blondie slid the salad in front of me and set the plate of wings in front of Sean. My mouth immediately watered.

"You brought a friend coffee, that's all." He pushed the plate toward me. "Feel free."

I shook my head. "Oh, I don't want one, but thank you."

"You sure? You were starting to drool."

I touched the sides of my mouth.

Sean laughed. "I was kidding, but you can have one if you'd like."

"I'm good, thanks." I stuffed a too-large forkful of salad into my mouth, embarrassing myself even more, but at least I didn't have to make any more excuses about my strange visit. One I couldn't even explain myself.

Sean filled me in on why the Braves were the team to beat this season, and I argued my defense of the Cubs. His points were valid, and I had to explain that whether the

Cubs had their shit together or not, a diehard fan was a diehard fan.

"I can understand. I guess I'm that way about the Falcons."

"What about the Hawks?" I asked.

A slow smile crept across his face.

"Who are they?"

I returned the smile. "Valid point. Does anyone watch NBA anymore?"

"Not in this neck of the woods."

"I haven't watched since Jordan. I know people say LeBron is better, but I don't agree."

"I couldn't say. I don't know anything about the sport. But I know Jordan was good."

"Jordan averaged more points than LeBron, and his free throw percentage was considerably higher. That and LeBron's asshole personality put Jordan on the top of the GOAT list."

"Goat list?"

"Greatest of all time?" I smirked.

He nodded. "I did not know that. Tell me, do you have any sisters?"

"Nope."

"I can tell."

I was surprised at how easy it was to casually talk once we had our food. The conversation was superficial and unimportant, but it was sort of comfortable.

I tossed a twenty on the table. "I hate to eat and bolt, but I really need to get back to work."

"Please, a gentleman pays when he has dinner with a lady."

"This lady is currently carrying two loaded weapons and she knows how to use them."

"Yes, ma'am."

He stood by my Jeep as I unlocked the door. "I only walked you to your car because I'm a nice Southern gentleman."

"And here he goes with that again."

He smiled. "Listen, I like you. I think you know that, and I'd like to take you out on a date if you can break away from work for a few hours again sometime."

Way to make a girl feel like shit. "I've got this investigation, and I'm still trying to prove myself to my peers...I just don't—"

He stopped me. "I got it. Just riding lessons and random coffee chat, then." He reached out to hug me, and I let him. "For now."

A Malibu revved its engine a few cars from me.

30

I said goodbye to Sean and watched him walk to his vehicle, then focused on the Malibu. It was the red one again. The driver kept his head turned away from me, and his black baseball cap left me no option for any above-the-neck recognition, but I caught enough of a glimpse of the black jacket that the hairs on my arms popped to attention.

It was Hernandez. I kept him on my tail and called my partner. "I've got eyes on Hernandez."

"I'm three minutes out," he said.

"I'm not at Taco Mac. How about we meet at Senorita Taqueria instead of here?"

"You got it."

"Red Malibu, Kentucky plate."

"You sure it's Hernandez?"

"Call it a hunch."

"Fuck. I'm coming."

There were advantages to having a cruiser with a laptop, but in this case, I appreciated having to call dispatch for the check. They were faster and more efficient than I was when it came to technology, and I couldn't afford the distraction.

I stayed just a few cars ahead of the Malibu.

"The plate matches a 2014 Toyota Camry from Kentucky," dispatch said.

"Was it reported stolen?"

"No, ma'am."

"Do we have any recent reports of a stolen late-model red Chevy Malibu?"

"Nothing in the system, ma'am."

"I suspect it will be."

The vehicle turned left onto Old Milton Parkway, then made a right onto Haynes Bridge Road.

Bishop called. "I'm three cars behind you."

"He got behind me."

"You think he knows he's busted?"

"I don't think so. I'm going to turn toward Senorita Taqueria and see what he does."

"I'm on him now."

I watched him maneuver through traffic in the right lane and finally drop behind the Malibu. "That's ballsy."

The Malibu didn't seem to notice, stopping behind a vehicle in the left turn lane headed to the restaurant. I made the turn, but he had to wait for traffic.

"I'm feeling lucky." Bishop opened his window and placed the cherry just above his head.

"Shit!" I waited for traffic to move to make a U-turn.

Seconds later, the Malibu swerved right, slammed a compact car over two lanes, and kicked his speed up.

Bishop took off after him as I called dispatch requesting available LEO in the area. I threw my cherry on my roof, paused to allow the surrounding drivers a second to gather their senses, then whipped out in pursuit.

He weaved in and out of traffic for half a block, then swerved onto the entrance ramp to State Route 400. My heart raced, pumping a mix of adrenaline and blood through my body. Two Alpharetta PD cruisers sped past me, their sirens and lights sending traffic to the side of the road. I stayed on their tails.

Bishop spoke over the radio on my shoulder. "He's exiting at Mansell."

Someone from the Fulton County Sheriff's office identified themselves and spoke. "Exit ramp is blocked. Proceed with caution."

I pounded my fist onto my steering wheel. "We've got him!"

Bishop yelled at the sheriff's deputy blocking me from entering the restricted area. "Let her through!"

I flashed my badge. "Detective Ryder, Hamby PD."

The cop let me pass. I jogged over to the kid handcuffed and sitting in the Fulton Sheriff's cruiser. He lifted his head, and I pounced. "You piece of shit!" A strong arm yanked mine and whipped me away from Hernandez. "What the—"

Bishop's face was beat red. "You want to lose him! Is that what you want?"

I bent over and tried to catch my breath. "I'm not going to lose him!"

"Calm down, Ryder. You make a mistake on this, and you're fucked! Do you understand?"

"It's him." My heart raced, and I was struggling to breathe. "It's fucking him!"

Bishop put his hand on my shoulder. "I know."

I stared into the cruiser, my face hot as a fire, and jabbed my finger at Hernandez. "What's he paying you?" When the kid didn't speak, I asked again, only louder. "What's Petrowski paying you!"

"Fuck you, bitch!" He spat at me.

Bishop yanked me away again. "Away! Now!" He flung my arm toward the red Malibu.

I jerked it away, telling him where he could shove it, but still stepped aside. I hated admitting he was right, but if I didn't play nice, I could ruin my case against Petrowski. I leaned against my Jeep, watching the tow truck arrive, connect the red Malibu, and leave. Bishop paced the Fulton County cruiser housing Hernandez, talking to law enforcement I hadn't seen before.

I pulled my cell out of my pocket and pounded on it to call Garcia, not bothering with a hello when he answered. "We fucking got him!"

"What's he saying?"

I pressed my free palm into my forehead and walked a circle around my vehicle as I spoke. "I don't know. Bishop won't let me near him."

He laughed. "Smart man."

"Fuck you, Garcia."

"Calm down. You're less effective when you're heated like this. Bishop probably knows that by now. Get yourself together."

I took three deep breaths.

"Better?"

"No. I want him."

"You have time. Petrowski's not going anywhere."

"That's too bad. If he comes here, I'm taking him out."

"No doubt." Bishop signaled for me to come to him. "Gotta go," I said, and disconnected the call.

"We're taking him in. Chief will be there. Don't screw yourself with this, partner."

I jogged back to my Jeep and beat them to the department.

I waited for Bishop in the interrogation room. I knew he'd bring Hernandez there and then look for me, but I didn't want to waste any time.

He shook his head when he saw me leaning against the back wall.

"What took you so long?"

"We stopped for tacos." He escorted Hernandez to a seat at the table.

I chewed on my finger and paced from one side of the room to another. I eyed Hernandez, who refused to make eye contact with either of us, keeping his head down, staring at the table. I mouthed, "Jimmy coming?"

Bishop flicked his eyes toward the one-way mirror, telling me the chief was behind the glass. I wanted at the kid, and Bishop knew it, so was his silence a green light?

When he spoke, I realized it wasn't. He pulled out a chair opposite Hernandez and sat. "So, here on vacation?"

Hernandez angled his eyes up to Bishop and then retreated back to the table stare.

"Because I can name a lot better early spring vacation spots. Miami, maybe? Or were you worried the stolen tag wouldn't get you that far?"

Hernandez stared at Bishop. "Tag?"

"License plate," I said. "Came off a vehicle registered in Kentucky. What'd you do, switch plates?"

"I didn't steal no plate."

"The VIN's not scratched off the black Malibu, just like the one you crashed the other day," I said.

He glared at me. "I wasn't drivin' no black car. I just got here today."

"That's bullshit, and you know it."

The door opened and Michels walked in. He handed Bishop a file, smiled at me, and then left. Bishop motioned for me to hold off, then flipped through the file. "Looks like there's some truth to his story." He handed me the file.

I skimmed the two pages, then steadied my eyes on Hernandez. "You got a problem telling time, don't you?" I tossed the file on the table. "You flew into Atlanta from Midway four days ago. Time sure flies when you're stalking someone, doesn't it? Petrowski pay for your flight?" When he didn't respond, I stretched out and bent over the table, grabbing him by the shirt collar. "Answer the question, asshole!" I released my grip and stood up. Bishop glared at me. "I'm fine," I said, straightening my shirt.

Bishop must have sensed the good cop, bad cop thing wasn't going to fly, so he cut to the chase. "Why are you here?"

Hernandez jutted his chin toward me. "That bitch killed my brother."

"I should have reloaded and dropped another magazine in him. My bad."

Hernandez spat at me again. "You got nothing on me, bitch."

"That's where you're wrong, asshole. I got evading an officer, speeding, reckless driving, assaulting a police officer —twice." I pulled out the chair and sat. "You think Cook County's backed up? You should check out Fulton. Our judges like to take a lot of vacations. It'll probably be six months before you're even seen." I smiled as I stood. "When you're ready to talk, you let me know. I might be able to call in a favor and get you your own cell."

As I walked to the door, he caved. "I should have killed you when I had the chance."

"Yeah, well, we all have regrets. Like I said, I should have emptied another magazine into your brother." I knocked on the door. When it opened, I nodded to the officer and said, "Take him to lockup."

31

"Let me see." Jimmy walked around his office with his finger pressed against his lip. His calm voice didn't fool me. "Either you've got a plan, or you've lost your fucking mind." He turned and stared at me. "What the hell was that? You think we're going to get him to talk? He'll lawyer up now, especially if Petrowski's footing the bill."

I swallowed hard. "I got this, Chief."

"Really?" He kicked his small garbage can. "Jesus, I don't know what's worse, you pissing me off like this, or me feeling like Cochran."

If he'd meant to slam me, he succeeded. "I'm sorry."

He exhaled, then leaned against his desk. "We have procedure for a reason."

"I know."

"If you'd followed it, we might know who sent him."

"Petrowski sent him, Jimmy."

"How do you know? What evidence do you have to prove that?"

I opened my mouth to speak but stopped. The truth was,

I didn't have any evidence supporting that, but it was true anyway.

He nodded. "Just what I thought. What about his mother?"

"I don't understand."

"You killed her son. Maybe she sent him? Maybe he's doing it on his own to avenge his brother's death. Maybe busting that drug ring screwed with their income and they sent him. Think we'll find out now?"

I nodded. "I'll find out, sir."

"No, you won't. You're not working this. You're too emotional. I need a clear head on it."

"What? No! You can't take me off this case."

"Like hell I can't. Go home. Take a breather. Come back in two days."

"But—"

"Go home, Ryder. Now."

Bishop gently grabbed my elbow. "Come on."

I stormed out, snarling and dropping an F-bomb under my breath.

He followed me to my car. "You okay?"

"Do I look okay?"

He inhaled, pulled his pack of cigarettes from his pocket, and offered me one. I took it and lit it up. He did the same. "Let me handle this for the next few days. Give Jimmy a while to cool off. He'll come around. He knows you know this better than any of us. He'll let you stay on it."

"No," I said, shaking my head. "He won't. He's too green, and he wants to keep his job. I'm off."

"I'll follow you home."

"You can't leave, Hernandez is—"

"Hernandez will be there in the morning."

"No. Stay. Please. I'm fine. You need to talk to him again.

Start over. Maybe he'll talk to you. We need him to admit Petrowski sent him."

He finished his cigarette, dropped it on the ground, and smashed it with his foot. "You sure you're going to be okay?"

I nodded. "Andy's probably still at my place anyway. I doubt I'll be alone." I headed toward my car. "Call me if he says anything."

"I will."

I hit every red light from Haynes Bridge to the intersection just before my townhome community's entrance, where I slowed enough to watch the light change and the arrow turn green for me. As I drove forward to turn, a black SUV sped through a red light, swerving enough to miss T-boning me. I glanced in my rearview mirror and said, "No plate." I shook my head. "Asshole."

Andy's pickup was still parked on the side of my driveway. It made me sad for him. I'd left four hours ago. He'd probably decided to retile my entire guest bath so he wouldn't have to go home and think about his brother.

I pulled into the garage, hit the button to close the door, then hit it again. I needed a cigarette. Hell, I needed the whole pack. I lit up as I walked out of the garage, staring up at the night sky.

"The stars are much brighter out here, aren't they?"

I recognized his voice immediately as the hairs on the back of my neck stood. I placed my hand on my weapon.

"I wouldn't do that if I were you. Three against one is a losing battle, don't you think?" Chris Petrowski stepped from the side of my garage, a sick, twisted smile covering his pockmarked face. "Looking good, Rachel. But you always were a looker, weren't you? Too bad you're such a fucking bitch. I could have had fun with you."

Someone to my right laughed.

I bit back my snide comment and glanced up at my garage light. It was out. Damn it. How did I miss that?

"Remove your weapons, please. You know the drill. One hand, two fingers. Isn't that how they teach you in cop school?"

His two thugs approached me. I held up my hands. "I'm not carrying."

"The one in your boot?" Petrowski asked.

I slowly held up my ankle to reveal my boot. "That'd be a worthless gun, don't you think?"

He wiggled his gun toward the thug on my right. "Pat her down. Give her a little extra love while you're at it."

The slimeball smiled as he sauntered toward me. He patted my waist and up my torso, then squeezed each of my breasts. I inhaled to keep my mouth shut as his hands traveled back down my sides, around my waist, and to my crotch. He smiled when he squeezed. But he totally missed the switchblade. Maybe there was a god, after all.

"You're not my type, asshole." I spat in his face.

He raised his hand.

"Leave her," Petrowski said.

I glared at him. "This isn't Chicago. These people hear a shot, they call the cops."

"Who says I'm going to shoot you? Besides, I'm not worried. Your boyfriend's been dead a few minutes already." He cupped his ear. "No sirens."

"My—" Fuck! I eyed Andy's car. "You son of a bitch!" My heart raced. I forced myself to calm down. It wasn't easy.

Petrowksi laughed. "I'm surprised you've moved on so

quickly. You seemed so distraught over that detective husband of yours."

I furrowed my brow. "Wait. You think I'm, what? Involved with someone?"

He shrugged. "Like I said, I was surprised." His tone was humored, like all of this was just fun and games for him.

I spoke through gritted teeth. "You know nothing about me."

He laughed. "Oh, my dear, I know more than you think. For example, I know sports, though I'm surprised you'd give up your love for Chicago baseball for the Braves. Sure, they have a nice stadium, but didn't you and Detective Mancini love a game in the bleachers at Wrigley?"

"What the hell are you talking about?"

"Your new guy likes the Braves. I'm told he wears that hat everywhere he goes. His farm, that bar you like to go to with the guys from work, this Taco Mac. Shall I go on?"

Shit. The Braves hat. Both Sean and Andy had the same hat. Petrowski or his minions must have confused the two and thought Andy was Sean. "You're not as smart as you think you are, asshole."

He sneered. "Everyone's allowed their opinion."

Three men. The one who patted me down was short, maybe five eight with his boots on. Approximately 180 pounds with big arms, a thick neck, and a wide chest. His legs disproportionate to his upper body. He liked the gym but must have hated squats. His weakness would be below the belt, which was good for me. I wasn't afraid of squats, and my legs were my strongest muscles. The other guy was maybe a few inches taller, at least twenty pounds less, and not exactly someone who hit the gym, but he didn't need to. The evil in his eyes said he got his kicks hurting people. He liked to torture them.

Petrowski didn't do his own dirty work, so if I had to guess, torture guy shot Andy.

The two men stepped back, put away their weapons, and clasped their hands in front of them.

Petrowski wiggled his gun toward my townhouse. "Let's take this inside, shall we?"

I took note of my surroundings, but nothing appeared out of place. No car parked on the side of the street, no engine running nearby, nothing.

The bulkier of the two men removed his gun and shoved it at me. "Go."

"Gee, you're a sweetheart, aren't you?"

"Through the garage," he said, nudging the barrel into the middle of my back.

Someone hit the garage door opener behind me. I closed my eyes for a second and took a deep breath.

Andy's body sat against my built-in bookcases. One shot to the forehead. Execution-style. His Braves hat lying on the floor beside him.

"Keep moving," the thug with the gun said.

I moved toward the back wall, and my sofa table. A quick look below the top told me Tommy's Sig was still there. I held my hands above my head, turned around, and leaned against the table. "Can't go any farther, big guy."

He took two small steps back, but I needed him farther away to access the gun or knife.

"The couch," Petrowski said. "Sit."

"I prefer to stand."

Buff thug with the gun yanked me by the arm and shoved me toward the couch. I caught myself before I could fall—a position no one wants to be in with this scenario. I watched the two thugs carefully. The big guy was the bruiser. He brandished his weapon like he knew what he was doing, but I knew better.

He was holding the gun with his knuckles up. Not only was it wrong, it was stupid. His hand shook slightly, and if he took a shot, he'd struggle to get the gun back in position to shoot me again. The problem I had was distance. The closer he was, the easier he could get off two shots that could hit me in two different spots. And one might accidentally end up a kill shot.

I needed that gun, and I needed a distraction. I glared at Petrowski as I sat down. "What's the plan? You just going to shoot me and leave? Pretty boring, don't you think?"

He walked over to my bookshelves. He stepped over Andy's remains, clearly adding his prints to the crime scene after the fact. He didn't do that on accident. He picked up the photo of me and Tommy at Navy Pier. "I thought he was a pain in my ass, but I'll admit, he had nothing on you."

"It's Tommy's investigation that put you in jail, asshole."

He opened his arms, palms facing up. "Yet here I stand, years before I was to be released."

"You won't get away with this. Too many people know you're here. Sanchez's brother will give you up to keep from doing hard time." I caught the questioning look in his eyes. It was brief, but it was there. Had he not used Hernandez?

The thinner of the two thugs stood with his hands clasped in front of him again. He had a weapon secured to a belt on his waist. Not holding it meant he was confident enough to think he didn't need it. I didn't recognize him or the other guy, and because of that, I couldn't determine how they might react.

Damn it! I glanced over at Andy. If Petrowksi didn't have me killed, Bishop would do it himself.

I'd strategically placed weapons throughout my home,

but none were in a spot I could easily access, and grabbing the switchblade from my pants would get that gun aimed straight at my head.

I needed to keep him talking, which, given what I knew about the POS, shouldn't be hard. "You must have loved those first few months in prison. I heard you got a lot of flak for being tough on crime. Bet you were someone's bitch from day one."

The thinner thug took a step forward. I clenched my jaw. I needed off that couch. "Listen, I'm all for hanging out and shooting the shit, but I gotta pee." I slowly stood.

Thug with a gun held it up sideways again. I glanced at the other guy. I could smack the gun out of the thicker thug's hand, grab the knife and stab him, then grab the gun and shoot the other, but time wasn't on my side. I held up my hands. "Who's my escort?"

The two men stared at Petrowski. He nodded to the one pointing his gun at me.

He shoved it into my back as he followed me to the bathroom. I listened closely, hearing additional shoes hit the floor. Damn. I had an audience. The switchblade was small. I could easily cover it with my hand, and the clip holding it to my thong was easily manipulated. I'd practiced removing it hundreds of times.

I smiled at the men as they stood and watched me drop my pants, careful to grab the knife without them seeing. I pulled my shirt over my waist as much as possible and slipped the knife into my sleeve, barely holding it with my hand. As I zipped my jeans, I kept my wrist slightly bent so they couldn't see the knife.

A knife was no competition for a gun, let alone three, but it was the best I had.

We walked back to the family room. On the way, I eyed

the secret gun compartment on my kitchen wall. If I could get to that or Tommy's Sig, I had a shot. I needed to keep myself between those weapons.

"Anyone want a beer?" I asked.

"Keep moving," the thinner of the thugs said.

I noted his accent immediately. Russian. Petrowski wasn't messing around. The Russian mafia infiltrated Chicago in the early 2000s, ranging from former prison members to corrupt officials and businessmen. Tommy found no connection between Petrowski and the Russians, so it had to come from prison. I could work with that. "Love your accent." I stopped near the back of my couch, a few steps away from the sofa table against the wall.

"Sit," the Russian guy said.

"I'd rather stand. Sciatica."

The other thug jabbed his gun into my back. I held my arms high over my head. "You want to cop a feel?"

"Leave her," Petrowski said.

I rested my hands on the cushions of my couch. Keep him talking, I thought. "Now I get it," I said. "You lost your Mexican connection in prison, but the Russians knew you could help them." I watched the man with the gun walk around the couch and aim it at me. Someone really needed to show him how to hold the thing. I tilted my head to the left. "Was there actually any piece of your soul left to sell? I mean, let's be honest here. Their loyalty comes with a price. So, tell me, how'd you do it?"

He walked to the photo of me and Tommy and removed it from the shelf. He stared at it, then set it back where he got it. "You think you're smart enough to play me?"

I didn't respond.

"Your husband did, and look what happened to him."

"And look what happened to the guy you hired to kill

him." I smirked at the guy pointing the gun at me. "Were you in prison with the commissioner here?"

He didn't respond. In fact, his face didn't even twitch.

"He ever tell you what happened to the guy he hired to kill Detective Tommy Mancini?"

Still nothing.

"I'm sure you heard about the twenty-some other people arrested, right? Took out a major portion of the Mexican cartel." I smiled. "It's a great story," I said, looking straight at Petrowski. "Made all the papers. County commissioner taken down by murdered detective's wife." I paused for effect. "Good times."

No one else found my story as wonderful as I did.

"Yet again, as I said earlier, here I stand."

"Yeah. With two thugs to go down for your dirty work." I stared at the scarier of the two, the one without the weapon. "Here's how this is going to play out. Brutus here with the gun is going to shoot me, but you'll go down for the hit too." I scanned the room and focused my eyes on a vase on the bookshelf near the French doors.

The thug without the gun eyed Petrowski. Petrowski nodded, and the thug walked over to the vase. I held my breath as he passed Herman. He grabbed the vase, examined it, then held it up over his head and slammed it toward the floor.

I laughed when it didn't break. "Can't break fake glass." I smiled. They thought I had a camera on them, and though I wished I did, I could work with the illusion. "It's all on camera." I stared into the thug with the gun's eyes. "Let me guess. You pulled the trigger on my friend."

He didn't move.

"And you," I said, flicking my head toward the other guy. "You watched." I stared back at Petrowski. "Anger is a powerful emotion, isn't it, Chris? You're not the only one with connections. You couldn't cross the state line without someone seeing."

Petrowski's jaw tensed.

"And now here you are, doing exactly what you promised in front of a whole courtroom full of cops."

He smirked. "Many of whom report to me."

"Ah." I smirked back. "But not all."

The thug searching for the cameras passed the couch and headed down the hall. I had a chance. It was slim, but it was all I had. He'd be a better aim than Petrowski and the other thug, so I went for it. I kept my hands on the couch, careful not to show the knife, then took two steps toward the right. "It's going to be a long night. May I go ahead and sit?"

The thug guarding me jabbed his gun toward me.

Petrowski stepped closer as he retrieved his weapon from his pocket.

I made it to the right side of the couch. These thugs were idiots, and Petrowski wasn't much smarter. The thug kept his knuckles up, the gun pointed at me without his finger on the trigger. Mistake number two, I thought. I lifted my left arm with the knife, clicked it open, then knocked his right forearm with the side of mine and circled my arm back before driving the knife into his gut.

I pulled it out as fast as I jabbed it in, hearing his grunt as he went down. The gun fell to the ground, hitting the carpet. I quickly grabbed it, stood, then turned toward Petrowski. I stepped forward on my right foot, drew my left knee up, pivoted my hip, and kicked his weapon from his right hand. It flew across the room toward my front entrance, the farthest point from both thugs. I jabbed the gun into Petrowski's gut, took a step behind him, then wrapped my right arm around his neck. I moved the gun to the side of his head. "I've waited a long time for this!"

The other thug stood with a gun aimed at me. I tightened my grip on Petrowski's neck. "Give me a fucking reason!" I didn't care. In that moment, the asshole could shoot me if he wanted. I'd get a bullet into Petrowski's head before he could hit me. I'd die knowing the man who ruined my life would never breathe again.

My front door burst open. "Police!" Bishop yelled.

The thug with the gun turned and aimed at Bishop, but my partner was too fast. He let loose one, two, three shots. Two in the chest and one in the gut. Michels rushed in, checked the other thug bleeding on my floor, cuffed him, then got on his radio.

I couldn't let go of Petrowski, tightening my grip around his neck. He scratched and pulled at my arms. Bishop yanked him off, and Michels cuffed him.

"You okay?" Bishop asked me.

I stared at the two thugs. The one I'd stabbed groaned, but he was in too much pain to move. The other one wasn't going anywhere. I bent over and tried to catch my breath.

"Ambulance is on its way," Michels said.

"Let him die," I said, staring at the thug still alive.

Bishop walked over to Andy.

I turned to Petrowski and charged toward him. "That wasn't my boyfriend, you piece of shit! You're going back to prison, and you're not getting out this time."

He smiled. "Your cameras will prove he was already dead when we arrived."

I laughed. "Then lucky for me I don't have any cameras."

Two slick sleeves charged in. The first one stopped in his tracks the moment he saw Andy Pruitt's body, making the sign of the cross over his chest. "Jesus, Mary, and Joseph."

Bishop hadn't moved. I turned toward him. "We need to keep the scene as clean as possible." When he still didn't move, I yelled, "Bishop, booties and gloves, now!"

My voice shook him into action. He retreated to his vehicle, then returned and slipped on booties and gloves.

"Chief's on his way," one of the officers said.

I stared at Michels. "How'd you know?"

"Bishop called and texted. When you didn't answer, we came. He saw the broken garage light and knew something was wrong. I was watching through the French doors." He smiled and nodded. "You got some killer moves, Detective."

"Something's not right." I exhaled, then chewed my nail. "The SUV!" I gave what little details I had on the black SUV that had almost hit me. "It had to be coming from here."

Michels nodded. "I'll get a BOLO on it now."

"It's not much to go on, but it's a start," I mumbled under my breath.

Bishop tossed me a set of booties and gloves, which I struggled to get on. Get your shit together, Ryder, I repeated in my head. "We'll get whoever did this," I said.

"And they're going to burn in hell." He offered a string of curse words my Italian grandmother would have found insulting, and she swore like a sailor. He walked over to Petrowski. "We got you, motherfucker."

The bastard just smiled.

I swallowed hard, forcing myself to focus on my surroundings. The two patrol officers just stood there, watching me. "Get your booties on, then come back in and start taking photos of everything."

They stood frozen.

"Now!"

I took a second to breathe, then forced myself to look at

Andy and remember his face. I turned to Petrowski. "Something's not right. You took a life for nothing."

He stared at me.

"Here we are, you in cuffs and me standing over you, smiling. Feels like old times, doesn't it?"

He didn't say a word. I nodded toward one of the officers standing near my front door. "Take him outside and throw him in a cruiser. Don't let him out of your sight."

I examined the room carefully. Nothing near Andy's body was out of place. Blood splatter covered the shelves and knickknacks with a trajectory that told me the shooter was less than a foot away when he pulled the trigger. The bullet entered right above the bridge of Andy's nose. My mind flashed back to the night Tommy died. Same bullet entry location. I dropped back to the ground and searched for the shell casing on Andy's left side and found it under his thigh. Before touching it, I asked Bishop for his phone and photographed the area, then I picked up the casing and studied it. I recognized it immediately. The same type of bullet was used to kill my husband.

32

I glanced at the photo of Tommy and me and then the men lying on the floor.

The EMTs arrived. One went to the dead guy, checked his pulse, turned, and said, "He's dead."

The shorter of the EMTs quickly examined the guy I stabbed. "Only one entrance and exit wound. Right side, near his kidney."

They both looked at me.

"I stabbed him," I said. My hands shook as I stared at the knife on the floor. "With that."

The chief walked in. "Shit."

"Yeah," I said.

He placed his hand on Bishop's shoulder, both of them staring at Andy sitting on my floor. "I'm sorry."

Bishop didn't say anything.

Jimmy slipped on a pair of booties and gloves. "Start from the beginning."

I retraced the events of the evening.

"Why was Andy still here?"

I shrugged. "He wanted to keep busy."

"I should have been here," Bishop said.

"It's not your fault," Jimmy said.

"It's mine," I said. "I should have made him leave."

"And Petrowski says he didn't do it?"

I nodded.

"You think he's lying?"

I shook my head. "My gut says he didn't do it."

Bishop glared at me.

"Whoever shot Andy did it the same way Sanchez shot Tommy." I walked over to Andy's body and crouched down beside him. "Weapon used was a 9mm. The shell is under his left thigh. +P ARX."

"Shit," Jimmy said. "That's some serious ammo."

"Manufacturer claims it's the most lethal, and it's exactly what was used on Tommy," I said. "And these guys aren't Hispanic. That means something went down between the Hispanics and Petrowski while he did time. Something that forced him to align with the Russians. Unless they researched what happened, this isn't their MO. They like to have fun before they go in for the kill."

Bishop's chin dropped.

"Was the type of bullet made public?"

I shook my head. "But it's common among the Mexican cartel crowd."

"And not the Russians?"

"I'm not sure. Let me get my cell out of my car." I removed my booties and gloves at my garage door and grabbed my weapon and my cell. Walking back in, I noticed several missed calls from Bishop, but also nine from Lenny and five from Garcia. I checked the list of texts too.

I called Garcia immediately. "I'm okay."

"Jesus, you scared the shit out of me not answering."

"I was a little busy fighting Petrowski and two Russian guys."

"Shit. Wait, Russians?"

"Yup."

"Explains why no one saw Petrowski with the Mexican cartel."

"Right."

"You okay?"

"Yeah." I sighed. "Physically anyway. I had an opportunity to take out Petrowski, but I didn't. I fucking didn't, Garcia. What the hell is wrong with me?"

"Nothing. You're a good cop, and a decent human being. You did the right thing. Tommy wouldn't want Petrowski's blood on your hands, Rach. You know that."

He was right, but I didn't care. I wanted Petrowski's blood on my hands. I wanted to stand over his body with a gun pointed at his head, saying my dead husband's name as I pulled the trigger. Hell, I fantasized about that, but when push came to shove, I couldn't do it. I was too weak.

"I'm sorry. I tried to get in touch with you when we learned he left the state."

"He didn't drive, did he?"

"Private jet."

"Let me guess, owned by a Russian."

"I'm sorry, Ryder. I didn't know."

"It's okay."

"So, no casualties?"

"My partner took out one of the thugs. I got the other in the stomach with my knife, but he'll live. And someone killed my handyman."

"One of the thugs?"

"I don't think so." I stepped toward Andy. "Any idea if Russians favor the +P ARX?"

"You think it's the Russians?"

"I'm working a theory."

"Ammo's hard to get these days."

"So they'll use whatever they can."

"Pretty much," Garcia said.

"I'll get back to you, okay?"

"Sure thing. I'll check around about the ammo. See if I can find anything."

"Thanks," I said, and disconnected the call.

Dr. Barron arrived at the same time as Ashley. She hit the ground running while the rest of us analyzed the scene from an investigative angle.

"I'm guessing the shooter was under six feet. Maybe five-seven, tops," I said.

"Explain," Jimmy said.

I walked over to the built-in bookcase Andy designed and died against. "Stand with your back against the shelves."

He stood, and I moved close enough to stretch my arm fully, aiming an imaginary gun at his head. "The casing dropped to the left, which leads me to believe the shooter is righthanded, and it didn't go far, which tells me its pathway was blocked, at least to some degree." I extended my arm out again, allowing about an inch of space between my fingers and Jimmy's forehead. "I'm five-five. If you look at the blood pattern behind me, it's just past my shoulders. The guy was taller than me, but not by much."

"What's the average height of a Russian man?" he asked.

Bishop checked his phone. "Five-foot-seven to nine."

"What about Mexican?"

Bishop slid his finger over his screen. "Five-seven." He was incredibly calm. I didn't know if that was good or bad, though I leaned toward bad.

Jimmy rubbed the top of his head. "So, it could be either group."

Ashley tapped on the door. "Sir?"

We turned around.

"I found it behind the body." She held up a gold chain with a skull pendant attached.

I swallowed hard. "Petrowski's not an idiot. If he wanted me dead, he wouldn't waste his time with symbols and messages. Those aren't his. That's not his MO. Sure, he's messing with me now. He showed up just to fuck with my head because he knew I wouldn't kill him." I dropped my head back and exhaled. "Fucker knows me better than I know myself."

"He wanted you to suffer."

I shook my head. "I was wrong. He wouldn't waste his time with that. Besides, it would leave too much of an evidence trail. It's not Petrowski." I walked over to the couch and stared at the blood on the carpet. "Savannah set me up tonight. Did you know that?"

He nodded.

"Sean was there, and he was wearing the same Braves hat as Andy. I even pointed that out to him."

"It's the Braves. Most of the men in Georgia have one of those."

I shook my head. "No. Whoever did this knew I met Sean at Taco Mac. They saw us together, saw the hat." I pressed my lips together, then spoke as my brain processed it all. "They must have come to my house, saw Andy, and assumed he was Sean. They killed Andy because they thought it was him hugging me outside of Taco Mac."

Bishop exhaled.

"I need someone on Sean."

"I'll handle it," Jimmy said. He stepped away for a

moment but returned quickly, nodding once to me. I took that to mean he'd taken care of it.

Bishop continued his train of thought. "The SUV that almost hit you was coming from here."

"Michels called in a BOLO."

"Black SUV," Bishop said. "Half the state drives one of those."

"Shit," Jimmy said.

Petrowski was telling the truth. "Someone's entered my home twice now. The first time was a warning made clear by leaving everything in place and destroying the framed photo of me and Tommy. Andy was here that day, but he left. Tonight, Sean and I sit together in a crowded sports bar, then some kid in a Malibu drives by and distracts me." I lifted my foot to step forward but moved back when I realized I hadn't put on another pair of booties.

"Chief," Barron said, standing over Andy's body. "I'm ready to have the body transported for autopsy."

Bishop exhaled. "Allison. I need to talk to her."

"I'll call the patrol with her," Jimmy said.

Bishop nodded, then looked me in the eyes. "We need to find the bastard who killed my best friend."

I fought back tears. "We will."

Joey Angelini picked up on the first ring. "Do you ever sleep?"

"Do you?"

"Right. How's it hanging, Detective?"

"Probably lower than yours."

"Ouch! That's harsh."

"My bad. Listen, I need a favor."

"You tell me my dick is small and then you ask me for a favor? That's class for ya."

"It's about Petrowski."

His voice dropped an octave, turning his tone serious. "Damn, girl, you got some major balls."

"So I'm told. Listen, I need phone records and emails. Can you get that?"

"Shit. I mean, yeah, sure. What's going on? I mean, other than the shit you've already told me. Did something new happen?"

"My handyman was shot execution-style." I paused and exhaled. "In my house, with the same type of bullet used to kill Tommy. Petrowski insists he's not involved."

"Wait. You talked to Petrowski?"

"He showed up here with some big Russian dudes."

"And he's still alive?"

"It was a mistake on my part, but I need to know if he's got a connection to any of these players."

"And you think he'd use his cell phone? Petrowski's cocky, but he ain't stupid."

"I have to check whatever I can."

"Motherfucker's got to go down. I'll do whatever I can. Tommy was my man, you know that." He coughed. "I heard you found Sanchez's half-brother too. Damn. Is he mixed up in this? You think Petrowski brought him in as some kind of mind-fuck revenge?"

"Who told you?"

"I know a guy."

I laughed. "Hey," I said as a thought occurred to me. "Can you hack hospital records?"

"The right question would be, what can't I hack?"

"Right."

"Let me guess, you want me to check Sanchez's mom's medical records, right?"

"You'd make a good cop, Angelini."

"Nah, I like working outside the law."

I laughed. "Let me know what you find, and put a rush on it, will ya?"

He laughed. "Who needs sleep? But yeah, I'll get what I can ASAP."

"Thanks," I said, and disconnected the call.

Bishop knocked on my cubby wall. I set my cell face down and waved him in. "How are you?"

"I'm fine."

His red cheeks, tired eyes, and obvious effort to keep his shoulders back proved he was lying. I understood. We needed to hit this hard and fast. If we didn't, we could lose leads, and I knew he'd never forgive me or possibly himself.

"Bishop, I just want to say I'm—"

"Don't. Andy wouldn't go to the safe house."

"But if I'd figured this out sooner, maybe things would be different."

"Does that mean you've got it figured out now?"

I shook my head.

"Then don't dwell on the could haves." He stood in front of my desk and tapped it with a pencil. "We didn't have anything solid connecting you to those pendants, no matter what you wanted to believe. You did everything right. This isn't on you, so don't carry that around."

"Easier said than done."

"Understood." He tapped the pencil on the corner of my desk again. "You got a place to stay?"

"Yes, my bed."

He crooked his head to the right. "What?"

"It's my home."

"It's a crime scene."

"That's been examined and recorded." I straightened in my chair and gently removed the pencil from his hand. The tapping drove me crazy. "Besides, if we're going to catch this person, the best way to do it is to use me as the bait. He'll come for me soon enough."

Bishop sat in the chair across from me. "Allison's a mess."

"I can imagine."

"Thanks for letting me go to see her on my own."

"Is she staying there?"

"No, but I convinced her to go stay with a friend in Alabama for a while, so there's that."

My past ruined Allison's life, and I'd carry that monkey on my back for the rest of mine.

"I wish there was something we could do for her."

"We need to find the person who did this. I don't want her back until we do."

"I'm not wrong about this."

"I don't think you are, but we can't shove the pieces of the puzzle together and make them work. We have to consider the possibility we're dealing with three separate crimes here."

"Brad's murder, Petrowski coming for me, and Andy's murder."

Jimmy gave us until four a.m. and forced us to set our watch alarms. He warned us if we stayed any longer, he'd pull us off all three cases and put us on desk duty. It took us almost two hours to convince him to do that much, and we weren't going to push him.

A good defense attorney could use our involvement in the cases to their advantage, and we spent two hours in an emergency meeting with the district attorney pleading to stay involved. We played out every possible outcome, assuring her we'd work by the book. Jimmy had been effective in keeping it out of the news, but that wouldn't last. When a drug addict dies, it's sad, but add in a family member's death and it becomes news.

The LED lights in the investigation room and ridiculous amounts of caffeine kept us going, but I hit the wall just before four o'clock. I dipped my head back in the rolling chair and closed my eyes. "We have nothing to connect Parra to Hernandez, and unless one of his cronies killed Andy, there's no way he did it from a jail cell."

Bishop stood and put on his coat. "I need a shower and a clean pair of underwear."

"Ditto." I checked my watch. "Two minutes before our alarms go off. Jimmy will be proud. At least we have a game plan for tomorrow."

"If you can call it that."

"It's better than flying blind." I grabbed my things, and we walked out together.

The moon hung in the middle of the sky, its normal brightness blurred by clouds.

Even though no one was on my tail, I took an alternate route home. Traffic was sparse, and I was the only one going my direction. I rolled down my window and lit up a cigarette. The rush of nicotine immediately calmed my nerves and, along with the cold air, chipped away at my exhaustion. I studied the area around my townhouse before pulling into my garage. After assuring myself it was clear, I closed the main door and walked inside.

An immediate wave of sadness swept over me. I leaned against the dining room wall and stared at the bookcases. Andy's blood splatter flooded my mind with images of him propped against the very things he built. That sweet man didn't deserve to die. It was all my fault. All of it. I should have known something like this would happen. Tears flooded my eyes. I should have killed Petrowski after he murdered Tommy. Fuck the law! Look where it got Andy.

My legs collapsed beneath me. I slid down the wall, covering my face with my hands as the sadness took over. I cried uncontrollably until the sadness turned to rage and the tears dried. I stared at the yellow tape blocking my fresh start, my new life, the one I promised myself I would live to honor Tommy.

This would never end. Petrowski would keep coming for me, keep torturing me until I broke. I laughed at the thought, wiping the tears from my face. "I'm already broken."

There was only one way for this to end, one way to keep the people in my life safe.

I took a deep breath, gathered every ounce of strength I could muster, and stood. I pressed my hand against my chest as my breath caught in my lungs.

Breathe, Rachel. Breathe.

I ripped the crime scene tape off the wall and walked to Herman's bowl, picking it up gently and placing it on my kitchen counter. I fed him some extra pellets, feeling guilty knowing he'd witnessed Andy's death, adding him to the list of lives affected by mine. "You okay, little guy?"

He preferred the pellets over my company.

I walked to my bedroom and plugged my phone into my charger, realizing I hadn't returned any of Lenny's calls or texts. He hadn't attempted contact in several hours, which led me to believe he'd talked to Garcia, but just in case, I sent him a text telling him I was fine and would call soon. He didn't respond, but I assumed he was asleep. That confirmed Garcia spoke to him.

I stripped down to my bra and thong, then tossed the ripped underwear into the garbage. Yanking the knife out had ruined it, but it was a small price to pay. I turned on the shower, then stared at myself in the mirror as the water heated. I stepped into the shower and washed the night from my skin, but I couldn't wash away the pain. I leaned my head onto the tile and cried.

34

"If Sanchez's mother has more kids, she gave birth under a false name," Joey said. "Or she went back to Mexico to give birth."

"Can't see that happening."

"Me neither, but didn't want to rule it out."

"Thanks, Joey."

"I got those phone records for ya too. How do you want them?"

Joey didn't like a paper or digital trail, but I needed my own eyes on the records, and there was no other way to get them.

"Can you email them?"

"To your undercover address?"

"Yes, please."

"They'll come from a Russian email."

I laughed.

"I'm hilarious."

"And awesome. Thanks for the help."

"Any time, Detective."

I checked my email, and sure enough, up popped a new

mail with an address I couldn't begin to read. As I scrolled through the lists of names and email addresses with time and date stamps, another email arrived with text messages, and then another with emails.

I broke my promise to the district attorney. Accessing these without a warrant would make them inadmissible in court, but I didn't care. Joey was the only person I knew capable of pulling this kind of information, and I knew he could make it disappear just as easily. I printed everything out and headed back to the department.

Bishop leaned against my cubby door. "You find something?"

I glanced from the papers to Bishop's concerned face.

"I'm reading Petrowski's text messages."

He walked to my side and studied the papers. "You get a warrant for those?"

I laughed.

"Damn it, Ryder. We promised to follow the book on this!"

I looked up at him, noting the red creeping up his neck and face. "Joey's good. I promise."

He walked back to the chair in front of my desk and dropped into it. He was tired. The puffy circles below his eyes were darker and more prominent than yesterday. His scruff was more of a beard now, and his bent collar told me he'd thrown on a shirt without fixing it in a mirror. "We could have gotten those, you know."

"Doubtful. Petrowski's attorney is crooked, and he's been around a hell of a lot longer than our baby district attorney."

"We'll still need them if we want to use any of it."

I smiled up at him. "There are ways to use information with no one knowing, partner."

He raised an eyebrow. "Did you find anything useful?"

"Not yet." I gathered the papers and stuffed them back into their folder, then shoved it into my bag. I checked my watch. "I need real coffee."

"Dunkin'?"

I nodded. "After we talk to Hernandez. Barron hasn't called with the autopsy report." I placed my hand on Bishop's shoulder. "Should we call him first?"

He shook his head. "We know Hernandez and Parra didn't kill Andy. We can fake it until we have more details."

"Sounds like a plan."

Bishop stopped just outside my door. I noticed a few of the patrol hanging out watching us. He tilted his head toward me. "Can I ask you something?"

"Sure."

"How'd you manage to stab the one guy and get Petrowski in a chokehold?"

I smiled. "Muay Thai."

"Mai Tai?"

"Thai boxing. It's a combat sport."

"You're a boxer?"

"No, but Tommy was. He taught me everything I know."

"He did good."

I glanced at his legs. "If you could balance on one of those stumps, you might be able to kick someone's arm."

He laughed. "I doubt I could get my leg a foot off the ground."

I laughed too. "Don't worry. I got it covered." We stopped at the front desk of the department's jail. "One sec, I want to check something."

"Meet you there."

I nodded, then spoke to the jail officer, showing him my badge. "May I have Hernandez's bag, please?"

He slid a clipboard under the partition. "Signature."

I signed and returned the clipboard to him. He set it aside. "One minute." A few moments later, he unlocked his door and handed me a small plastic bag. "Return it when you're finished, please."

"Hold up, I just need one thing, and you can have it back." I opened the bag and removed the skull pendant and gold chain, then handed him the bag. "Thanks."

"Whatever floats your boat."

I walked into the room with Bishop and Hernandez. They both sat silently. "Well, looks like you're having a party in here. Glad I showed up." I kept the necklace in my hand.

"I'm supposed to have an attorney."

"Right. About that. There's a bit of a backup. It might be a few days."

"This is bullshit," he said.

"This ain't Chicago, Hernandez." Bishop leaned back in his chair and sucked on a toothpick. It was a brilliant Southern-style move—appear relaxed and calm. "We do things different down here."

I set the skull pendant on the table and slid it between me and Hernandez. "Nice necklace."

Sweat appeared on his forehead.

"Popular too."

"Tell us about it," Bishop said.

"It's a necklace. Fuck you."

I smacked the table with my hand. "We got three dead and five skull necklaces just like this with each victim or at scenes related to them. It's more than a fucking necklace, Benny. It's a fucking message, so tell us what the hell it means!" I snatched the pendant and held it up by the chain. "All of them look exactly like this one. You're going down for three first-degree homicides, Hernandez, so you'd better start talking."

"Those ain't mine! You think I'm stupid? I wouldn't leave shit on a dead guy!"

"Then I guess someone's trying to frame you."

He cussed under his breath.

I softened my tone. "Who sent you here?"

"No one."

"You're lying."

"Fuck you."

"Thanks for the offer, but I'll pass." I leaned back and crossed my arms.

"I want my attorney."

Bishop closed his notepad and stood. "Come on."

We left the room, closing the door behind us.

"He's not going to talk," Bishop said. "And he's asked for a lawyer twice. We can't sweep that under the rug."

He was right. Heat flushed through my body. "We need to flip him."

"We do, but this isn't the way to go about it."

We made sure his public defender was en route, then returned the pendant to the jail officer and left.

Bishop leaned against his Charger and lit up in the Dunkin' parking lot. He offered me one.

"No thanks." I chewed my fingernail. "He's not smart enough to execute a plan this detailed. Someone used him to distract us, then went to my house and killed Andy, thinking he was my boyfriend."

He stomped out his cigarette with his boot. "You kept telling me the pendants meant something. I should have listened."

"If I can't go back and blame myself, you can't either."

He turned to me, gave me a look I didn't quite recognize, then nodded. "Hernandez is a gopher. He's low-level crime. Smash-and-grabs, tire slitting, purse grabs, not multiple murders. I think you're right. Whoever's doing this is using him as an assist, and they chose him because of his connection to Sanchez."

"Manipulated his anger about his brother's death."

Bishop nodded. "We need to get the DA back out here before the public defender's shitstorm we both know is coming."

I nodded.

He picked up the cigarette butt and spat on it, then pressed it together and walked over to throw it in the trash.

Jimmy caught us on the way through the pit. "My office, now!"

Bishop and I eyed each other. He mouthed, "Shit."

Jimmy held his door open and waited for us to walk in, then slammed it behind us.

"Are you trying to ruin this case or are you just stupid?"

I assumed that was rhetorical.

Bishop must not have been sure, because he said, "We're just doing our job, Chief."

"Like hell you are!" He glared at my partner. "You're a good cop, Bishop."

It wasn't the right time to ask if he meant that for me too.

He jabbed his finger at me. "And you! You want to catch these bastards?"

I pressed my lips together, thinking that was probably rhetorical too.

"Then get your shit together and do it the right way." He stormed to his chair and crashed down into it with an exasperated groan. "Son of a bitch!"

Bishop and I sat, and since I had the bigger balls of the

two of us, I went for it. "I'm assuming you've spoken with Hernandez's attorney?"

He responded with flared nostrils and slitted eyes.

"Jimmy, we believe he's connected to Petrowski. Our plan was to flip him and then hit Petrowski with it in the balls," Bishop said.

Jimmy narrowed his eyes at my partner. "Petrowski's gone. While you two were on your little coffee break, his attorney pulled him."

My eyes widened. "He hasn't even appeared in front of the judge!"

He pinched the bridge of his nose. "Apparently this guy is above the law."

"He tried to kill a police officer," Bishop said.

I cracked my knuckles. "Anthony Rossi is a dirty lawyer; he bought the judge."

"Maybe so, but it's out of our hands," Jimmy said. "And you withholding Hernandez's rights to an attorney just adds to this shitstorm."

I pressed my lips together as a thought pushed to the front of my mind. "What if Petrowski's not responsible for this?"

"No way," Bishop said. "His name's all over this."

I sighed. "I think we're wrong. I think I was wrong. Of course I'd blame Petrowski, but think about it. He's out what, two months, and comes for me like this?" I shook my head. "It doesn't make sense."

"He was at your house when Andy was killed," Bishop said. "He held you fucking hostage. If you hadn't one-upped him, you'd be dead."

I couldn't explain Petrowski's appearance at my house, but the more I thought about it, the more I began to believe he wasn't responsible for Andy's murder. "He told me he didn't kill Andy."

Bishop laughed. "And you believe him? The guy's a sociopath. You've said it yourself. He promised to come for you, and he has, dropping people I love in the process."

I swallowed.

Bishop stood, then began pacing the small office. "I'm sorry. I didn't mean—"

"No, you're right. And he did come for me, that I can piece together. But you don't know Petrowski like I do. The guy's one-hundred-and-fifty-percent ego. If he planned to kill me then, he'd want me to die knowing he killed Andy. He'd brag. Bishop, that's what I missed. He didn't kill Andy. That wasn't part of his plan."

"So, what? He has good timing?"

"If Petrowski wanted to kill me, I'd be dead."

"Maybe he doesn't want you dead," Jimmy said.

"Maybe he wants you to lose people so he can watch you suffer," Bishop added.

My gut told me otherwise. "No," I said, shaking my head. "This isn't Petrowski. This is someone else. And I think Hernandez is working for the killer, not Petrowski."

"He's lawyered up. He won't talk," Jimmy said.

"He's already sitting on ten years easy. We get the DA to push on all charges, then offer him a deal, and his lawyer won't want to take it to court. He'll make him talk."

They both thought about that for a minute.

"Listen, I know I've screamed Petrowski this whole time, but my head feels clear now. I'm telling you, pendants and small-time crooks aren't his thing. He brought Russian mobsters with him to my house and let me live. He's leveled up. This shit isn't his. You have to believe me. We get Hernandez to flip and we find Andy's killer."

"I'll call the DA," Jimmy said.

Fifteen minutes later, we spelled out our plan for Stacy Mayor, the district attorney. She walked around the investigation room and examined the evidence on the walls. "You really don't think Petrowski's involved?"

"No," I said.

"Then why show up like he did?"

"I'm still working on that."

"Doesn't that lead to the possibility that he's killed the others to watch you suffer?"

I shook my head. "He expected one of the Russian thugs to take me out. If he'd killed Brad Pruitt or even Jeffers, he would have told me right away. He'd want me to die knowing what he'd done."

"Your report says he told you that your boyfriend was dead."

"Yes, but he didn't say he killed him, and inside he said he didn't."

She chewed on her pencil eraser and nodded. "You know this guy better than any of us."

"I do, and with all due respect, Anthony Rossi is about twenty-five years older than you, and he's tried and won a lot of tough cases with big-time crooks in Chicago."

"So you're respectfully saying I wouldn't have a chance in hell of beating him in court."

"Respectfully, yes."

"I'm not going to agree or disagree, but I'll take note." She read the notes on the board under Benny Hernandez. "How many Fulton County sheriff's deputies were at the scene the other night?"

"At least five," Bishop said.

She nodded. "I'm not sure the pendants are strong enough to link him to the murders, but we just need his attorney to think they are." She turned and faced us. "Since you haven't charged or arrested him for the murders, technically you didn't violate his Sixth Amendment rights, but that's a shaky leg to stand on." She smiled. "Thankfully, I have excellent balance."

I decided I liked Stacy Mayor. I liked her a lot.

35

The public defender stormed out of the secure area of the jail and charged toward Mayor. "You harassed my client and withheld access to an attorney? What the hell kind of ploy is this?"

"Nice to see you too, Shelly."

Huh. I'd thought the public defender was a man. Was this an archnemesis thing, or were they law school pals?

"Don't give me that crap, Ms. District Attorney." Disdain oozed from Shelly's lips. "You just screwed yourself on this one, and you know it."

Mayor smiled. "How about we take this into the interrogation room and discuss it privately? We have something we think you'll want to know." She turned around and mouthed, "I'll do the talking."

The fact that she was even letting us in the meeting surprised me. The Chicago DA's office never went that route unless they were desperate. Mayor didn't strike me as the desperate kind.

The DA sat across from Benny Hernandez and his public defender. We stood behind her.

"Mr. Hernandez—"

"Don't answer any questions," Shelly said.

"Mr. Hernandez," Mayor repeated. "We have"—she counted the offenses in his file—"fifteen charges stemming from the night of your arrest. Two counts of assaulting an officer, each carrying up to ten years. Driving with a stolen tag, reckless driving, endangering the safety of others by speeding, not to mention grand theft auto, resisting arrest, and evading multiple officers, which, if your attorney hasn't mentioned, is more like five additional charges." She held up a typed document from our files. "Shall I go on? The list is quite long, and I'm certain we can make it longer."

Shelly huffed. "You can't be serious."

"Sure, I can. He evaded multiple officers. Just that alone gets him most of his life behind bars, not to mention the ten he'll get for stealing each Malibu." She straightened the papers in her file and closed it, then removed the bag holding his skull pendant. She slid it into the middle of the table. "We also have your signature."

"Signature for what?"

I tried not to smile.

"Your client here is under investigation for three homicides." She smiled at Hernandez. "Did you fail to mention that to your attorney, Mr. Hernandez?"

Shelly spoke before he had a chance. "Don't answer that." She glared straight at the DA. "I need a minute with my client."

Mayor nodded. "Very well." She stood, but before walking out the door, she turned back around and said, "We have three murders, and one of those pendants on each victim's person. Your guy tells us who he's working with, or he's going down." She closed the door behind her.

"Damn!" Jimmy said. "I should have been an attorney."

Mayor laughed. "That would be fun to watch."

We waited in the hallway. Bishop paced the hall, clearly jonesing for a smoke, while Jimmy and Mayor talked, and I replayed in my head everything that had happened over the past few days. "Someone's been watching me for a while. Hernandez has been in town less than a week." I'd chewed my nail so low the tip of my finger was raw. I continued chewing on it anyway. "Andy lied to us."

Bishop stared at me. "About what?"

"He said he hadn't seen his brother, but how else would they make the connection? Whoever Hernandez is working for had eyes on me for a while, assumed Andy was my boyfriend, then followed him. When they saw Brad, they decided he was the perfect choice to leave their little pendant messages, and their first hit."

"Why not Allison?" Bishop asked. "Why not take her out first?"

"I don't know. That part doesn't make sense, but I'll figure it out. And whoever saw them together wormed his way into Brad's hotel room where he left the pendants."

"But why take out a homeless addict?" Mayor asked.

"They didn't. He did that himself. They planted the skull pendants knowing an addict would lift them and we'd find the one on Brad. They knew I'd fall for it, immediately think Petrowski was involved." I sighed. "Fuck. I walked right into their trap."

"And then Petrowski shows up at your place right after they killed Andy," Bishop said. "That can't be a coincidence."

"They knew Petrowski was headed here. And if for some reason I survived, they knew I'd blame him for the murders, too."

"That would mean Hernandez would have to know Petrowski was in town."

"Or the person he's working with knew."

"The missing link," Mayor said.

I nodded. "We need Hernandez to tell us who brought him to town. It's someone close to Sanchez."

The public defender opened the interrogation room door. "Let's talk." She pointed to Mayor. "Just you."

Michels walked through the door to the secured hallway. "Caroline Bryant's been attacked. It's bad."

My body stiffened. "Where is she?"

"Northside Forsyth. She's asking for you."

I eyed Jimmy. He nodded. "Go. I'll fill you in."

Bishop flicked his head. "I'll drive."

We made it to Northside Hospital in twenty-five minutes and parked outside the emergency entrance in the designated spots for law enforcement and personnel. The woman at the emergency desk directed us to Caroline Bryant's room. She looked like she'd been hit by a semi. Her left arm was wrapped in cloth and ice packs. Blood seeped through in sections, leaving a dark pink stain on the cloth. They'd shaved half of the left side of her head where they'd stitched up a laceration. I didn't count the stitches, but it looked to be well over ten. She had two black eyes, a swollen lip, and a broken nose. She had to be in a lot of pain, and I hoped she'd been too stoned to feel it, though by the looks of her, I doubted any amount of drugs could numb that kind of pain.

She opened her eyes when Bishop pulled up a chair beside the bed. She tried to smile at him, and when she did, I noticed most of her front teeth were broken or missing.

She turned toward me, and a soft groan slipped through her swollen lips. "Water."

Bishop held a glass of water to her mouth. She took a small sip, then another, and coughed. The machines connected to her lit up and beeped. "They're coming for you," she whispered, her voice raspy and soft.

"Did you get a look at who did this to you, Caroline?" Bishop asked.

She shook her head slowly.

"Was it one person? Two? More?" I asked.

"Don't know." She swallowed. "I didn't see them."

"How many voices did you hear? Two, three?" I asked.

"Three, maybe?" She coughed. "I'm not sure."

"What did they say?" Bishop asked.

She pointed at me. "Her. They want her." She closed her eyes.

"Fuck!" I backed up and bumped into a machine attached to a computer that lit up like a firework. It beeped and flashed red and yellow. I stood in a panic, trying to figure out how to make it stop while keeping an eye on Caroline.

A nurse walked in, gently pushed me aside, then did some karate-style moves with her arms. Tubes and wires flew, and the beeping stopped. She turned to me, her round face angry. "Please keep away from the equipment."

"Ma'am," Bishop said. "Can you provide us with the circumstances surrounding Ms. Bryant's case?"

Bishop's eyes shifted my direction. I swallowed hard. As a detective, I knew I could be intimidating, but that nurse was utterly terrifying.

Her eyes trailed up and down my body, landing on my weapon in its holster and my badge clipped to my belt. "My patient needs her rest," she said. "And I don't know what happened. I came in this morning, and she was here. I just treat their condition, Officers. I don't get involved in their lives. I don't have time for that."

"Yes, ma'am," Bishop said.

I handed the woman my card. "We would like to talk to her again when she's feeling better. Would you please ask her to contact me?"

She stared at my card, and then at me. She set the card on the rolling cart beside a glass of water and a box of tissues. "What this woman needs is her family, not pressure from the police."

Bishop spoke softly. "I'll contact her family, ma'am, but it's important we talk with her."

"And we'll be sending someone from the county sheriff to keep an eye on her room," I added.

She examined me carefully. "She's in danger?"

"She's part of a murder investigation, ma'am."

She glanced at Caroline and sighed. "You send that deputy right quick. I'll do my best to watch her, but I can't make any promises."

The woman was at least six inches taller than me and double my weight. She might have looked scary, but guns and knives don't know fear. "Thank you," I said.

She nodded once. "Now get on out of here. You're not making things any better for her."

We walked out of Bryant's room.

Bishop whispered, "That woman's got Nurse Ratched's blood in her veins."

I knew he was trying to lighten the mood, but it didn't help. I'd just received another message, and it was time to play hardball.

36

Jimmy waited for us in our investigation room. We walked in to him staring at the boards on the walls. He turned around with his hands on his waist and exhaled. "Shit on a stick, this is seriously fucked up."

"Any word from Mayor?" I asked.

"Not yet."

Bishop closed and locked the door behind him, then tossed his bag onto the table, removed his jacket, and tightened his shoulder harness. "Fucked up is putting it mildly."

Someone knocked on the door. "Pray it's Mayor," Jimmy said.

Bishop opened the door.

The scowl on Mayor's face wasn't good news.

"Hernandez didn't flip," Bishop said.

"Nope."

"Shit."

I leaned my head back. "Dammit!" I flattened my palms on the tabletop. "We need to force their hand. Make them come for me."

"I think you're right," Bishop said.

"We do that, we put a lot of people at risk," Jimmy said.

"I agree," the district attorney said.

"It's our only option, and I know a guy." I grabbed my cell phone from my bag and dialed Garcia, putting the call on speaker.

Garcia came in hot. "How'd Petrowski get out?"

"How do you think?"

"Damn, corruption is deep."

"You have no idea," Mayor said.

"Detective Garcia, meet Fulton County District Attorney Stacy Mayor."

"Pleasure," Garcia said.

"Also got the chief and Bishop with me."

"Obviously this isn't a social call. What do you need?"

"I need your CI to spread that Hernandez flipped. Say he dropped names."

"Shit, did he?"

"No."

"You're setting a trap."

"Bastard won't budge. It's our only option."

"You're hedging a bet you could easily lose, Ryder," Garcia said.

"Yeah, well, I'm feeling lucky."

And five hours later, our plan was in motion.

"I'm not comfortable with you being alone," Jimmy said.

"I've gotten pretty good at being alone, Chief." I smiled. "Besides, Bishop and Michels are on their way to my place now, so I won't be alone." I tightened my Kevlar vest around my sides, then slipped into my shoulder holster.

"No, you won't. I've got Harry and Sanders in their

undercover vehicles. They'll take turns keeping tabs on you."

I smirked. "I bet that's killing them inside."

He chuckled. "One hundred percent."

"Michels needs to be a detective."

"He's getting there. Maybe your Garcia can transfer here and show him the ropes?"

I laughed. It felt good. "That would be so fun to watch."

He chuckled, then attached the wireless microphone to my vest. "The earpiece on?"

I nodded.

He walked out of the room, closed the door behind him, and spoke softly into my ear. "Savannah will kill me if something happens to you."

I smiled. "Grow a pair, Chief."

He walked back in. "You ready?"

I nodded. "This is nothing compared to what I've done in the past."

"I don't like putting my men—team—in harm's way."

"We got this, Jimmy."

"I know."

I smiled and then walked into the pit to head back home. At least ten people stood there watching me. One of them smiled and said, "Good luck, Detective."

I blushed. "Thank you."

Several others wished me well too. Damn them. I walked out of there with a stupid smile on my face, which did nothing for my tough-girl reputation, but it did make me feel like they had my back.

I called Garcia from my Jeep. "Anything?"

"Word's out. That's about all I know."

"Your informant doesn't know who's responsible, right?"

"Seriously? You're seriously asking me that?" He swore in Spanish.

"Sorry, partner."

He sighed. "Bishop got your back?"

"I'll be fine, Garcia."

"You'd better be. Call me when it's done."

"I will."

I turned left out of the department instead of right, the easiest way back to my place. The point was to give a small amount of time for the information to travel as quickly as possible. Whoever was responsible for these deaths knew Petrowski hadn't killed me, and hearing that Hernandez flipped meant they'd have to work fast to finish the job themselves. They had an advantage on us, only they didn't know it. They thought we knew who they were, so they'd tread carefully. The advantage was we didn't, and their carefulness would only make our job harder.

I turned left at the light onto Highway Nine. I glanced in my rearview mirror, but there were no cars behind me. "Shit. Nothing," I said.

"It's okay," Jimmy said in my ear. "Give it time. Our guys are all in place."

I looped back around at Windward, turning left on the green arrow, and left into the Chick-fil-A drive-thru. I ordered a small Diet Coke, paid, and headed back out to Highway Nine.

I picked up a black SUV a few cars behind me. "Bingo!" I smiled. "Black SUV."

"I'm three behind," Sanders said.

Don't screw up, I thought.

"House is clear," Bishop said. "I gotta say, I'm surprised you have so many outfits."

"Are you in my closet?"

He laughed, and then the others on the radio laughed too.

"Door from the garage is unlocked," Michels said. "We cleared the area, and I'm across the street."

"SWAT is in position," Jimmy said.

"Ten-four," I replied.

The SUV kept straight when I turned right at the intersection of Mayfield and Providence roads. "You see that, Sanders?"

"Ten-four."

Either I picked up another tail, a white crossover of some sort, or a soccer mom liked her windows tinted darker than the law allowed. "White crossover's got dark tint on the front window. Can't make out how many inside."

Harry spoke. "Black SUV coming my way."

My heart raced. I trusted Bishop, and I was pretty close to trusting Michels. I knew Jimmy had my back. I just didn't have a whole lot of faith in Sanders or Harry. But it didn't matter. I had to trust them. And I had SWAT, so if this went bad, they were the experts.

The black SUV met me at the intersection. I waited; it waited. Since I was on its right, I drove straight through the intersection. I glanced in my mirror and saw Harry on its tail.

"I'm two out," I said into my mic.

"Ten-four," the guys all said sporadically.

I pulled into my community, grateful to be able to get out of my car even though I knew my life was at risk. I was more comfortable taking a bullet in the vest than sitting in a vehicle with it and my shoulder holster squeezed under the seatbelt. I just couldn't guarantee I'd take a bullet in the vest. I stepped into my house, set my bag down on the kitchen counter, and walked into the family room. I stared at the spot where Andy died.

A sweet man who was paid to do work in my house had his life taken from him, all because of me.

I went about my business, even going as far as removing my shoulder holster and hanging it in my closet. Bishop took note and shook his head.

It was really hard not to laugh when he handed me a sweatshirt off a hanger. He whispered, "You hang these up?"

I whispered back, "Don't you?"

"No."

I shrugged. "You should."

I putzed around the house, sending Lenny text messages, apologizing repeatedly for worrying him, and promising him we had this handled. I watched *CSI*, thinking Ashley would love a job like that, and she'd probably be excellent at it too. I poured a small bottle of vinegar into a bucket, added a few cups of water, and began the process of cleaning the blood off the shelves.

This could have been done professionally, but I'd wanted the shelves left to me. Andy had worked so hard on them, and I wanted to treat them, and his blood, with the respect he deserved.

Bishop sat on the couch. "It's after midnight. I'll get Michels inside, and we'll take turns keeping watch. Get some rest."

"I'm not tired."

"You look like shit."

"Thanks, partner." I scrubbed at a blood stain. It wouldn't disappear. I kept scrubbing, fighting back tears. "Damn it!"

Bishop placed his hand on my shoulder and gently removed the cloth from my hand. I turned around and hugged him, tears falling onto his shoulder. "I'm so sorry!" Bishop let me cry it out. I gathered my emotions and released him, sniffing and wiping my nose.

He tilted his head. "Rachel, it's—"

I shook my head and covered my mouth, speaking through my fingers like an idiot. "No, please. I fucking hate crying in front of people."

"I'm not just people."

"I know." I put my hand out. He stared at it, then handed me the cloth. I tossed it in the bucket on the floor.

"We'll get someone out to take care of that after this is finished."

"It's okay," I said. "I want to do it."

"Rachel, we're going to get them. We'll get Andy's killer."

"I know."

37

I awoke to the smell of coffee. After taking a second to clear the fog in my head, I jumped out of bed. I'd slept in a pair of Tommy's sweats and one of his sweatshirts, and Bishop's eyes widened when he saw me.

"Nice."

"Bite me." I walked over to the coffee pot and poured myself a cup of Costa Rican heaven.

Bishop leaned against the opposite counter. "Why two coffee makers?"

"Normally I use the Keurig for myself, and the pot for people like you."

He nodded once. "Interesting."

"A pot's a lot for just a grab-and-go in the morning."

"Depends on the size of the cup." He sipped his drink. "SWAT left at about three. I sent Michels home an hour ago, and Harry and Sanders are long gone."

"Not surprising." I sighed. "I thought for sure something would happen last night."

"Me too."

"They played us again. They knew we were waiting."

Bishop's cell rang. He glanced at it, said, "It's Jimmy," and answered on speaker.

"We're good, Chief."

"I know. Just got word that Caroline Bryant died this morning."

I tipped my head back and sighed.

"Cardiac arrest, I'm assuming due to her injuries," Jimmy said.

I ran my hand through my messy hair. "We can add another homicide to the list." I chugged my already luke-warm coffee and slammed my cup onto the counter. It shattered into pieces. I caught my breath as blood appeared on my hand. I stuck it under the faucet and let cold water run over it. It wasn't a big cut, but hands were always heavy bleeders.

"You all right?"

I held my hand above my heart. "I'm fine. I'm taking myself off the case."

His eyes widened. "What?"

"I've handled this wrong from the start. My gut's been off, my questioning of witnesses is awful. I'm too emotional. People are dying because I can't get my shit together."

"People are dying because someone wants you on your knees."

"Well then, they've won."

He stared at me in confusion. "No." He shook his head. "Whatever's going on, whoever's killing people you know, people I know, they want you. You can't walk away. You'll never forgive yourself if you don't see this through."

I'd shown Bishop a side of myself I allowed so few to see, and it made me feel weak and vulnerable. I hated that, but I had nothing left. They'd won. They'd taken me without even touching me. "I don't know if I can do this anymore."

He held my shoulders and stared into my eyes. "What did you say? Are you being a fucking wise guy with me?" His upper lip twitched.

I almost smiled. "Oh my God, did you just quote De Niro?"

He held out his chin and smiled. "You've seen *Goodfellas*?"

"I'm Italian. It's the law."

"How's my accent?"

"Just don't quit your day job and you'll be fine."

He made me another cup of coffee while I stewed on my inability to figure out how to catch this killer. "Listen, could we have handled this case better?" he said. "Sure. But what's done is done. We finish what we started and learn from our mistakes."

"The mistakes are mostly mine."

"Then we learn from your mistakes."

"You're an asshole, Bishop."

"And that's why you love me." He gave me a once-over again and handed me the coffee. "You look like shit, but we don't have time for you to primp. Caffeinate and then get dressed. We got a killer to trap."

"I could really use a cigarette right now."

"Don't tell me you're trying to quit in the middle of all this?"

"Okay."

He exhaled, pure annoyance filtering out of his nose. "Fine. I'll try too."

A smile crept across my face. "Two cops in nicotine withdrawal? This killer doesn't know what's coming."

"Damn straight. Now come on."

"Give me five."

Jimmy pulled us into his office as we walked into the station. "You look like shit."

I shrugged. "It's part of the job."

"I wasn't talking to you."

Bishop's jaw dropped. "Thanks, Chief."

I took a deep breath and exhaled. "I'm sorry."

"Don't be. This is probably the most excitement these guys have seen since, well, your last investigation."

I tried to laugh, but it wasn't as funny as Jimmy had hoped. Or maybe I just wasn't in the mood.

"You think Garcia's informant messed up?"

I shook my head. "He's good. He does what he says."

"Then we missed something."

"You mean I missed something."

Bishop crossed his legs. "She's wallowing in self-pity."

Jimmy made eye contact with me. "You're not a mind reader. It's not easy to predict what a killer's going to do."

"But it is. I just screwed up. Again."

He sighed. "Put it in a box, Ryder. We got a job to do."

I nodded.

"Okay then." He rubbed his palms together. "Let's figure out where we went wrong."

"For starters, thinking they'd come back to my house was my first mistake."

"Actually, that was my call," Bishop said.

"And I agreed. I should have known better. They'd already come there. They'd know it was a set-up."

Bishop nodded. "Mayor couldn't flip Hernandez. What does that tell us?"

"This is personal," Jimmy said.

"Yes, and I guarantee our guy is pissed. He's got two

choices now. Sit on this or act. With his fall guy, a fucking corrupt politician, walking away without a slap on the hand, he'll have to act. He sits on this and that's just asking to be caught."

———

Michels kept close to our sides. We spent hours in the investigation room analyzing and overanalyzing everything we had, but we just couldn't come up with a hit for the second killer. Sanders and Harry, as well as all available patrol, kept their eyes out, but found nothing.

Bishop brought lunch. "I spoke to Allison."

"How's she doing?" I asked, sipping my Diet Coke.

"Not good, but she's safe, and that's all that matters." He checked the bag. "Damn, no ketchup. Be right back."

My cell phone rang. I didn't recognize the number. "Ryder."

"Detective, it's Captain Bradwell."

"Captain Bradwell, what's up?"

"I understand Caroline Bryant was beaten and died as a result of her injuries."

"Yes, unfortunately. And Andy Pruitt was murdered also."

"I am aware. How's Bishop?"

"Pissed off. Determined."

"As expected. My informant believes he's got some information regarding your investigation. He'd like to meet to discuss."

"When?"

"Midnight, tonight."

"We're sitting on a timebomb here, Captain. If he knows something, we need it now."

"I tried, but he's pushing back. Claims he's being watched by the people responsible, but he's assured me his information will lead to an arrest."

"I can't guarantee that," I said.

"I've explained that. He's still willing to meet, but in a private location."

"Go ahead."

He gave me the location. "I understand you had SWAT at your home last night. Make sure you're alone tonight, Detective."

"Bishop will come."

"Alone. Too many police and he'll bail."

"Will you be there?" I asked.

"Yes, ma'am."

"Done."

"Detective?"

"Yes?"

"I've been by your department. I left the CI file for your review."

"The one with you the other day?"

"Correct."

My eyes widened. "Thanks, Captain."

I disconnected the call and fist-pumped the air. Captain Bradwell had just dropped a whopper of a gift in my lap.

Bishop walked in with his ketchup.

"Your friend Bradwell is a fucking badass."

"What happened?"

"I think he just gave me our guy." I typed Morales's name into CODIS.

"Morales? We cleared him."

"He said Morales wants to meet. Said he knows the killer."

"Shit."

"Bradwell said he left his CI file at the desk."

"I'll go get it."

"Bishop, it's not a red file."

His eyes widened. "Holy shit. He's been investigating his informant."

I smiled. "Fucking badass."

He took a waffle fry, dipped it in ketchup, and stuffed it in his mouth. "Be right back," he said, walking out the door.

"No DNA on file," I said to myself. I switched over to AFIS, then ran any possible matches for Morales's prints. He was in the system, so the prints available were clean. If he had any family in the system too, AFIS would pull similar prints within a twenty-five-percent match and higher. No fingerprints matched exactly, even from finger to finger on the same person, but similarities could help verify family members.

I watched the screen as it ran through millions of possible matches. It stopped and showed twenty-two possible connections. I flipped through the prints, stopping when I hit gold. I stared at the mugshot. "Holy fucking shit."

Bishop walked in with the file. He stared at the screen. "Damn? How the hell did we miss that?"

"Morales is good."

I redialed Captain Bradwell's number.

He answered and said, "My phone is dying. Can you call on the non-emergency line?" He gave me the number.

"This is Detective Rachel Ryder from Hamby PD. I need a private video connection with Captain Bradwell, please."

"One moment." She placed me on hold but returned to the line quickly. "Here is the number and passcode."

I jotted it down. "I'm calling now."

"He's waiting."

I set up the call, and Bradwell answered immediately. "You read my file quickly."

Bishop was currently skimming through it.

"Not yet, but I had a hunch." I explained what I'd done.

He nodded. "That's impressive."

"How long have you known?"

"I told you I read about your case. What I didn't tell you was how seriously I vet my CIs. When I ran his prints for possible matches, your husband's killer appeared. I recognized the name, but it didn't make sense until Morales said you'd showed up at Good Times."

"Why didn't you share this earlier?"

"I had nothing but that. I needed to plant the seed with Morales, and now that I have, we can move forward."

"And you still couldn't share this on the phone earlier?"

"My line isn't safe."

"You're playing along."

He nodded. "I've been working Morales for over a year. I established a relationship, provided intel on some very small cases, and earned his trust."

"And what? He just asked you to help kill a cop?"

"I might have mentioned the cost of private school for my daughter, and the lack of pay to cover it."

I smiled. "Brilliant. Tell me about the location."

"I will be there first, making sure you haven't brought anyone prior to our arrival. We'll need your men outside. The building is abandoned, and it would be easy to see if someone was inside."

I tapped into the computer and pulled a GPS satellite map of the location. After reviewing the lay of the land, I said, "There's a wooded area behind it. We can put our guys back there. We'll need mics."

"I can't guarantee Morales won't check me, but I'll go without."

"I've got a mic disguised as a heart-shaped pendant, and the earpiece is easily hidden by my hair."

Bradwell pointed to his high and tight haircut. "I don't have that ability."

Bishop laughed. He reviewed the property on the satellite. "I'll have our guys in place an hour before go time."

"That works. Just stay invisible."

"You won't even know we're there."

38

I killed my Jeep's headlights as I pulled into the empty parking lot. One dim light illuminated the abandoned building. I adjusted my vest and removed my jacket. Morales would see the gun in my shoulder holster as well as the one on my waist. I checked the earpiece, making sure it wasn't going anywhere. "Looks like one light is on," I said.

"Ten-four," Bishop responded. "Bradwell confirmed six people in the building including himself."

"Location?"

"No mic, Ryder. Not sure. He approached the window and gave the signal. Best we can do."

"Ten-four."

"We got eyes on you from across the street."

I checked the rearview mirror. "The trailer?"

"You got it."

"Where else?"

"Four lining the woods, two on each side. The back side is a warehouse. If you can, face the loading dock doors. Something happens and you can't speak, Michels or I will see."

"Got it." I checked my watch. "Time to roll."

"Stay safe, partner."

"Copy that."

I scanned the area outside the building. If Morales had men there, they knew how to hide. I stepped out of my Jeep slowly, shutting the door without hitting the lock, then walked up to the center door and knocked twice.

The door opened, and Bradwell smiled. "He's in back." He rubbed his face with his thumb and index finger in the shape of a gun.

I swiped three fingers over my lips, then carefully pointed to my left boot.

He winked.

He escorted me through the building toward the back. I paid careful attention to my surroundings, noting the garbage on the floor, the broken desks shoved against the walls, the hanging lights. Bradwell opened a door to what appeared to be the warehouse section of the building. Perfect, I thought sarcastically. Big enough to hide people and small enough to get hit from multiple bullets.

A scattering of windows lined the walls of the large space, with four loading dock doors as Bishop mentioned, and three regular doors between them. There were two makeshift offices, likely built after the fact, on opposite corners of the room, each with fenced decks on top. I'd seen the setup hundreds of times. Warehouse managers would stand on those decks watching the workers. It gave them a view of their process, and it gave a shooter the perfect spot to take me out. I showed no emotion. I knew what I was walking into. I knew Morales wanted to kill me for taking out a family member.

Morales stood in the center of the room, forcing me to stand right in the middle, the perfect spot for anyone with a gun aimed at me. I wasn't worried about the shooters. I knew they were there only in case things got out of hand. Morales didn't want his shooters to kill me. He wanted to take care of that himself.

I smiled. "So, tell me, how are you related to Sanchez? Cousins?"

He laughed. "You are good."

"Rumor has it." Bradwell was standing next to Morales. I looked him in the eyes. "I knew the moment I saw the file."

"Everyone has a price."

My heartbeat kicked up a notch.

"Her guns, take them," Morales said.

Bradwell looked me in the eyes as he removed the guns from my shoulder holster and waist. He dropped the magazines and emptied the barrels, then slid the guns across the floor. He left the Sig in my boot. I stared at him. He smiled and walked back over to Morales.

Morales was holding a gun in one hand and pulling something from his pocket with the other. He beckoned to me. "Come closer. I have something to show you."

I took two steps closer, eyeing the deck in the back corner. I knew at least two men were up there, but I couldn't see them.

He held out a skull pendant and gold chain. "For you. Please put it in your pocket."

I eyed the pendant. "Thanks, but I prefer silver."

He sneered, then handed the necklace to Bradwell, who stuffed it in my jeans pocket, making eye contact again.

Morales showed no expression. No anger, no anticipation. He didn't need to. The gun pointed at me said it all. Bradwell stood beside him, his weapon on his waist. He'd take it out if Morales told him to. He was probably a good shot, and if he had to shoot, he'd aim low on purpose.

"When someone in my family dies, we unite." Morales laughed. "Imagine a family torn apart, shipped off, person by person, to a strange country, to work hard just to send money back home, and then die because of that hard work."

"Sanchez killed my husband."

"It was not personal."

"It was personal to me."

"And you have made it personal for my family now also, amiga. You killed my cousin, and now you are trying to destroy another with your lies."

I laughed. "You might want to get your facts straight. Hernandez is an idiot. We know he couldn't pull any of this off himself, and if I'm being honest, you're starting to look about as stupid as him."

"Fuck you, bitch." He lifted his arm and raised the gun. "You will pay for hurting my family."

A bullet rang through the warehouse, its explosion like lightning striking the metal roof. I covered my head and ducked as I dropped to the ground. I grabbed my weapon and aimed it at Morales, but his expression told me he wasn't the shooter. He looked me in the eyes, dropped his weapon, and touched the blood pouring from his chest. Another shot hit him less than an inch from the first. Two more shots ripped through the silence. Bradwell went down.

I glanced up at the back deck, then quickly whipped around to check the other one. I moved toward the side wall while shots flew at me from above. I rolled to the side to cover my head as best I could and took a bullet on the side of my thigh. "Fuck!" I brought my leg to my chest. The pain was unbelievable, sending shockwaves up and down my body. I grabbed my leg with one hand and checked the wound, then went for cover, aiming my weapon behind me and running on my injured leg toward the other office for cover. The pain overwhelmed me, searing through my leg and up into my side. I dropped to the ground and dragged myself toward the office.

But I didn't make it. The pair of men's black dress shoes just inside the door stopped me. I scooted back with my good leg, holding my gun toward the office door. The dress shoes stepped out of the office. Chris Petrowski aimed his gun down at me and smiled. I squeezed the trigger, once, twice, three times.

Petrowski went down, blood pooling in a circle on his chest.

The warehouse lit up as the doors between the loading docks crashed open. Bishop hollered, "Police!"

I crawled past Petrowski, grabbed his gun, and slid it into the office, then hid behind the office wall as gunfire tore up the warehouse. I stayed behind the wall, checking the action as I removed my shirt and ripped it in half, then tied it over my leg to stop the bleeding. I checked Petrowski, who was lying on the ground inches from me. His chest wasn't moving. If he wasn't dead, he was close.

I felt no remorse.

The shooting stopped.

"Ryder!" Bishop yelled.

I held my necklace up to my mouth and whispered, "Leg shot, it's bleeding bad."

"Paramedics are already here," he said.

"Check Bradwell," I said softly. I wasn't sure Bishop heard. I was tired, weak, going into shock. "Move, Rachel. Move," I told myself. I crawled over to Petrowski and checked his pulse, then stared into his eyes. "Gotcha." Then I lay on my back, breathily heavily, pain piercing my entire body.

Bishop rushed over. "Fuck!" He hollered something else,

but his words were muffled and faded, and then they were gone.

I woke to two Bishops standing beside me. "Hey, partner." He smiled, but it quickly faded. "You look like shit."

"Two," I mumbled, trying to say I saw two Bishops, but speaking more than one word at a time took too much effort. My lips were dry, my throat drier. "Water." I raised my right arm to rub my eyes, but he stopped me.

"That one's connected to a bag."

My eyes flitted around the room. All white. Machines buzzing. I was tired. So, so tired. "Bradwell."

He nodded. "He's alive, but it was close. Needed a hell of a lot of blood and three hours of surgery, but he'll pull through."

Every breath brought stabbing pain to my left side. "Why does my—" I reached over with my right arm, wanting to cry from the pain. I felt the bandages around my side, then blinked until I could see my leg. It was still there in one piece. Relief washed over me.

Bishop patted my hand. "You took three shots. One to the leg, one to the spleen, and one grazed your left side." He sighed. "They had to remove your spleen, but you were lucky. That bullet only broke two ribs."

"Hurts." Pause. "To breathe."

"It will for a while."

One of the machines beeped loudly. Bishop checked it, then smiled. "Oh, you're going to love this."

A familiar face walked in. "How's our patient this afternoon?"

I glanced at Bishop. He smiled. "Yup, Nurse Not-So-

Ratched."

She hushed me before I had a chance to speak. "You're at North Fulton Hospital, sweetie." She adjusted the bag attached to my arm. "And you're a lucky gal. I took a new job here just in time to treat you. Your friend here's been by your side since you arrived. He told me what happened. You are one tough cookie, that's for sure."

I tried to laugh, but it hurt like hell. I swallowed, and that hurt, too. "Water, please."

She placed a straw to my lips. "Just a little."

I took a sip, and she smiled. "Good job. See that chart over there?" She pointed to the wall in front of me. "Tell me where your pain level is based on that chart."

"High," was all I could manage to say.

She huffed and did something to the tubes in my hand. The pain disappeared, and I was instantly sleepier. "Hmm."

Bishop laughed, but if he said something, I had no idea what.

The lake's waves slammed against the rocks, sending splashes of cold water toward us. Tommy wrapped his arm around my shoulder and pulled me close. "Look at that moon."

I admired its brightness, the way it illuminated the night sky, casting shadows onto Lake Michigan. I shivered.

"Here." Tommy moved behind me and pulled me close, bending his legs and pressing them onto my sides for added warmth. "Better?"

I leaned back against his chest. "I'd prefer if we were naked."

His warm breath tickled my neck. "That's easily done."

I laughed. "We don't need an audience, baby."

He whispered in my ear. "We don't have one, babe."

39

It took me six months to heal. Six long, excruciatingly painful months, and most of that pain was mental, not physical.

Five people died the night of the shootout, and the one who lived filled in the holes to a case that looked like a pound of Swiss cheese.

Benny Hernandez's story coordinated with the survivor's, an employee of Petrowski. Both tried to cut a deal for giving the truth, but the DA wouldn't budge.

Hernandez found out I was in Georgia. He contacted his cousin Raul Morales, and they set up a plan to first taunt and then execute me. They wanted me to suffer, Hernandez said, just like Sanchez's family suffered.

Morales had eyes on me for a month before Hernandez got antsy and showed up. He saw Andy at my place multiple times and, as I thought, mistook him for Sean, who he'd seen with me once or twice. When he figured out Andy's brother was an addict, he decided to play that angle, not knowing Morales was Brad's dealer.

As we determined, Jeffers's death was an accidental overdose. Hernandez buddied up to Brad, purposely leaving pendants in his hotel room. We could only assume Jeffers saw them and grabbed one for himself. Hernandez insisted Jeffers wasn't part of their plan.

Hernandez had no connection to Petrowski, but Morales did. He made contact through an inmate when Petrowski was in prison. The survivor worked for Petrowski, not Morales. He said the plan was for Morales to kill Sean, but he'd screwed up by letting Hernandez follow me and get busted. That lack of organization sent Morales to my house, where he'd planned to finish it, but instead came upon Andy. Where we were wrong was in thinking they'd shot Andy because they thought he was Sean. Morales shot Andy because Andy recognized him.

Petrowski wasn't directly responsible for any of the deaths. His shooter claims he'd come to my place to get a lay of the land, because he had every intention of killing me himself, but whether it was that night, he didn't know. He said when Petrowski saw a black SUV rushing out of the community, he thought I'd been eliminated already. He got cocky, the guy said, though he wasn't exactly sure why Petrowski stuck around. Without being there, he couldn't offer more than that. The taller of the Russians survived that night, but he lawyered up and hadn't said a word.

We might not have known for certain Petrowski's intentions the night Andy died, but we did know his plan for the night at the warehouse. According to his shooter, the plan was to take out Hernandez in lockup and clean up the rest at the warehouse. When Bishop learned Hernandez was at risk, he had him immediately put into solitary just in case, where he was still hanging out awaiting trial. Someone—we thought from Alpharetta PD—leaked the fact that Bradwell was playing Morales, and Petrowski's shooter said the end game was to eliminate both Morales and Bradwell but leave me for Petrowski.

He wanted the kill shot.

And he almost got it.

The shooter got me in the leg, a bullet shot from the opposite side of the warehouse grazed my side, and as I shot Petrowski, he nailed me in the spleen. I never felt the third shot, but the doctor insisted the pain traveling up my side that night wasn't from my leg. It was from the bullet snapping my ribs and blowing up my spleen.

Petrowski didn't die on that warehouse floor. He lived long enough to make it to the hospital, long enough, the ER doc said in his statement, to say my name.

I still felt no remorse. Petrowski deserved to die, and in my book, so did Morales and the cronies. Brad Pruitt and Caroline Bryant were rage beatings given by Morales, all because he wanted to hurt me from all angles. Hernandez confirmed Brad Pruitt, and ultimately, Barron was able to connect Morales to Caroline's death from a small bite mark on her inner thigh.

Bishop told me he'd asked Hernandez why Morales didn't touch Allison. His response? Because he'd made a promise to her. I laughed when he told me that, and it hurt like hell.

Bishop wheeled me to Andy and Brad's joint funeral under the strict promise I would be returned to the hospital immediately. Allison had their ashes buried with their parents, and only a few people were asked to attend.

I arrived early on my first day back. The pit was empty, with patrol tied up in their entry and exit meetings. I'd brought a coffee and got to work finishing the last read-through of the final report on the events. For the first time, I didn't add something new. I stared at the unopened pack of cigarettes on my desk. I kept a pack there, one in my Jeep, and one on my coffee trunk. All served as reminders of my strength. That two weeks in the hospital, the pain, the constant in and out of a drug-induced sleep, got me through withdrawal, so in a weird way, I was grateful.

I promised myself I'd never smoke again.

Bishop walked in and sat across from me. "Chief would like to see us in his office."

I stood, a familiar dull pain tickling my thigh.

"Still hurts?"

"Not exactly, but it doesn't not hurt either. I can't explain it. I think it's more mental than physical."

He raised an eyebrow. "A reminder."

I shrugged. "Something like that." All eyes were on me as we walked across the pit to Jimmy's office. I didn't think it was because they were wondering about my sexual prefer-ence, and honestly, I didn't care. I hadn't thought about that in months. I was alive, and Chris Petrowski wasn't. That was all that mattered. If my being a badass meant they'd gossip about my sexuality, so be it.

Jimmy smiled and suggested I sit. I chose to stand. The more circulation I had in my leg, the better it felt.

"I have some news." He smiled at Bishop, then pulled out a file. "Ninety-six." He tossed the file at my partner. "Congratulations, Sergeant."

My eyes widened. "Holy shit! You passed the exam!"

Bishop shrugged. "Did you have any doubt?"

I punched him in the arm. "Tons."

He laughed.

Jimmy laughed too. "One of our officers passed his

detective exam too. He'll start training this week."

"Michels?" I asked.

He nodded. "Initially, I'd planned to have him work with you two, but it looks like it'll just be Bishop for a while."

I blinked. "What? I'm back. I'm cleared for full duty. Please don't stick me behind a desk. That will kill me."

"This place would implode with you behind a desk. You spent five months living in my house. I refuse to put myself through that same kind of hell again."

Bishop chuckled. "Better you and Savannah than me."

I glared at him. "Watch it, partner." I looked at Jimmy. "I don't understand."

He leaned back in his chair and crossed his arms over his chest. "Seems you made an impression on Agent Olsen."

It took me a minute to remember who that was. "DEA Agent Olsen?"

Jimmy nodded. "He's asked us to loan you out for a special task force. If you're up for it, you'll start tomorrow. If you're not, then we're all going to be living in hell with you digitizing case files—"

I cut him off. "I'm in."

"How about you wait until you learn the details? He's on his way here now." His phone rang. He checked the caller ID. "I need to take this."

Bishop walked me back to my cubby. "Provisional task force with the DEA. That's big stuff, partner."

"Sergeant Bishop. Sounds good."

He smiled. "Sanders won't think so."

"I wonder if he passed?"

"Doesn't matter. Jimmy told me two weeks ago if I passed, the job was mine."

I punched his arm. "You asshole, you didn't tell me that!"

"He asked me not to."

"I'm your partner! You're supposed to tell me shit."

"You were living with my boss. I'm not as stupid as I look."

I laughed and instinctively held my side, not because it hurt but because I'd grown used to expecting it to.

"You sure you're okay?"

"I'm fine. I promise."

"What about the therapy?"

"What about it? I went through it as required. I got my sign-off. It's all good."

"Did it help?"

"I did what I had to do. I don't regret killing Petrowski, and it was a clean kill. Am I sorry to see him dead? No, but I've let it go. That's what Tommy would want."

He nodded, knowing there wasn't anything he could say. "Guys are going to Duke's tonight. It'd be great if you showed up."

"I'll think about it," I said.

Agent Olsen showed up an hour later. It was a slow day in Hamby, and I'd actually spent the morning cleaning my cubby, so when he arrived, he got a dose of my sense of organization. Jimmy brought us all to his office.

"Two weeks ago, a freshman at the University of North Georgia OD'd on a highly potent version of carfentanil," Jimmy said. "He graduated from Hamby last year."

Special Agent Olsen added, "He's the second in three weeks."

I cringed. "Carfentanil is serious shit. Garcia and I worked on a federal bust in Chicago a few years ago. Biggest arrest I've been involved in."

"I know," Agent Olsen said. "That's why we want your help."

"I'm in, no question."

He looked to Jimmy.

"She's cleared for full duty," he said.

"Very well." He pushed a box on the floor toward me. "Here's what you need to know. I'll send someone for you at 0800 hours."

"Here?"

He nodded, then stood and shook Jimmy's hand. "Thank you, Chief Abernathy." He smiled at Bishop and then turned to me. "Welcome to the DEA, Detective. We'll deputize you first thing in the morning."

"Thank you," I said, shaking his hand so hard he laughed.

"Nice grip."

I slipped on my favorite black ankle boots and did a final check in the mirror. "Not bad," I said to my reflection. I walked into my family room, feeling the wave of sadness rushing through me. Bishop had a plaque made for a shelf in remembrance of Andy, and it sat on the bookcase where he died. I wasn't sure there'd be a day I wouldn't feel that rush of emotion from looking at his name.

I tapped on Herman's glass house. He swam over and popped his head to the top of the water. I dropped in a pellet and told him I'd be home soon. I glanced at the box of information on the floor, feeling prepared to hit the ground running in the morning. But tonight, I was ready to enjoy myself with the people who'd stood by me and helped me heal.

Savannah charged toward me as I walked into Duke's.

I held out my arms. "No hugging. It hurts."

"Liar!" She hugged me anyway. "I'm glad you came." She took my arm and dragged me toward the bar. "Look! Bishop's here."

I stopped and stared at the corner table and Sean sitting with his back against the wall.

She shoved me ahead. "Don't be so obvious."

"I'm not being obvious. I just want to say hi."

"Honey, that man tried to visit you for three months, and you turned him away each time. He's moved on. Don't ruin his relationship by messing with his head."

"We left things on good terms."

"Really? You sent him a text and told him things wouldn't happen, and you call that good terms?"

"I said I wanted to be friends."

"And you've ghosted him ever since." She all but shoved me onto a barstool.

"I was busy healing."

I looked back at Sean and the pretty blonde sitting across from him. "He looks happy."

"He is. Now leave him be."

I'd meant what I said, but Savannah was right. Telling Sean over text was selfish and cowardly, but in my defense, it wasn't because I didn't have feelings for him. It was the opposite. What if we got involved and someone hurt him because of me? I couldn't take that risk. Sean Higgins didn't deserve that, no matter how much I'd thought about him over the past six months. I turned around again and caught him staring at me. I smiled and shrugged a little. Maybe someday I'd explain it to him.

He looked away without returning the smile.

The End

OVERKILL
Rachel Ryder Book 3

With a suspected drug ring operating in the local school system, Rachel must go undercover to help bring them down.

Deputized as a Drug Enforcement Agent and working with a provisional task force, Rachel Ryder takes on her toughest case yet.

Caught between multiple agencies and working undercover from inside the local schools, Rachel lays it all on the line to protect the youth of her new community.

Get your copy today at
CarolynRidderAspenson.com

KEEP IN TOUCH WITH CAROLYN

Never miss a new release! Sign up to receive exclusive updates from Carolyn.

Join today at CarolynRidderAspenson.com

As a thank you for signing up, you'll receive a free novella!

YOU MIGHT ALSO ENJOY...

The Rachel Ryder Thriller Series

Damaging Secrets

Hunted Girl

Overkill

The Chantilly Adair Paranormal Cozy Mystery Series

Get Up and Ghost

Ghosts Are People Too

Praying For Peace

Ghost From the Grave

Deceased and Desist

Déjà Boo

The Holiday Hills Witch Cozy Mystery Series

There's a New Witch in Town

Witch This Way

Who's That Witch?

Another Witch Bites the Dust

Greatest Witch of All

The Lily Sprayberry Realtor Cozy Mystery Series

Deal Gone Dead

Decluttered and Dead

Signed, Sealed and Dead

Bidding War Break-In

Open House Heist

Realtor Rub Out

Foreclosure Fatality

The Pooch Party Cozy Mystery Series

Pooches, Pumpkins, and Poison

Hounds, Harvest, and Homicide

Dogs, Dinners, and Death

The Angela Panther Mystery Series

Unfinished Business

Unbreakable Bonds

Uncharted Territory

Unexpected Outcomes

Unbinding Love

The Christmas Elf

The Ghosts

Undetermined Events

The Event

The Favor

The Magical Real Estate Mystery Series

Spooks for Sale

Selling Spells Trouble

Cloaked Commission

Join Carolyn's Newsletter List at

CarolynRidderAspenson.com

You'll receive a free novella as a thank you!

ABOUT CAROLYN

Carolyn Ridder Aspenson is the USA Today bestselling author of the Rachel Ryder thriller series and numerous sassy, southern cozy mysteries.

Now an empty-nester, Carolyn lives in the Atlanta suburbs with her husband, two Pit Bull-Boxer mix dogs and two cantankerous cats, but you'll often find her at a local coffee shop people-watching (and listening.) Or as she likes to call it: plotting her next novel.

Join Carolyn's mailing list at
CarolynRidderAspenson.com